# BLAIR DENHOLM
# **MOVING TARGET**

## By Blair Denholm

The Fighting Detective

*Fighting Dirty*
*Kill Shot*
*Shot Clock*
*Trick Shot*
*Shot to the Heart*
*Drop Shot*
*Point Blank*
*Moving Target*
*Cold Shot*

Vinci Books

vinci-books.com

Published by Vinci Books Ltd in 2026

1

Copyright © Blair Denholm 2023

The author has asserted their moral right to be identified as the author of this work in accordance with the Copyright, Designs and Patents Act 1988. This work is a work of fiction. Names, characters, places and incidents are the product of the author's imagination or are used fictitiously. Any resemblance to actual persons, living or dead, places and incidents is entirely coincidental.

All rights reserved. No part of this publication may be copied, reproduced, distributed, stored in any retrieval system, or transmitted in any form or by any means, including photocopying, recording, or other electronic or mechanical methods, nor used as a source for any form of machine learning including AI datasets, without the prior written permission of the publisher.

The publisher and the author have made every effort to obtain permissions for any third party material used in this book and to comply with copyright law. Any queries in this respect should be brought to the attention of the publisher and any omissions will be corrected in future editions.

A CIP catalogue record for this book is available from the British Library.

Paperback ISBN: 9781036708290

The EU GPSR authorised representative is Logos Europe, 9 rue Nicolas Poussion, 17000 La Rochelle, France

contact@logoseurope.eu

*I am not afraid of the darkness. Real death is preferable to a life without living.*

            Vasco da Gama

## Chapter One

THE DARK, brooding rain clouds that had been hovering over London for the last two days finally opened up. Light drops quickly turned into a steady drizzle. Fitting, Jack Lisbon thought, as he pulled his daughter closer to his side. His ex-wife Sarah, the reason they were all gathered here today, was always complaining about the English weather.

'Daddy, when is the funeral service going to start?' Skye sobbed. 'I just want it to be over.'

'Soon, love.' Jack clicked the little button that locked the top of the umbrella into place. 'I think the vicar's still waiting on a few people to turn up.'

'Who? Everybody mummy knew is already here!' She pointed at the large crowd of mourners huddled in the gardens and around the doors of St James Church in Croydon, South London.

'Just a couple more, sweetheart.' Jack estimated the crowd at around sixty people, not including the vicar, funeral director and attendant staff. An equal distribution of black and white faces, predominantly female. Sarah had been one of the most popular hairdressers in the area, her customers encompassing all ages. Handkerchiefs were in abundance as the mourners failed to hold back the tears. *Fair play to you Sarah*, Jack thought to himself. *You had the common touch and the people loved you.*

If Jack got a third as many punters turning up to his farewell gig it would be a miracle. He could count on the fingers of one hand those who truly cared. Claudia at work, a couple of the uniforms, Trevarthen in particular. Micky Knox here in London. Oh, and his dog Daisy. True friends were few and far between. But that never really bothered Jack. The one who cared the most for him – and the one he cared for the most – shivered under his wing like a frightened little bird; her mother cruelly snatched away by cancer way too young.

Now it was time to step up, to be a real parent, not just exist as Skye's abstract notion of a father. Or the image she held dear – the heroic detective who lived in the exotic tropics of Far North Queensland, Australia. He would earn her trust and love after the grieving and the healing was over. Given his shady work history in the UK – sprinkled with suspensions and reprimands – it had been a battle to prove he was worthy of custody. When the decision in his favour finally came through, his heart nearly leapt out of his mouth. It could have gone the other way, with a particularly nasty government bureaucrat arguing that Jack was a bad man with a record of absenteeism, alcoholism and aggression, and that Skye should remain in Britain under the care of the state. Even though past troubles in the UK were a black mark against him, Jack proved he was a changed man. His unblemished and stellar record as a criminal investigator in Australia – with a number of high-profile cases even making the news in the UK – certainly didn't harm his cause.

As they waited for the remaining stragglers to arrive, random people approached father and daughter, offered their condolences. Touching, Jack thought, since only a few of them knew Jack from Adam. And those who did, mutual friends of his and Sarah's from happier days, probably hated him deep in their hearts for abandoning Sarah and Skye when his own life started to spiral out of control. Running away from his responsibilities, they'd be thinking. An irresponsible wastrel of a man.

If only they knew the truth. Or perhaps it was better they didn't. In reality, Jack had run away from some serious trouble that could have seen him sentenced to life in prison. Outwardly, he'd fled the country because he was given an ultimatum by the London Met – resign with some dignity intact, or face being sacked for corruption. But the biggest motivation for his escape was the fear that someone would discover he'd committed a brutal murder. And stolen a shit-load of cash from the victim's safe. Because if today's sympathisers knew that, they might not be extending their hands for Jack to shake.

'When are the rest of the people coming?' Skye blurted. 'I'm sick of waiting. I'm cold…and…I'm…' she burst into a flood of tears, Jack hugged her tight. 'Why did mummy have to die?' she wailed, her head snuggling into his chest.

'There, there, sweetheart. I know, it's not fair.' He stroked her mop of curly hair. 'It's just your cousins from Jamaica we're waiting on now,' said Jack gently. 'They won't be long, I'm sure.' He felt his breathing had become constricted, loosened his necktie. He hardly ever wore the damn thing; it usually hung out of sight in the back of the wardrobe, only seeing daylight for court appearances.

'I've never even met them,' she pouted and stamped one foot on the damp grass. 'Why are they so important that the whole funeral is being held up?'

'Come on, love. You're twelve years old, a big girl now. We have to be patient with other people. Maybe they were held up in traffic? Let's give them the benefit of the doubt.'

Lips pressed hard together, she looked up at him with moist eyes but said nothing. Her petulance was perfectly understandable. Jack had only heard Sarah mention these cousins once or twice in passing. Perhaps they were thinking there'd be an inheritance waiting for them? If so, they were going to be sorely disappointed. Sarah was known for donating far too much of her meagre beautician's wages to charity, but she always made sure there was enough left over to pay for Skye's needs. In other words, she died virtually penniless.

A black cab pulled up outside the church, sending a spray of water from a puddle in the gutter. Two people dressed head to toe in black alighted. 'Look, love,' said Jack, pointing at the latecomers. 'Here they are now.'

Ida and Lenny, daughter and son of Sarah's older brother Marcus, who himself died a decade ago from cancer, slowly made their way through the little graveyard towards the gathered guests. They must have recognised Skye from photos, Jack surmised, because Ida stopped midstride and the pair changed direction and made a beeline towards them.

A few words of introduction and sympathy were exchanged, Skye remaining the epitome of respect despite the harsh words she'd only moments ago said to Jack. The cousins, in fact, were friendly and gracious and came across as deeply sincere; Jack took back his unspoken words about the inheritance angle. Skye took an instant shine to them, too. She held out her hand to cousin Ida. 'Would you like to sit with me and dad at the front?' she said, the tiniest smile breaking out on her face. It was the first real positive sign in Skye's demeanour since Jack picked her up from a none-too-pleased Aunty Jocelyn and they'd gone to stay at Micky Knox's house in St Auburn. Jack's heart melted at the kid's sudden turn of generosity. Sarah may have been a temperamental hothead when it came to her relationship with Jack, but she always showed genuine compassion for others. It seemed Skye had inherited the caring gene from her mum. *Not a bad legacy to leave behind, old girl,* Jack said to himself.

'OK, everyone,' called the funeral director through megaphone hands. The bald, portly man waved his hand at the entry to the church. 'Let's all get inside now.'

---

JACK GLANCED down from the raised dais. It reminded him of the press conferences he'd run with Inspector Joe Batista, only the audience wasn't waving microphones and shouting questions at him. All the mourners' eyes were turned towards him expectantly. He singled out Skye, gave her a smile of encouragement and an awkward wave, mouthed the words "I love you." Giant teardrops rolled down her cheeks. He scanned the room: some folk were squinting disdainfully, knowing Jack only from the bad things Sarah had told them. Others wore more forgiving expressions.

The vicar had already spoken at length, a selection of traditional hymns and two rollicking gospel tunes had been sung. Sarah's sister Jocelyn, her best friend Ramona from the salon, a handful of women Jack didn't know, had all had their turn, saying glowing things about Sarah as a mother, a friend, a family member, a pillar of the community. Skye was praised as the perfect child, which drew some laughs.

Now, it was Jack's turn. As an ex-husband who hadn't enjoyed the most convivial relationship with the deceased, the job wasn't going to be an easy one. The room was so quiet, when he cleared his throat it sounded like a chainsaw starting up. He took a sip of water, then looked down at the piece of paper he'd written the speech on, which was totally unnecessary since he knew by heart all the words he'd composed on the plane from Dubai to Heathrow. Despite their years apart, and the knowledge that he and Sarah had been at each other's throats far more often than they'd spent in each other's arms, he put the best spin on it that he could. A joke here and there, recalling Sarah's volatile temper by mimicking her Jamaican accent but with respect, not in a mocking way: *You're guilty as a cat in a fishbowl! Dere will be hell to pay, Jack Lis-bon!* Skye could barely keep it together as Jack busted out her mum's favourite phrases.

Then, no words left to say, he took a deep breath and stepped down. He felt he'd done justice to the woman's best qualities and people weren't staring daggers at him. At any rate, it was a relief to have finished.

The burial ceremony was the hardest thing Jack had had to endure in his life. Watching his daughter's tiny hand tossing soil over the casket, streams of tears indistinguishable from the slanting rain, brought tears to his own eyes. Conscious of his chest rising and falling as the vicar spoke the eulogy, he prayed he wouldn't faint from the emotion of it all and topple into the grave and land on Sarah's coffin.

As everyone filed out of the churchyard on their way to the wake in a nearby community hall, Skye holding the hands of her cousin Ida and her dad, Bob Marley's classic "Three Little Birds" boomed out loud and clear from speakers inside the church. Skye sang along like it was a memory of her favourite nursery rhyme. No doubt her mum had The Wailers on a loop at home. Jimmy Cliff and UB40 were other favourites Skye would be well acquainted with. As they exited the gate and headed for Jack's rented Opel, the entire crowd was belting out the song, telling each other not to *worry 'bout a ting!* When they got to the reception, the atmosphere could tempt Jack into hitting the booze, but he would stay strong as ever and stick to coffee. Years of sobriety behind him, he would never return to his bad old ways. He had a kid to raise and be a good example for, after all.

As Jack opened the passenger door for Skye, he looked at her with the deepest affection he had ever felt for another human being. So many missed years, so much to make up for. In a few days, after a number of boring but necessary legal formalities had been taken care of, Detective Sergeant Jack Lisbon of the Yorkville CIB, Queensland Police Service, would be winging his way back to the warm tropics. This time, with the most precious thing in his world keeping him company. If he ever returned to the UK, he reflected, it would only be on the strength of an extradition order. Who knew? Maybe a dogged cold-case investigator might figure out the truth, that Jack had offed the despicable Alex Gallagher. But that would never happen because Gallagher was a piece of scum, and, unlike Sarah, mourned and missed by few. And certainly not by any cold-case investigators.

But before touching down in Oz, they were taking a side trip to Jack's ancestral home of Portugal, where his father was born and learned his trade as a mechanic before migrating to the United Kingdom. The little break would give him and Skye the perfect opportunity to grieve in peace. They'd take a well-earned rest for a couple of weeks, soak up some sun and see all the famous sights, and prepare for their life together Down Under.

And while they were there, Jack would meet a cousin of his own and do his level best to stay out of mischief.

## Chapter Two

THE WOMAN WAITING inside the Humberto Delgado Airport terminal's crowded greeting hall held a cardboard sign above her head displaying the words "Lisbon welcomes the Lisbons!"

'*Bom dia*,' said Jack in the most appalling Portuguese. 'Nice touch with the sign. Very droll. Mirabella Coelho, I presume?'

'*Bom dia*, Jack,' said the woman, delivering a white-toothed smile that gleamed like a camera flash. 'You presume correctly.' Mirabella, who spoke English with only a trace of an accent, glanced at Skye, to be met with an expression of curiosity mixed with suspicion. 'And you must be Skye! Your father has told me *so* much about you in our little chats.'

Skye, wide-eyed, said: 'Only good things, I hope.'

Mirabella laughed. 'More than good, young lady. You've been through a lot, he tells me. A kidnapping a couple of years ago, for goodness' sake. And now this awful tragedy with your mum...' She reached out slowly to touch Skye on the shoulder, but the girl shrank back into her father's one-armed embrace.

'Oh, I'm terribly sorry!' said Mirabella, her hands cupping her reddening cheeks. 'I've said something wrong. I didn't mean anything by it.'

'No, no.' said Jack. 'I…ah…just a second.' He placed his carry-on bag on the floor. 'That thing's darned heavy.' It wasn't – the bag contained a paperback and a change of underwear. He needed time to regroup mentally. 'It's just that us Brits have a tendency to dodge the emotional stuff.'

Mirabella nodded, as if satisfied with the explanation.

Jack scratched the back of his head. He wasn't flustered merely due to the awkwardness of the unfolding situation. There was a more superficial reason. Mirabella, whom Jack had met online through a genealogy site but never seen before, looked like she could have been the twin sister of his work partner back in Australia, Detective Claudia Taylor. Mirabella's eyes were brown instead of Taylor's deep forest green, and her hair – tucked into a scrunchie, yellow like Taylor often wore – had more of a wave to it. She stood a couple of inches shorter than Taylor and weighed perhaps a kilo or two more, with a bit of extra padding on the hips. There were some minor differences in facial features, too, but overall the likeness was uncanny. He even wondered if Skye's initial standoffishness had something to do with the woman's close resemblance to Taylor, whom the kid had spoken to on Zoom calls. Skye had formed a kind of bond with Taylor, liked her a lot, even viewed her as her father's potential new girlfriend. And maybe Jack did too.

Jack took a deep breath. 'Like you said, she's been through a lot. We just have to give her some time, don't we sunshine?'

Skye peeled herself away from Jack's side, rubbed a

wrist under her nose and gave a little sniff. 'Yes.' She gazed up at their new friend, forced a smile. 'I'm sorry for my reaction, Mirabella. It's not your fault what happened.'

'No need to apologise, my dear.' She winked. 'Let's get to the car and back to my place. I have a couple of rooms set aside for you two. It's cool here in the terminal, but believe me, it's nice and warm outside. Feel like a swim?'

Skye nodded rapidly. 'Are we going to the beach?'

'No. I have a pool at my place.'

'Well,' said Jack, tossing the backpack over his shoulder again like it was empty, drawing a look of astonishment from Mirabella. 'What are we waiting for?'

---

THE OPULENCE of the woman's home took Jack's breath away. Located in a secluded pocket of the leafy Belém district, the three-level house contradicted the one thing he thought he knew about the local people. That they were dirt poor. With Portugal having one of the lowest per-capita incomes in Europe, he half expected Mirabella to take them to a modest little flat way out of town. The drive from the airport had already set Jack's expectations low: crumbling facades with tiles missing here and there, pathways and traffic islands overgrown with grass and weeds, graffiti prolific on the walls of all kinds of buildings. Yes, she had a nice car, but for some reason Jack assumed it was rented.

'Please, follow me.' Mirabella waved her guests into the brightly lit atrium, dotted with deep-green plants. They gawped around at their surroundings, cool air from a powerful air-conditioning system washing over them. Sparkly clean and tidy as a pin, the tile and glass interior put the airport terminal to shame.

Mirabella showed Jack and Skye upstairs to their rooms. Five-star luxury all the way: king size beds with expensive sheets, ensuites in both bedrooms, wide-screen TVs, bar fridges. As he was unpacking his meagre supply of clothes, Jack wondered if this lavish home could really be Mirabella's property. She'd be lucky if she was forty and, as far as he knew, the woman was single. Perhaps she inherited it? Or maybe she was renting in a share arrangement with some other people. Or was she some kind of protégé, like his mate Mickey Knox, the drop-shipper extraordinaire? When he and Skye had changed into their swimming gear and the dressing gowns that were laid upon their beds, they met up again with their host in the vast sitting room.

Jack fired from the hip. 'Have you owned this place for long?' It was a direct question loaded with an assumption. A classic detective's ploy.

'One year. Actually, not even that. I'd say nine months. And,' she dragged the word out, 'before you make any wild guesses, because I can see it all over your face, I'll tell you how I can afford it.'

Over fresh orange juice and a platter of walnuts, olives, sliced carrot and celery, Mirabella explained how her website had recently enjoyed a stratospheric rise in popularity, especially in the last year. Apparently, there were loads of millionaires in Brazil who were prepared to fork out lots of money to find out if they were related to a famous explorer from centuries ago. Having a lineage that goes back to Vasco da Gama, Ferdinand Magellan or even one of their crew, brings a ton of street cred in the backrooms of Rio's business enterprises.

'But you only charged me,' Jack did a quick back calculation from Australian dollars using his fingers as an imaginary calculator, 'about two-hundred euros to track down my cousin Paulo.'

'You have a cousin here, Dad?' Skye exclaimed, spilling juice over the counter top. 'That's so exciting. Why didn't you tell me?'

'It was going to be a surprise.' He grinned and flicked her under the chin. 'But now I've let the cat out of the bag.'

Mirabella magically produced a dishcloth and wiped up the spill. 'Finding your dad's cousin was so easy for a genealogist like me it would have been criminal to charge him a lot of money.'

'Who is this person?' Skye nibbled on a stick of carrot.

'Paulo Lisboa,' said Jack. 'He lives in the south of the country, in a region called the Algarve, where there are more beaches than you can imagine, sunshine.'

'Yeah?' said Skye. Her demeanour had brightened considerably since arriving at the Belém mansion. 'When are we going there?'

'Soon,' said Jack.

'You can stay here with me as long as you like,' said Mirabella, pouring more juice into everyone's glass. 'Come and go as you please.'

Skye screwed up her face as she posed a question to Mirabella. 'Not that I'm ungrateful or anything, but how come we're staying here with you and not in a hotel?'

The tone in her voice confirmed for Jack what he'd half suspected: his daughter was jealous on behalf of Claudia. He was about to invent some reason for their choice of accommodation but was spared the trouble.

'Because,' said Mirabella. 'Having a famous detective staying in my house is an honour, and, this is my selfish side speaking, a terrific marketing opportunity for me.'

'But he's not famous here,' countered Skye. 'Just in Australia, and a little bit in England.'

'I'm not famous anywhere,' Jack protested.

Their host shook her head. 'You'd be surprised. A Portuguese backpacker touring Australia a couple of years ago, who happened to be in North Queensland at the time, wrote a short blog piece about a detective with the same name as our capital city who solved a mysterious crime.'

'You're kidding.' Jack raised an eyebrow.

'No. It was the one about the basketball coach getting killed in a hit and run murder.'

'I remember that one. I know all of dad's cases inside out,' Skye boasted. 'Who got killed – this one was the American coach Dale Collins. And the murderer was Dieter Baumann. He was sentenced to life in prison.'

Jack stared at her open-mouthed, then said: 'What the actual…?'

'Call it a gift.' Skye offered a smug smile before grabbing a handful of walnuts.

Silence reigned for a moment as the adults came to grips with the child's savant-like knowledge of Jack's career.

'Here, look at this.' Mirabella broke the silence and flipped up the lid of a laptop on her table. She pulled up a webpage, spun the device around for Jack and Skye to see. 'It's Rodrigo Ferrão's post.'

Jack squinted to read the article, but soon gave it up as a bad job. 'Oi,' he said. 'I recognise the pictures OK, but I can't understand a word of the text. It's in bleedin' Portuguese innit.'

'Sorry?' said Mirabella. 'Innit? What on earth does that mean?'

Skye sighed. 'I apologise for dad. It means "isn't it".'

'Wow. I never would have guessed.' Mirabella shook her

head before translating the article, which had gone viral in a matter of weeks. 'So, although three years have gone by, at one time everyone was talking about the Australian cop from England with the Portuguese name. Even now the post gets a couple of hundred views every day.'

'I wonder why the bloke never asked me for an interview?' Jack mused aloud. 'Then again, I can be quite intimidating when I want to be.' He puffed out his chest like a peacock and winked at Skye who rolled her eyes.

'Oh, boy. Cringey,' she laughed.

Mirabella closed her laptop and said, 'Since Rodrigo failed to get your words into his article, perhaps you would like to do an interview for me, Detective Lisbon? You know, as a favour for letting you stay in my house?'

'So that's been your angle the whole time?' Jack grinned.

Mirabella shrugged. 'I neither confirm, nor deny.'

'Hmm. Spoken like a lot of suspects I've arrested. You ain't been in trouble with the law yourself, have you?'

'I can only repeat my previous answer.'

*'Very cagey.' Jack glanced at Skye, who was blushing like a peach and staring at her hands. Oh my God, the kid's embarrassed, thinks her old man is flirting. The thing is, could she be right?*

'So, you agree to my request?'

He nodded. 'The pleasure would be all mine.'

Mirabella clapped her hands. 'Excellent. But first, a swim.'

Skye was out onto the patio and racing to the infinity pool, feet slapping on the tiles, before Jack had time to grab his towel.

## Chapter Three

JACK WIPED crumbs and a smear of custard from his lips. He and Skye had spent a pleasant hour cruising the local neighbourhood on foot, checking out the famous attractions – the Tower of Belém and the Monument to the Discoveries on the embankment by the majestic Tagus River, and, most important in Skye's opinion, the old bakery the Pastéis de Belém, where they make the famous custard tarts using a secret monks' recipe created two-hundred years ago. Or so the legend went, according to the woman conducting the walking tour they'd latched onto. There were so many things to see in Portugal, and this was just one tiny part of it. Jack had scheduled three weeks for this holiday, but would it be enough? If not, they could always come back for another visit.

The clear blue skies, warm sunshine and abundance of smiling faces on the streets seemed to be lifting Skye's mood. 'It's kinda cool here, dad. Thanks for bringing me.' She gave a feeble smile that belied the positive words she's just spoken, then nibbled the edges of a *pastel de nata* before putting it back on her plate. She dabbed at the corners of her eyes with a napkin as a trickle of tears ran down her cheeks. 'Oh...I'm sorry. It just happens without me even thinking about it.'

'Don't apologise, love.' Jack reached out and placed his hand on the top of hers. 'You're allowed to cry wherever and whenever you damn well like, OK?' He stroked her wrist. 'You've just lost your mum, no one's gonna think badly of you for grieving. It's only natural. C'mon. Let's head into the city and ride that famous Tram 28.'

Skye nodded slowly. 'OK.'

Still technically the off-shoulder season, throngs of people choked the esplanade by the glistening water of the broad river. What would the city of Lisbon be like in the peak of summer? Jack wondered. The atmosphere today, though, was idyllic, topped off with picture-postcard perfect weather. A few more touristy distractions downtown and Skye's mood would improve again.

They jumped on the sleek and modern tram No. 15 that would take them to Lisbon's Baixa district via the riverfront. Jack felt a tingle of indefinable pride that his roots could be traced back to this place and its ramshackle, shabby beauty. A minnow of a country, Portugal's brave explorers had opened up many parts of the new world. It shook off a cruel dictatorship in 1974 and resumed its seat at the table of civilised, democratic nations. *Well done, little Portugal*, Jack thought to himself as he gripped Skye's hand.

He cast his mind back to his childhood in South London, and his Portuguese migrant father, a wife-beating drunkard who barely had time for his son. And maybe that was a blessing. It's what led Jack to the gyms and boxing as an outlet for his frustrations. The boxing skills learned in his youth held him in good stead today: quick fists were often the key to escaping hairy situations and sometimes, just sometimes, the only way to get the nastiest of villains to fess up to their crimes. Was all that something to be proud of? It wasn't Jack's place to judge – his ways got results and justice got served. The tram came to a squeaky stop at the city's main square, the bustling Praça do Comércio.

After five minutes hunting about, they found a place to eat next to an industrial-age wrought-iron structure, the Elevador de Santa Justa. Skye reckoned it looked like something out of an H.G. Wells novel. Jack was astounded – not by the comparison, but by the fact the kid knew who H.G. Wells was. He could only shake his head in wonder. She was going to be all right.

'I've got a feeling you'll end up liking this place so much you won't want to come with me to Australia,' said Jack, sipping an espresso coffee strong enough to revive a corpse.

'I do like it. But I think Australia's going to be even better. At least I'll be able to understand everything since the people speak English there. I know 'cos mum and I used to watch all the Australian soap operas, like *Neighbours* and *Home and Away*.'

'Oh dear,' Jack chuckled as he plucked another – his third – *pastel de nata* from the long rectangular box that contained ten of the mind-blowing egg tarts. He'd bought them to compare with the originals they'd tried at Belém, but his palate failed to distinguish even the slightest difference. A long run along the waterfront tonight would be in order to burn off the calories. 'Don't be too sure about understanding everyone in Oz, sunshine. I've had to learn a whole new vocabulary to make myself understood. Crikey this, fair dinkum that. It's like bleedin' Chinese until you get used to it. Then there's the godawful accent.'

'Hmmm,' Skye murmured. 'I reckon I'll get by.'

Jack frowned as he handed over the cash. A ridiculous five euros each to take the short trip to the viewing platform at the top of the elevator and back down. At the top was a wonder that made the expensive but brief 45-metre vertical ride worth it. The whalebone-like remains of the Carmo Convent, wrecked in an earthquake in 1755 that killed ten thousand souls, caused fires and a tsunami, took his and Skye's breath away.

With a hundred selfies on Jack's and Skye's mobile phone cameras, they decided it was time to enjoy the number one highlight on every tourist's wish list – ride the Number 28 Tram, or "elétrico" as the locals called it. With the help of an online map they found their way to the closest stop on the route. A long line confronted them.

'Dad, is it really gonna be worth it?' said Skye as they shuffled another half metre closer to the start of the queue. 'We'll be here ages before it's our turn.'

'Of course it's worth it.' Jack had no idea how frequently the trams ran. He'd give it fifteen minutes, otherwise they'd come back another time. He'd read it was best to try early in the morning or late in the evening. Now seemed to be bang in the middle of the busy period.

'But look,' Skye pointed at the next rickety tram car to start the journey. 'There's no way we'll get a seat. They're packed in like sardines.'

A woman in her early to mid sixties, with a walking stick and a string bag full of red onions, gave a jolly laugh. 'A very appropriate comment.' She laughed again, like it was as natural for her as breathing, her eyes aglow with mischief. 'Did you say that on purpose to make a joke?'

'What do you mean?' said Skye, arching an eyebrow.

'Sardines are pretty much our national dish.'

'They are? Yuk! I'd advise you to switch it to those custard tarts. They taste much nicer.'

The woman looked at Jack. 'Your daughter?'

He beamed with pride. 'Sure is.'

'A wise head on such young shoulders. I too, would recommend changing it. The *pastel de nata* is a much more worthy candidate for the role. Sardines are, how do you say, very overrated.'

'If you don't mind my saying so, your English is amazing,' said Jack. 'Does everyone in Portugal speak it so well?'

She shook her head. 'Not in the countryside. But in the bigger cities like Lisbon and Porto, and in the touristy areas, definitely. The generation coming through now will be speaking it the best. As well as the Scandinavians do, I'd bet. My name is Anna, by the way.'

After Jack introduced himself and Skye he said: 'Tell me, are we wasting our time queuing up for this tram? There are a lot of folk waiting to get on.'

'Not at all. It's well worth the experience. I ride it every day. The trick is to get on at a different stop. Come with me.'

Anna took off like a startled hare, her walking cane clacking on the ubiquitous white cobblestones. Jack wondered how she didn't slip over, the surfaces of the little blocks were so shiny and slippery. They wended their way up a steep street, Anna as nimble as a woman half her age.

'Here. This is the best spot.'

Soon, the yellow and white rattler rumbled up to the stop. Anna clambered on board first, Jack and Skye right behind her. A gracious young man stood for Anna, but there were no other spare seats. Skye was right – it was like a sardine can inside. The plucky little tramcar rolled along narrow roads, its metal wheels screeching on the rails on the tighter corners. Standing passengers lurched as the driver applied the brakes on steep descents. At some points the tram got so close to the walls of buildings you could almost reach out and pluck drying clothes from washing lines.

'You want to get off here?' Jack asked as the tram stopped at the top of a steep hill.

'All the same to me,' said Skye. 'I can barely see out of the windows with all these people in the way.'

'This is Alfama,' said a smartly dressed middle-aged woman standing behind Jack. 'A very famous part of Lisbon. The oldest part, in fact. Well worth checking out.'

'Thanks. I think we—'

But there was no time to carry the conversation any further as an ear-piercing scream echoed inside the tramcar.

'Help!' A woman's voice yelled out. 'Someone's stolen my purse!'

Jack looked at Anna pleadingly. 'Will you keep an eye on my daughter for me?'

A rapid nod of approval. 'Anyone tries to touch her and whack!' The old dame gave her walking stick a shake. She then said something in Portuguese to the overweight man sitting next to her. He smiled, stood, and gestured for Skye to take a seat.

Meanwhile, Jack picked his way through the crowd, saying another couple of words he'd learned: *com licença*, then "excuse me", then the Portuguese phrase again. It seemed to do the trick as passengers leaned sideways to let him through. He reached the hysterical woman, standing right behind the driver. She was bawling worse then half the mourners at Sarah's funeral.

'Don't go anywhere,' Jack yelled at the back of the driver's head. The man at the controls spun around, a peeved look on his face.

'I cannot stop the tram for too long,' the swarthy man behind the controls, reeking of nose-hair-curling body odour that somehow penetrated the plastic partition separating him from the passengers, spoke in a lilting tone. 'There is another one right on my tail. Congestion on the line is not good, sir!'

'You have to stay put until I've established what's going on here. I believe a crime has been committed.'

'And you are a policeman?' said the driver challengingly. 'You don't look like one. Where is your badge, sir?'

'Oh dear,' said the woman who had cried for help, her voice shaky to match her trembling body. An American tourist judging by her accent. 'I think I made a big mistake.'

'What do you mean?' said Jack.

'Ah...my purse is here. I couldn't see it under this souvenir I bought.' She held up a long woollen red-and-green scarf. 'See!' The tears had dried up already. 'I do apologise. It's just that I was warned about pickpockets on this route and I guess I assumed the worst when I saw—'

'It's fine.' Jack held up his hand to cut her off before she got on too much of a roll with her blabbering. He offered the driver an apologetic grin. 'Sorry, mate. I actually am a policeman, but not a local one. Drive on, sunshine.'

'Dad!' Skye leapt out of her seat excitedly when her father returned. 'Did you catch the thief?'

'No, sweetheart. But I could have charged someone with wasting police time.'

'No you couldn't, silly. You've got no jurisdiction here.' She crossed her arms, oozing pride at knowing such a word.

'A lawyer now, are we?' Jack shook his head. 'Bleedin' wonders will never cease.'

'I watch a lot of cop shows, what can I say?'

Anna stood as they approached the next stop. 'This is me here. Miradouro Santa Luzia.'

Skye held out her elbow, which Anna leaned on before standing. '*Obrigada*. Thank you. And nice to meet you.'

'And you!' The old woman shuffled a few steps before turning around. 'If you want I can show you something very special close to this stop.'

Ten minutes later, Skye was chasing peacocks around the walls of St George's Castle, Jack was sipping a coffee and, for one precious moment, all was right with the world.

## Chapter Four

THE PLAN WORKED A TREAT. Skye was exhausted after Jack ensured they packed into their program just about every tourist attraction the city of Lisbon had to offer. They finished off by eating an alfresco dinner in the cool and hip Graça district. Grilled fresh sardines – which Jack suggested on a dare – was not what either of them expected, and they both loved the meal.

Tomorrow they would take a drive in a rented 4x4 to the southern end of the country where they would visit cousin Paulo. Mirabella had set everything up to make sure Paulo would be there when Jack arrived. For some gut-felt reason, Jack wanted no preliminary chit-chat with his relation; he wanted the experience to be real and raw, even though the suspense was killing him on the inside.

There was plenty to see along the way before they got to the Algarve. He'd play it by ear. He smiled to himself – Operation Distract Skye was going pretty well. She'd only cried a couple of times today thinking about her mother.

The girl snored softly as they hummed along the track,

the No. 15 tram whizzing them back to Belém and Mirabella's house. His heart ached every time he looked at Skye, her head bouncing ever so gently on his shoulder.

Twilight descended over the glimmering expanse of the Tagus, streetlights began to flicker and glow brighter as the sun prepared to dip over the horizon. To Jack's surprise, this evening tram was full of passengers. Not so much tourists this time; he assumed by the business attire many were wearing that these were commuters heading home after a long day at the office.

Three more stops, then he envisaged carrying Skye in his arms through the darkened backstreets of Belém, stopping regularly to check his bearings. Nope. She was way too big for that now. He'd done enough exercise today, hiking up and down the city's precipitous inclines. He pulled out his mobile, scrolled until he found Mirabella's number. She might agree to pick them up at the tram stop, assuming she hadn't gone out for the evening. Thumb poised to make the call. And then, all hell broke loose.

BANG!

Jack instinctively shielded Skye with his body, head turned to the right, ears straining towards the source of the noise. His eyes darted left and right, bulging like ping pong balls.

Skye jolted awake. 'What's happening?'

BANG!

Unmistakable. Gunshots, emanating from the first of the two carriages.

Piercing screams, people ducking for cover and holding briefcases over their heads, the screech of brakes.

Jack's heart rate kicked into overdrive. The screaming continued unabated. Apocalyptic noises. Men and women hysterical with fear.

*Would there be another shot?*

Skye wriggled under the protection of her father's strong arms. 'Daddy!' she squealed. "I'm scared. What's happening?'

He pulled her tight to his chest. 'Shhh. It's OK.'

'But people are screaming!'

He grabbed her head with both hands, stared into her eyes. 'Nothing will happen to you. Understand me? I let you down before, never again!'

The doors of the tram hissed open, passengers pushed and shoved and roared at each other in their haste to escape the danger inside. Jack's instinct was to follow them out and run as far away as possible, but his training and years of experience told him to wait and assess.

Despite all that, he had doubts. Run or stay?

*Christ, Lisbon, what to do?* The answer, as always, was listen to your gut. *Stay put.* The shooter could have been the first out the door when they sprang open. He could be waiting to pick off victims as they tried to flee.

Wait till the carriage clears, then inspect if safe to do so. *DO NOT LET THE CHILD OUT OF YOUR SIGHT!*

'Daddy! Please, we have to get out of here,' Skye wailed.

'No.' Jack felt his pocket for a non-existent weapon. 'Trust me, sunshine.'

The sound of a third shot rang out and the pair instinctively ducked their heads. Then Jack realised – that shot had been fired outside the tramcar.

Then a fourth shot, fainter again. The shooter was on the run.

'Come with me.' Jack stood, led his daughter by the hand. Skye clung tighter to his side than she'd ever done before as they made their way to the nearest exit – the rear door of the second carriage they'd been sitting in. Jack shielded her with his body so she wouldn't see the bloodied victim at the front end of the tramcar. Outside, not a soul within a hundred metres of the tram. They collapsed on a patch of grass behind a big, shady tree. Jack dialled Mirabella, she answered on the fourth ring.

'Thank God you're home,' he said. He realised his breath was ragged. 'Can you come to the tram stop opposite the monastery?'

'I'm a little busy with a project right now. Can you wait five—'

'No!' He drew a deep breath. 'I'm sorry. There's been an incident and I need you to come and collect Skye.'

'An accident?' her voice sounded genuinely panicked.

'No, an incident. Someone's fired shots in the tram.'

'What! Are you both OK?'

'Yes. We're unharmed. But please, can you hurry?'

'On my way.'

'Wait!'

'What?'

'Be careful. Keep your eyes open and don't open your car door for anyone. And call the police. I'm sure they're being flooded with calls, but do it anyway.'

'Got it. Wait by the front gate of the monastery.' She disconnected the call.

He hated to abandon the crime scene unsecured, but his daughter was the priority and the local cops would surely get there soon. They walked briskly for four minutes before reaching the agreed spot. Mirabella was just pulling up as they arrived.

'Drive straight home, don't stop for anyone.' Jack bundled Skye into the front passenger seat, thumped on the roof of the car with the flat of his hand. The vehicle tore off with a screech of tyres. Jack watched for a moment as it turned a corner and disappeared before sprinting back to the tram as fast as his legs could carry him.

---

TWO MINUTES LATER, Jack rang Mirabella again. They were just entering her underground garage. Skye was safe. He thanked the woman profusely for her quick action and heaved a sigh of relief. *What a holiday this is turning out to be.*

In detective mode now, he bent at the waist to examine the body of the young woman. Aged early to mid twenties, dark complexion and wiry jet-black hair like Skye's. Jack wondered if she was North African, perhaps Arabic. Or maybe she was native Portuguese; many of the locals had olive complexions. She was slumped over the two front seats on the lefthand side of the tram. At a glance, he determined bullet entry points in between the shoulder blades and in the back of the skull. The shot to the head had exited and lodged in the perspex window. The killer had dispatched his victim quickly; the shot in the back was likely a mistake, the one to the head was the square up. Not surprisingly, the driver had fled the scene along with everyone else. And with two shots heard outside the tram, they would have kept on running. Jack snapped pictures on his mobile phone from several angles – just in case – careful not to get too close and contaminate any evidence.

His guess was that the woman had died quickly. The city's police department, in whatever configuration it was organised, would have the technical wherewithal to figure all the forensics stuff out. From what he could gather, gun crime – and crime in general – was low in Portugal, nevertheless there would be experts able to do the necessary ballistics analysis. He'd be the reliable witness for a change, although he didn't see the killer at any stage so his value to any investigation was a moot point.

The combination of sirens wailing and anxious voices at the side door made Jack stop his examination and pocket his phone. He stood and turned to see what was up and to offer his assistance. A burly man in a dark uniform and baseball cap barked something at him in Portuguese. Behind him, a couple more uniformed cops and a man and a woman in plain clothes. Jack sniffed the latter out as detectives. He held up both hands, palms out and said calmly, 'I'm an Australian police officer and—'

'Get on the ground, hands behind your back!' The cop switched to perfect English. Before Jack could argue the point, the cop produced his service pistol — a Glock 19 — and pointed it at Jack's head. The only smart thing to do in the circumstances was to comply. He felt sure hands apply snap-tie handcuffs and haul him to his feet. 'Stand over there!' The officer pointed at the metal pole running floor to ceiling in the middle of the carriage. The officer followed Jack, spun him around and shackled him to the pole, with metal cuffs this time.

'Are you going to leave me like this for long?' said Jack. 'Only I'm late home for tea as it is.' He smiled at the grim-faced officer who resembled a shaved gorilla. 'And I really am a cop. We'll all have a good laugh about this later.'

'Shut up,' said the gorilla. 'Be quiet until Detective Da Silva questions you.' As he spoke, the officer patted Jack down and extracted his wallet and mobile phone.

'You don't seriously think I'm a suspect in this crime do you?'

The gorilla didn't answer, turned and ambled to the murder scene. He exchanged a couple of words with a short moustachioed man whose receding russet mane matched the colour and texture of his wiry facial hair. Jack assumed this was Detective Da Silva. Next to him was his matronly partner, a middle-aged woman in a dark pantsuit. Both wore protective blue booties and rubber gloves. The officer handed over Jack's belongings to the detectives, before stepping outside to speak to a couple more uniforms who were dealing with a gathering crowd of curious onlookers, suddenly a lot braver with the law on hand. Among them could be witnesses who had returned, in addition to the sticky beaks hoping to capture some images for their social media pages.

'Oi!' Jack called out. 'Don't let him go. That ape's got the keys to these cuffs!'

'One moment sir, while we check out your identity,' said the woman. Her accent was so heavy on the long vowels she almost sounded Russian.

That won't take long, Jack thought. As predicted, the gorilla soon returned. A quick word from Da Silva and the officer freed Jack from the cuffs – metal and plastic. He then handed gloves and booties to the local investigators, and with a smile gave a set of the protective gear to Jack. 'I apologise for the way I handled you, Detective Lisbon,' said the gorilla. 'However I would have acted the same way even if it was our famous footballer Ronaldo who was standing over the victim's body. Rules are rules.'

'Perfectly understandable,' said Jack. 'No hard feelings, Officer…?'

'Mendes. First name Luca.' The two men shook hands respectfully.

When Mendes had again stepped off the tram, Jack snapped on the gloves and said to Da Silva, 'If you ask me, your man was gentle.'

'How would you have responded in the same situation?' said the female detective.

'I'd rather not say,' Jack hitched his thumbs into his belt. 'Let's just leave it at that.'

Da Silva gave Jack a knowing smile. 'I'd like you to tell us what you saw while Detective Quintal and I briefly examine the scene. Our forensics team will be arriving...' he checked his watch... 'in about three minutes.'

'Right.' Jack rubbed a spot on his left wrist where Mendes had pulled the snap-tie cuffs on a little too tightly. 'I was returning to a friend's place after a day sight-seeing with my daughter when I heard a shot, followed by another...'

'How long between the shots?'

'Less than two seconds. In fact, I'm guessing the perpetrator squeezed the first into the back, then finished her off with the second slug to the back of the head. Once the compartment had emptied, which didn't take long as you might imagine, there were two fainter shots fired outside.'

'When?'

'Maybe half a minute to forty-five seconds after the first two. Do you know if anyone else was shot outside?'

'Not that we have seen in the nearby vicinity. Perhaps they were warning shots, him telling people to get out of his way?'

Jack nodded. 'Sounds logical. Have you ID'd the victim?'

Quintal held up a small plastic card with writing in Arabic and French. 'A Moroccan driver's licence. The name on it is Salma Farooq and the photo matches the poor woman here. Date of birth 29 September 1998. That makes her 25 years old. There's an older-model iPhone in her jeans pocket. There were other documents in her handbag, not stolen so we can rule out robbery as a motive.'

Jack had already ruled that out. Pickpockets on public transport don't usually execute their targets.

Quintal continued. 'The documents I found indicate she could be here in Portugal on a student visa. She's wearing a swipe card on a lanyard. Looks like she's interning in some capacity at the Department of Foreign Affairs. That needs looking into as soon as possible.'

'Extraordinary,' said Da Silva. 'Perhaps she's a dual national?'

'Is there a passport in her bag?' said Jack.

'No,' said Da Silva with a hint of disappointment in his voice. 'Just the Moroccan licence. We'll run her ID through all the databases once we get back to the station. I'm assuming you'll accompany us?'

'Whatever for?' said Jack. He remembered Skye's words. 'It's not my jurisdiction.'

Da Silva cleared his throat. 'Maybe so. But, if you don't mind helping us out…we wouldn't say no.'

'Don't tell me you've read the infamous blog post by that backpacker?' Jack asked incredulously.

'Indeed I have. The entire Polícia Judiciária has read it.' Da Silva quickly explained that this was the branch of the Portuguese police that dealt with serious crimes, such as murder and terrorism. And that Jack's exploits were quite well known among the troops.

Jack felt himself blushing. Being a minor celebrity in the land of his forebears was a humbling experience. He did a mental head shake to clear his thoughts. 'You said you guys also deal with terrorism. Would the fact she's possibly a Moroccan national make you think that's something you could be dealing with here? And the other fact that she's connected with the Ministry of Foreign Affairs?'

Quintal squeezed her lips into a fat circle. 'Who knows? To me it looks like a targeted execution. Yes, the passengers were scared, how do you say, shitless?'

Jack grinned. 'Or the more polite version – witless.'

'Ah yes.' She laughed uneasily. 'Forgive me. As I was saying, the killer injured no other people on the tram. A terrorist would be looking to create maximum chaos and damage. On the other hand, unless this was some random act of violence, the link with the Ministry could be key.'

De Silva made a pensive frown that accentuated the wrinkles on his high forehead. 'I agree. Who knows what a deep dive into Ms Farooq will turn up?'

Mendes hopped back on board to announce the arrival of the forensics team and to report that six witnesses had returned and were prepared to give statements about what they had seen. The fact the uniformed cop went to the trouble of addressing the detectives in English told Jack they were keen to have his input. Flattering from a professional point of view, but he wouldn't want the case to suck up too much of his time. He was on a mission to bring his daughter home, after all, not get drawn into a web of international intrigue. It was now after 7:00pm. 'I'll come with you out of professional curiosity, but I'm not staying more than a couple of hours. That suit you?'

Da Silva sighed, almost with relief. 'Perfect. Someone will drop you back to your accommodation once we're done.'

'I'll be keen to have a look at the CCTV from inside the tram,' said Jack. He popped a stick of mint chewing gum in his mouth and started mashing. 'I'm assuming you've got a coffee machine back at the station?'

'I can delight and disappoint you all at the same time,' said Quintal. 'We have plenty of coffee, but with the exception of the underground Metro system, much of the public transport in Lisbon isn't equipped with security cameras.'

'Let's hope one of the passengers close to the shooter had their camera running at the time, or filmed the geezer as he was fleeing the scene.'

Da Silva ran a hand over his moustache. 'I hope so too. Otherwise we've got a big job ahead of us.'

## Chapter Five

THE CRIMINAL INVESTIGATION police's headquarters at 174 Rua Gomes Freire rose into the night sky in geometric splendour. Spread out over nearly 100,000 square metres and reaching eleven storeys in one section, the HQ was located in a busy neighbourhood of Lisbon. Da Silva explained on the short ride over that the modern architectural masterpiece, inaugurated in 2014, had instilled a new feeling of pride in the force. Jack caught his breath when they entered the huge atrium, which would be flooded with sunshine during daylight hours. It made his own station in sleepy Yorkville look like a doll's house by comparison.

Detective Quintal had been right about the coffee. Perhaps a touch too bitter for his taste, but he wasn't going to complain about it. The local cops were treating him like royalty.

Unfortunately, she was also right about the CCTV. Inquiries to the transportation authority confirmed the tram in question had no cameras, including tiny concealed ones the police may have missed. With security camera footage often the key to catching the bad guys fast, not having it meant solving this crime would require all the smarts the Polícia Judiciária could bring to the table.

Jack finished giving his formal statement, thought about souveniring the police pen before placing it on the desk. He stood, tucked in a flap of his shirt that had popped out, plucked his jacket from the spine of the chair and donned it like a matador. He turned to Da Silva. 'All done. Now, about that lift home?'

'Just one more hour of your time please, Detective Lisbon.' Da Silva steepled his fingers and looked over the top of his glasses. 'An extra set of eyes on what we've gathered so far could prove useful. You may also look at things more objectively, not having your mind clouded by preconceived notions of our city as a local would.'

Jack frowned. 'So you're not just a cop, you're a part-time psychologist 'n all?'

Da Silva bowed his head, missing the sarcasm. 'Very observant. I do have a major in psychology from Coimbra University as it happens. Is it the way I ask questions?'

'No,' said Jack, slightly irritated. 'It's 'cos you talk like a bleedin' egghead academic trying too hard to impress.'

'Not sure I appreciate the tone, Detective Lisbon.' Da Silva spun a pen around on the table. A spark flickered deep in the man's eyes; it told Jack this fellow had a long fuse, but he could go off like a firecracker if pushed too far. His hands were rough and gnarly for an officer who probably rode his desk most of the day, the shoulders broader than an average white collar worker's, too. Jack intuited there was a lot more to Da Silva than appeared on the surface.

Jack sighed. 'No, I'm sorry. My fault. I'm tired and… well…it's been an ordeal, even for a jaded cop like me who's seen it all. Or thinks he's seen it all. And enough of this

Detective Lisbon nonsense. It's confusing enough as it is with me and the town having the same name. Just call me Jack.'

Da Silva's eyes brightened. 'Is that the laidback Australian coming out in you?'

'Maybe it is. I used to be an uptight Brit. No longer!'

'And you can call me Zé. Short for José.'

The men shook hands on the deal. 'Don't expect all the police here to be on board with such informality. The top brass, I mean. They tend to like their little titles and ranks.'

'Got it.' Jack paused for a moment, then said: 'But seriously, I've got a distressed kid waiting for me to give her a cuddle and some words of reassurance, plus a bleedin' long drive to the Algarve tomorrow. So no more than an hour, OK? I feel guilty enough as it is.'

'Agreed. Let's go over what our junior detectives have come up with short notice.'

Da Silva picked up his phone, gave a calm directive in Portuguese. Moments later a young woman wheeled in a trolley. From the top she lifted a thick manila folder and passed it to her boss and exited the room. He licked an index finger, began to flick through the pages, selecting a number of sheets and setting them aside to form a second, separate pile.

'What are you doing?' said Jack, sipping a fresh coffee an officer had brought earlier.

'Finding pages in English for you to read. As you would expect, the vast majority of the information is in Portuguese, but there is plenty in English too.'

'Not to be rude, but I ain't got time for reading. I said I've only got an hour to spare you. Perhaps if there's a summary you could, y'know, summarise?'

Da Silva put down his reading glasses, gave them a

polish on a handkerchief and put them on again. 'OK, but I would be grateful if you could read the material later, if you get the chance. Maybe while you're sunning yourself on the beach in the Algarve? Unless we crack the case quickly that is. It seems our victim was a writer of sorts. A journalist in fact. She's a…how do you say…stringer for a couple of magazines. Her articles have been published in English, as well as French, Arabic and Portuguese and–'

'Wait. Did she speak all of these languages?'

'Some could be translations, I suppose. But I'd hazard a guess and say yes, she was a polyglot. Why do you sound so surprised?'

Jack shrugged. 'I guess because I don't need to be a linguist where I come from to catch villains. English is more than enough for me to deal with.'

A triple-tap knock came on the door.

'Come in, Raquel,' Da Silva beckoned with a crooked finger.

Detective Quintal pulled up a chair next to Jack, placed a folder on the desk and got down to brass tacks with the initial findings of the forensic team. It didn't take Sherlock Holmes to figure out the victim died instantly from the bullet to the head, although the one in the back may have been enough to kill the victim on its own had the second shot not been fired. The slug retrieved from the perspex window was from a pistol that took 9mm Luger cartridges, which meant a wide open field in terms of the weapon used. Jack knew that a vast array of guns could fire this ammo – Glock, Sig Sauer, H&K to name a few.

'Has the body been moved from the scene?' said Jack.

'Yes. The forensics officers had to work quickly to get things moving again. The tram has been driven back to the depot at Alcântara, where we can examine it in relative peace without commuters getting in the way.' Da Silva gave a thin smile. 'The driver returned to the scene after running away. He was shaking like a leaf, but he insisted he be the one to take the tram to the depot. He was unable to describe the shooter at all.'

Jack rubbed his chin; he hadn't thought of the logistics of a mobile crime scene like this. It was a unique circumstance and a challenging one for the police. For some reason he half expected the tram to sit where it had stopped until the crime had been either solved or put into the too-hard basket. But that was nonsense – the world had to keep moving along.

Quintal took a sip of coffee. 'The body's at the mortuary. We are sure the bullet still inside the victim's body will be of the same type as the one retrieved from the window. But as usual, we must never assume anything.'

'Indeed,' said Da Silva. 'Does she have relatives in Lisbon?'

'Her mother lives across the river in Setúbal. Her name is,' Quintal consulted her notes, 'Suzana Farooq. The parents are divorced, the father is a Moroccan national and lives in Casablanca. As you suggested, she is a dual citizen.'

'Good work, Raquel. When we're done here, please take Detective Horta with you to inform the mother of the sad news.'

'Shall I take her to the mortuary to ID the body?'

'How does her face look after the coroner patched up the skull?' Da Silva screwed up one eye as he posed the question.

Jack knew exactly where Da Silva was going with this. A badly disfigured face can be horrific for a relative to identify.

'Not too bad.' Quintal tilted her head slightly.

'Fine. But don't offer to take the mother; only if she

asks. We can identify the victim officially by other means if we have to.'

Quintal nodded then proceeded with the rest of the primary findings. 'Spent casings found within 100 metres of the murder scene were of the same type found in the tram. A quick sweep of the immediate area around the body itself revealed a lot of hair, skin flakes and latent fingerprints, as one would expect on a tramcar travelled by hundreds if not thousands of people every day.' She looked up from the report. 'Unless there are matches between the huge number of samples taken at the scene and criminals logged in the system, the physical evidence may prove to be a waste of time and resources.'

'So, seems we're not going to solve this forensically,' said Jack, rubbing his hands together. 'My favourite kind of case.'

'It's "we" now, is it?' said Da Silva.

'Figuratively speaking,' Jack chuckled. 'But in reality it's "you", because I have other plans. Think of it like one of those legal documents, where the singular refers to the plural, one gender refers to all, and so on and so forth.'

The two detectives stared at Jack, barely comprehending his ramble, but they nodded just the same.

'Now,' Jack continued. 'Getting back to the file, what's in there that might give us some leads?'

Da Silva scratched his head. 'There's a lot here to digest. I'm going to get our top researchers in to, as you said, summarise what they found.'

'When?'

'Now.' Da Silva pressed a button on his phone and buzzed in junior detectives Bernardo Horta and Catarina Rebelo. 'These two are excellent officers, with a keen eye for detail,' he said a moment before the pair knocked and entered.

Jack pegged them as being in their late twenties to early thirties. Immaculately dressed and square shouldered, they exuded the supreme confidence of fresh cops yet to be jaded by the job. *Give them ten more years,* he mused. Horta and Rebelo stood at ease while the others remained seated. Da Silva waved a hand and Horta, 'Please, Bernardo. And no waffling, Detective Lisbon can't stay long.'

'Waffling?'

Da Silva translated the obscure word into Portuguese and the officer laughed.

'Of course. Definitely no waffling.' Horta smiled at everyone in turn before beginning. 'We've run the victim's name through all our databases and come up with the following basic stuff.' He counted on his fingers as he went. 'The victim is twenty-five years old, born in Lisbon. Mother living in Portugal, father in Morocco. No siblings. She's got no criminal record – clean as a whistle. Not even a parking ticket. She was in her final year of studying for a master's degree in international relations at the Universidade Nova de Lisboa. She had received top clearance to work as an intern at the Ministry of Foreign Affairs by the Serviço de Informações de Segurança.' He looked at Jack, hands spread and palms out. 'That's the Security Information Service, also known as SIS. I guess the equivalent of MI5. She worked as a freelance journalist for a couple of esoteric magazines that deal with international relations.' He took a deep breath. 'And that's about it, without waffles.'

Jack burst out laughing, gave a clap. 'Bravo, sir.'

Da Silva then beckoned for Rebelo to debrief. Perhaps conscious of the lack of time, she gave a rapid-fire report on the victim's social media presence. 'Salma Farooq was a very busy girl.' She coughed into her fist, rather daintily, Jack thought, before continuing. 'Not only did she study, work as an intern at the Ministry of Foreign Affairs *and* write articles for a number of publications, she managed to find the time to post frequently on Instagram and Facebook, and she often got into polemical arguments with people on Twitter. Her content was sometimes related to articles she'd written about international relations. Using a program developed by our techs here in Lisbon, we've been able to quickly home in on accounts with whom she had the most interactions.'

'Interesting,' Jack observed flatly, more out of politeness than anything. The extra hour he'd offered only had fifteen minutes left before it was time to skedaddle. Social media was more his partner Claudia Taylor's thing.

'Indeed it is,' said Rebelo. She handed around a printout with a number of names on it, a number next to each name, and information from the account profiles. 'These are the people she interacted most with over the last year.'

Detective Horta took up the reins. 'At the top of the list is her mother, Suzana. Liking each other's posts, communicating via the Messenger app several times a day. The woman is going to be devastated when she finds out what's happened.'

'That's an understatement,' said Da Silva. 'Have we cracked the phone yet?'

'We can't seem to get into it. I guess it's a job for tomorrow when Mario's on shift.'

Da Silva stood suddenly. 'Call him and get him in here immediately. I don't care where he is or what he's doing.'

'Sir,' said Horta meekly.

Da Silva resumed his seat. 'Social media is all well and

good, but experience shows us phone calls, texts and emails are just as likely to point us in the right direction. After we've unlocked her phone, located any other devices and got inside them, we can spread the net a lot wider.'

Jack nodded, knowing the man was bang on the money.

'First thing in the morning I'll be seeking a warrant to get the records of every person in her contacts lists.' His voice rose to a crescendo. 'Crimes like this don't happen often in Lisbon, and I don't like it when they do. I want this case solved FAST!'

A brief silence ensued before Rebelo ventured to speak. 'If I may continue with what we do have, sir?'

'Of course.'

'These are the other four people she had the vast majority of contact with online.' She cleared her throat. 'A person called Rafael Xenos, also known as "The Porcupine" on Twitter, who we suspect is a troll, a keyboard warrior if you will. Salma's posts were constantly under attack from this guy. Then there's Marina Ventura, her editor from the magazine *Euro Politics Today* – one article seems to be in the pipeline. Best friend Fernanda Brito – works as a bank teller and has known the victim since childhood. Finally, dissertation mentor at the university, a Professor João Grosso.'

'Good work, Detective Rebelo,' said Da Silva. 'We'll be talking to all of them.'

'Not sure about "The Porcupine."'

'Why?'

'He lives in Canada. My honest opinion, he shouldn't be considered a serious suspect.'

'Still, I want to look into him.' Da Silva scribbled something on a notepad. 'She may have pissed him off enough for him to organise a hit. Some people are quick to take offence these days.'

'Sir.' Rebelo nodded respectfully.

Jack sat forward in his seat. 'What about her address? Has anyone been to her home to check it over?'

'I plan to head there immediately after this meeting is over,' said Da Silva. 'Detective Rebelo, you are coming with me.'

'I thought I was going with Bernardo to inform the mother?'

'I've changed my mind. Bernardo can take someone else.'

'Who sir? said Horta. 'There's only Joana Costa in our section this evening and she was about to head home.'

'Too bad for her. Ready, Detective Rebelo?'

'Yes, sir.' She smiled broadly, clearly thrilled to be asked along for the ride.

'What about door knocking?' said Jack.

Da Silva rubbed the side of his nose. 'I've already sent a request for a couple of officers to be released from current duties to doorknock the apartment building. And, right now, we have detectives and uniformed officers randomly questioning people in the Belém area where the murder happened. As you say in English, it's a needle in a haystack, but you never know.'

'Very true.' Jack reflexively checked his watch again. A five-minute overrun on the agreed period. Not a hanging offence, but not getting home to Skye ASAP could be.

Da Silva must have sensed his guest's restlessness. 'OK, Detective Lisbon. Thanks for listening.'

Handshakes all round.

'I'm glad for the experience of...ah...experiencing...' Jack winced at his own verbal clumsiness. *These foreigners speak better English than I do, dammit...* 'another country's policing methods. Not sure I'll be of any use going forward. You lot seem more than capable.'

The local cops thanked Jack profusely for giving of his time.

'I might be able to claim it as a tax expense at the end of the financial year, so there's that,' Jack grinned.

'Mind if I grab your phone number, Jack?' said Da Silva.

The business card was already hovering within the man's reach. 'Call me any time for a consultation. I've got an Australian SIM in my mobile. Which means you'll be paying for an international call if you decide you want a chat.'

'The organisation will pay for any phone calls.'

'Yeah.' Jack scratched his head. 'Of course. Can't say I'll be able to front physically for any more chinwags, though.'

'Let's hope it won't be necessary.' Da Silva touched Jack gently on the elbow and steered him out of the office.'

'Necessary? I'm meant to be on holidays here, innit. You ain't thinking of subpoenaing me as a witness, are you?'

Da Silva winked. 'Heaven forbid.'

## Chapter Six

'IS this definitely the right address, Catarina?' said Da Silva, his eyes searching for a place to park in the broad, tree-lined avenue.

'Don't you trust the GPS, sir?'

'Not with my life, no. Did you hear the story of the American tourists visiting Cascais? They drove off the end of a pier because the satellite navigation told them to keep on going, even though they could see the folly of obeying the instruction?'

'Really?'

'Absolutely.' He wasn't sure if it was true or an apocryphal urban legend. He'd heard the story from a pal at the tennis club, but it sounded plausible. The device in his own modest Corolla had sent him on circuitous routes plenty of times, so perhaps there was a grain of truth to the tale.

'I think that might say more about the IQ of those tourists than the qualities of the technology.' Rebelo checked the details on her mobile screen. 'Anyway, this is definitely the right building.'

Da Silva found an empty parking space twenty metres from the big ugly pink block of flats in Avenida Dr. Alfredo Bensaúde.

'A bit on the austere side, don't you think?' said Rebelo, pointing at the edifice as she rounded the front of the vehicle. 'I would have thought she'd be able to afford something better than this. She's writing articles for popular magazines, yeah?'

'Freelance writers aren't exactly rolling in money, you know. The pay rates for their articles are lousy.'

'But *Euro Politics Today* is a pretty big magazine. They'd be able to pay decent rates.'

'No more than they can get away with legally, would be my bet. Especially when it comes to young stringers. Whatever money Farooq made would've gone towards accommodation and tuition fees, with not a lot left over for luxuries. Don't forget she was a student. They're too caught up in causes and whatnot to worry about material things. They don't mind a bit of squalor.'

'Maybe back in your day, sir. Not sure about the current soft generation.'

Da Silva grunted; she had a valid point but he was loathe to debate it.

They waited for a couple of cars to pass before trotting across the street. The first hurdle: the building could only be accessed by punching in a password on a wall-mounted console. Either that or by forcibly breaking in. They waited ten minutes on a bench near the entrance a couple of metres away – he chewing his lip, she scrolling her phone – before they saw a young man alight from a bus fifty metres up the road.

'If that fellow doesn't enter this building, I'm going to

bust our way inside,' said Da Silva. 'I'm sure there's a crowbar in the boot of the car.'

'Isn't that a bit drastic?'

Another grunt was his only reply.

Luck was on their side. The man shuffled up to the solid glass door, shoulders sagging under the weight of overloaded shopping bags. The detectives followed close behind. Da Silva tapped him on the shoulder.

'What the hell!' the man shouted as he spun around to confront the threat. 'Get away from me or I'll scream.'

'Sorry,' said the head detective gruffly as he flashed his ID. 'We need to enter the building on urgent police business. We need you to let us in.'

Once the man got his rapid breathing under control, shaking fingers tapped a 4-digit code and the three entered together. Da Silva made a mental note of the passcode. On the ride up the slow elevator to the sixth floor Rebelo casually enquired if the man had been a resident for long and if he knew a woman called Salma Farooq. The answers were, respectively, one year and no. The man asked if the cops could please explain why they were here. The blunt answer Rebelo gave nearly made him drop his shopping.

'Oh my God! Yes, I heard about that shooting. It's all over Facebook.' His face grew pale. 'Are you saying someone in my apartment block is the murder victim?'

'Yes, I'm sorry to inform you that Ms Farooq was registered as residing here,' said Rebelo. 'Are you sure you don't know her?' She pulled up a high-resolution photo on her mobile, turned it towards the man.

He nodded slowly. 'Ah, yes, that nice lady. What a shame! I have seen her about. In the courtyard. Smoking one cigarette after the other, on the phone a lot, chatting away.' He shook his head as his gaze flicked from one cop to the other.

'You think that chain smoking indicated nervousness?' said Da Silva.

'No. Often she was laughing as she talked on her mobile.' He paused, seemed about to cry. 'She seemed like a lovely person. I never spoke to her apart from exchanging pleasantries in passing. You know how it is these days, people are too wary of each other.'

'Have you seen any suspicious-looking characters hanging around the apartment block lately?' said Rebelo.

The man placed a forefinger to thin, bloodless lips. 'Not that I can think of off the top of my head.'

Da Silva handed him a business card and told him to call if he suddenly remembered anything he thought could be important.

The man exited the lift at the fifth floor, almost tripping over his feet in his haste to get away from the police. Da Silva wondered if there might be something dodgy in the man's shopping bags, immediately dismissed the idea of following it up. A bit of weed or some recreational drugs wasn't worth the bother with a full-blown murder enquiry on his shoulders.

At the sixth floor, the cops emerged from the lift into a gloomy corridor, cobwebs here and there where the wall joined the ceiling. Farooq's apartment lay diagonally opposite the elevator shaft. A quick count: five apartments on this floor. Eight storeys – forty apartments in the entire building. Easy enough to canvas them quickly once more officers arrived.

Da Silva peered at the lock before pulling out his trusty B&E tools. He picked the lock of Salma's apartment door within five seconds, pushed it open with the palm of his hand. Both he and Rebelo donned disposable gloves and booties at the threshold before going inside.

Rebelo located the main light switch with fumbling fingers and flicked it on. The small reception room, an open-plan kitchen-diner, was sparsely furnished with a round table and four chairs, a two-seater settee and a coffee table. By a window stood a desk with three drawers to the right of a gamer-style office chair; upon the desk sat a blinking Wi-Fi modem, a closed laptop, a printer and a multi-layer file tray holding various loose papers.

No sooner had their eyes taken in the surroundings than an unholy stench assaulted both cops' nasal passages. They instinctively covered their mouths and noses with their hands. 'What the hell is that?' said Da Silva through his fingers. 'A corpse from the depths of hell?'

'It smells like a cat's litter box. One that hasn't been emptied for a while. My sister has two cats and…oh Jesus…'

'I think I'm going to puke.' Da Silva doubled over, clutching his stomach.

'One second, sir.' Rebelo said through the hand cupped over her face. She power-walked through the small reception room to a small square window and flung it open. The evening air was totally still and the open window made no immediate impression on the stench. She shrugged as she looked back at Da Silva, removing her hand for a second. 'Not a puff of air. I'm not sure this is going to work.'

Da Silva, grumbling, propped open the front door with a broom he found in the adjacent utility closet. 'We need a cross breeze.' He made a gagging sound. 'Try the bathroom for air freshener,' he blurted. 'I'm going to be violently sick if we can't do something about this.'

She fetched an aerosol can. 'All I could find was deodorant.'

'I don't care if it's bloody insect repellent. Just spray!'

As Rebelo let loose and the chemically recreated odour of a pine forest battled with the dominant pong of cat faeces, she looked down to see a ginger feline rubbing against her legs.

'I hope that thing's apologising for nearly killing us,' said Da Silva. 'I'm tempted to toss it out the window.'

Rebelo stopped after a minute of solid spraying, placed the can on the kitchen bench. The befouled air finally started to be sucked out the window and into the warm Lisbon night, and the atmosphere in the apartment became slightly fresher.

'Seems like you've made a friend out of that beast.' Da Silva, a more humane tone in his voice post fumigation, nodded at the cat. It started to mewl, then switched to a prolonged purr. 'Do you think it's hungry?'

'Probably.' Rebelo opened two overhead cupboard doors before she found an open box of kibble. She poured a large portion into an empty double bowl, added a cupful of water to the second section. The cat started munching like it hadn't eaten for days.

'What shall we do with it?' Rebelo shook her head.

'I'll arrange for the animal to be taken to a shelter once we're done investigating here.' He checked in the small bedroom and found a cat crate in a corner. He brought it out and placed it by the front door.

Rebelo put the food bowl inside, ginger followed and the cage door closed behind. Then she located the foul litter tray, oddly situated next to the humming refrigerator. She grabbed the tray with the tips of her fingers and held it at arms' length. She disappeared into the lift, giving Da Silva the chance to snoop around. Four minutes later, his phone chirped.

'You lost already?' he said, placing his haul of documents on the desk. 'Try GPS.'

'Ah...I can't get back in the front door.'

He chuckled. 'Then it's a good thing I remembered the passcode. 3-7-9-2.'

When she returned with a sheepish grin plastered all over her face, Da Silva said in a deadpan voice: 'Did you inspect that tray for clues before you got rid of the contents?'

Hands on hips she replied: 'Are you joking?'

He furrowed his brows. 'Not at all. It could have contained valuable—'

She pulled out her mobile.

'Who are you calling?' said Da Silva, already seated at the kitchen table ready to dive back into the papers he'd collected.

'Forensics. In case you were right about the litter box and there's some vital clues in the...poop.'

'I *was* joking, Detective.'

'Oh.' Blushing, she said, 'But maybe you were right, you know, inadvertently, and there is something in it?'

'Yes, there was. Plenty. And believe me, the best place for it is the dumpster.' He beckoned her to the desk. 'I've found some correspondence crammed into the drawers and the in-tray. They're from a number of businesses and institutions, including the university she attended, the Ministry of Foreign Affairs, and two from this company called Entrega Rápida. You heard of them?'

Rebelo shook her head. 'No.' She shuffled through the pile of papers. 'It's unusual to have so much mail, isn't it? Just about everything is done online. Paying bills, buying stuff. I know I hardly get anything in the post. Once a year I might receive a postcard from my brother in Berlin, if I'm lucky.'

'A very good point, Catarina. The sheer volume of it tells me we need to check it out thoroughly.'

The pair spent the next fifteen minutes scanning the letters. First up for discussion, a letter from the Ministry of Foreign Affairs, dated six months ago, confirming that Salma Farooq had been accepted into its curricular internship program.

'It says here that her role was to assist with research in a specialised trade section that deals with Northern African nations, in particular Morocco,' said Da Silva.

'Interesting,' enthused Rebelo. 'Investigating a country she's a citizen of.'

'Kind of makes sense.' Da Silva nodded slowly. 'What also makes sense is this – her work at the ministry would have counted as credits towards the master's degree she was undertaking at the Universidade Nova de Lisboa.'

'A shame she won't get to receive that degree.' Rebelo shook her head slowly.

'Indeed,' said Da Silva. 'What have you found?'

'A couple of letters from the University. One's a boring one. Confirmation of her enrolment for the semester.' She held up a sheet of paper. 'This one is a lot more interesting. It's from her teacher, the Professor João Grosso we identified already as being in frequent contact with the victim; this is him responding to her request for an extension on her thesis deadline. The request was granted. The professor writes that he understands the internship is important and he's pushed the submission date out by another month.'

Rebelo glanced at Da Silva. 'Perhaps the research she

was doing had something to do with her death, led her in a dangerous direction?'

Da Silva nodded. 'Perhaps.'

'What about the Entrega Rápida letters?'

'Don't know, I haven't had a chance to look at them yet. There's a couple here, so…'

The sound of a phone ringing put a stop to the conversation. 'Where's that coming from?' Da Silva's eyes darted about, one eye squinting as he concentrated to locate the source of the sound.

'I think it's coming from the bedroom.' Seconds later, Rebelo returned holding up an off-white cordless handset. 'Found it under the blankets. Should I answer the call?'

Da Silva dropped a sheet of paper bearing the letterhead of *Euro Politics Today*. 'Give it to me, I'll take it.'

With the device extended in Rebelo's grasp, the phone stopped ringing.

'Did you see the…what do you call it… dock for the handset in the bedroom?' Da Silva's eyes scanned the kitchen-diner. 'I think it was on her bedside table.'

A nod of confirmation. The two inspected the base station. A light blinked. Someone had left a message, either from the call just missed or before that. Da Silva pressed a button, a woman's voice growled a couple of threatening sentences that could only be interpreted as a grim warning. The two cops exchanged looks of excited anticipation. There were three more messages. One from a telemarketer selling mobile phone plans, one from her mother just calling to say hello, and another that was ten seconds of silence before the caller hung up. Although the information could be confirmed via a phone log from the provider, to get things moving faster Da Silva made a note of all the numbers the calls came from and the times they were placed. He double underlined the first one with the warning.

'We find out who that angry woman is, and we've got our first prime suspect,' said Rebelo with a grin. 'Looks like we won't be needing that English cop to solve our case after all.'

'He's technically an Australian, but you may be right. Hopefully, he'll be able to enjoy the rest of his holiday in peace.'

Rebelo confided her disappointment that Jack Lisbon had even been granted access to their inner sanctum, let alone asked to assist the investigation. Da Silva could see her reaction for what it was – professional jealousy.

'That first message is potential dynamite,' said Da Silva. 'But don't jump to conclusions. Until we've questioned her and checked every piece of evidence, all we have is a motive. Albeit a strong one.'

The detectives perused two letters from Entrega Rápida: one confirming the company was planning to conclude a deal with a Moroccan textile company at the end of next month, the second declining Farooq's request to interview CEO Gorge Alvarenga. 'This definitely needs following up tomorrow.' Da Silva tapped the letter. 'One more thing before we wrap it up.' He checked his phone. The extra officers were minutes away. He flipped open the laptop that occupied a corner of the desk. 'Let's just see if, by some miracle, there's no password required to access her computer.' He let out a sigh. 'And of course there *is* a password!'

'Did you seriously expect otherwise? Our tech team will get in there no problem.'

'Yes, but I was keen to–'

A pounding on the door stopped the conversation in its tracks.

'I'm here to secure the apartment,' said Luca Mendes. 'I've got three other officers cruising the elevator making enquiries of the neighbours.'

'Excellent,' said Da Silva. 'Once they're done with that, get them in here to help bag up the items I would like taken back to the evidence room. There are quite a few.' He handed Mendes a list. 'And when you're done with that, I'd like one of them to drop off a special package at my place.'

'What's that, sir?'

'A present for my wife. A smelly ginger cat in a cage.'

## Chapter Seven

JACK JIGGLED Skye by the shoulder. She'd completed two bouts of sleepwalking in the night, twice stumbling into her father's adjacent room before he marched her back to her own bed. She was mumbling things about her mum but it was too incoherent to make out. She might need sessions of therapy once they got back to Australia: not only to work through the grief of losing a parent, but to help adjust to a new life in a strange land. Somehow, though, Jack knew the kid would take it all in her stride. 'Wake up, sunshine. Time to get on the road.'

'What? Where am I?'

'You're in Portugal, remember?'

'Hmmm?' Still half asleep.

'Do you remember what happened last night?'

'Something on the tram when we were coming home… a person was shot.' Awake now, her reply was calm and emotionless. Was that a good or a bad thing? Should this entire trip be called off? He'd book a flight to Brisbane right now if Skye showed signs of cracking.

'Did you see that person?'

'No, Daddy. But I know something bad happened. Something really bad. They died, didn't they?'

He sucked in a deep breath. He'd promised himself to always be straight up with her. 'I'm afraid so, sweetheart. I spoke with the police after the incident, did what I could to assist.'

She smiled weakly. 'Of course. They'll probably need you to solve it.'

He let her remark slide. The kid's wellbeing trumped the needs of the local cops. 'Now, are you going to be all right, sunshine? It's OK if you need to talk to a professional about what you saw.'

'Do you mean a shrink?'

He nodded slowly. 'A psychologist, yes.'

'Come off it, Daddy. I didn't really see anything.' She swung her legs out from under the blankets and sat up. 'Besides, don't you remember I was abducted, held captive in the Orkney Islands until you came and got me?'

'It's not something I'm likely to forget.'

'Me either. But I don't have nightmares about it or anything. Mum took me to a woman in Croydon to talk through it all, but somehow it hasn't really affected me like everyone thought it would.' She beamed. 'I guess that's 'cos I know I've got you looking out for me all the time.'

Her hero-worshipping was endearing, but he wasn't superman and there would be times ahead when he wouldn't be able to rescue her. He trusted her to be telling the truth, though. If she said these traumatic incidents weren't affecting her, perhaps they weren't. As long as he'd known her, Skye had never told him a lie. Not a serious one, anyway. *Wait till her mid teens, then that will change,* an inner voice warned. 'Are you up for that road trip to the Algarve to meet your uncle Paulo?'

'I though he was your cousin.' She narrowed one eye. 'Which makes him my…second cousin.'

'Bleedin' heck. I can't figure all that interrelational stuff out, but if you say so, I believe it. Now, come on. Brush your teeth, shower, get dressed, and we'll be on our way.'

Ten minutes later Jack greeted his daughter in the kitchen with a sizzling frypan of eggs and tomato, and a frown. 'Bad news, I'm afraid.'

'What is it this time?' Skye clambered onto a stool, elbows on the breakfast bar and cradling her chin in her hands. 'Oh dear,' she said, pointing an accusatory finger. 'Looks like you burnt the toast.'

Jack turned to see a thin trail of grey smoke emanating from the eight-slot toaster. 'Oh, shit.' He raced over to the smouldering machine, turned it off, and two scorched pieces of bread popped out.

'Make that two pieces of bad news. I found this on the fridge door.' He passed his daughter a handwritten note.

Skye read aloud. *'Bom dia! Your cousin Paulo has had to travel to Madrid to attend a business meeting with his partners. He'll be gone for three days. Sorry but it looks like you'll have to postpone your trip to the Algarve.'* Skye looked up. 'Doesn't he have a wife and kids down there? We could still go and wait for Paulo to come back.'

Jack stood over the sink, scraping black charcoal into a swirling stream of water. 'I think that would be a bit rude. Mirabella's teed up the meeting with Paulo, and *he's* my blood relation, not his wife, so…'

'But his children are your blood relations. Mine too.'

Jack's heart melted as the black specks of carbon circled the plughole and disappeared. He thought pairing Skye up with his new dog Daisy would be the panacea to her sadness. But this was an even better opportunity to inject some happiness into her life. She had no siblings, and this meeting with real, flesh-and-blood relatives would surely lift her spirits into the stratosphere after the sorrow of recent times. Having to delay the trip south was annoying, but no, it wasn't the end of the world. He turned, waved a dishcloth about, droplets of water flying. 'It's only a couple of days, love. We can do heaps of fun stuff in Lisbon – geez, it feels odd saying that – until Paulo gets back from his trip.'

'Why don't we fly to Spain, then?'

The kid had a point. It was a short flight across the border. But no. Bad idea. 'We don't know what kind of business he's conducting there. You and I could end up being an unwelcome distraction and put him off his game.'

Skye's shoulders slumped. 'Yeah, I guess…God, I miss mum…' The sobbing started again.

In a flash, Jack was beside his child, a comforting arm around her shoulder. 'Listen, kiddo. Once we're done visiting Portugal, let's hop over to Spain anyway. How does that sound?'

Her eyes brightened through the sheen of tears. Jack marvelled at how small the teardrops were, tiny little beads. As if a doll had produced them. She nodded. 'All right, Dad.' She looked into his eyes. 'Can we go and see FC Barcelona's stadium?'

'I never knew you were into football?'

'I guess there's a lot we don't know about each other.'

'You two OK?' came Mirabella's voice from the bottom of the stairs. She walked into the kitchen with a purposeful stride, stuck her head in the fridge and made noises of frustration. Then some hissed words in Portuguese that could only have been swearing. She closed the fridge door hard enough to make bottles rattle inside. 'I hate it when there's no yoghurt.'

'Wasn't me,' said Skye.

'Oi!' Jack flicked a tea towel over his shoulder. 'Those quick to deny are often guilty.'

'Honest, it wasn't me. I don't even like yoghurt…much.' A touch of panic echoed in Skye's voice until she saw her father's wink.

'No, no!' said Mirabella. 'No one's accusing you of…' She saw the conspiratorial look exchanged between her guests and burst out laughing. 'This British humour, I will never get it.'

Once the joke had finally worn off and the laughter ended, Mirabella organised coffees for herself and Jack, juice for Skye. When they were all seated, the hostess explained what had happened.

'Paulo apologised, but it was something he couldn't get out of. Turned out his architecture firm was competing for a contract in Madrid and only he could explain some of the technical details in the plans. If the job went to a rival firm, he'd lose out on a lot of money, might even have to lay off staff. Something he couldn't bear thinking about.'

Jack scratched his head. 'Maybe I should've just contacted him directly. I feel awful with you as the middleman…'

'Woman,' interjected Skye.

'Woman,' said Jack not missing a beat. 'I know I wanted our first meeting to be in-person and, y'know, special, but it's starting to feel a bit weird.'

Mirabella handed over a business card. 'I've already got one of those,' Jack said, waving the offering away. 'Besides, you're stored in my phone, innit.'

'It's Paulo's card. I think you're right. It does feel a little weird me being the messenger all the time.'

'Yeah,' said Skye. 'It's like in the schoolyard when two kids won't speak directly to each other and a third has to relay every word. I thought grown ups didn't need to do that stuff.'

Jack wrapped an arm around his daughter, pulled her tight. 'They don't, sunshine. I'll give the bloke a call, leave a message if he doesn't pick up.'

Skye licked juice from her top lip. 'I've calmed down now. We'll see Uncle Paulo when the time is right, hey, Dad?'

Jack nodded, noting she was happy to call second-cousin Paulo her uncle. 'Indeed we will. Just a few days to go.'

'Hey,' said Mirabella, looking at Skye with smiling eyes. 'How would you like to go on a girls' day out with me and one of my friends? I'll take you to the coolest shopping districts in town. Then a trip to the Aquarium. Let's give your dad a chance to catch up on some rest.'

'I don't need to—'

'Don't interrupt me please, Jack. Take some time out. I reckon you need it after that…incident last night.'

Jack sipped from the brutally strong coffee Mirabella had prepared. 'If Skye thinks it's a good idea then…'

'Of course it's not a good idea, Daddy.'

'Oh…'

Skye almost leapt off the stool. 'It's a great idea.'

---

HIS SHOULDER MUSCLES ached after swimming twenty laps of Mirabella's 25-metre pool. Despite having some beautiful beaches on his doorstep in Far North Queensland, the predatory crocs made swimming there problematic to say the least. The pool at his own gym was a chlorine-filled nightmare, with crowded lanes and cacophonous noise, constant whistles and echoes. You were either bumping into the person in front of you if they were too slow, or getting hassled by faster swimmers behind you. This morning's peaceful session was a reminder of what a pleasure swimming for exercise could be.

The downside – his deltoids and lats ached and pinched more than they would after a full-on boxing workout. Not having his mate Aden Trevarthen about meant he'd be training solo for the next little while. Unless he could find another workout partner. Perhaps Mirabella herself? Scratch that. Skye would automatically put two and two together and get romance. As he struggled with the settings on the strange space-age coffee machine – a serious advancement on his own modest Delonghi – his mind wandered. What if something developed between him and Mirabella?

No. Bad idea. Even if a connection blossomed, she had her life here, he had his in Australia. A short, hot affair with an attractive woman who looked a lot like Claudia Taylor seemed like fun, but the fallout in terms of Skye's mental health could be catastrophic. And her dad "hooking up" so soon after her mum was buried? It didn't bear thinking about.

After stacking and figuring out how to turn on the dishwasher, Jack flipped up the lid of his laptop on the kitchen bench. First thing – music. He pulled up a playlist of his favourite British punk tunes, kicking off with *The Damned* and "New Rose." With the thrashing guitars for background, he dove into news and gossip from back home. The sports results made for tragic reading. The Cowboys had lost their fourth game in a row and would struggle to make the finals. Perhaps he should abandon rugby league and jump on the FC Barcelona bandwagon with Skye? That lot were pretty good at winning. He clicked to bring up the tab for his favourite Australian news site.

Top story – the murder of a young woman on the Number 15 Tram in Lisbon.

*What the?*

Music off. Full attention required.

Jack's eyes raced through the article. The anonymous reporter provided the main details of the crime, including the rumour that an Australian national was on the scene when police entered the tram. Eyes darting back and forth in search of his own name, his heart skipped several beats. Only natural, when the word "Lisbon" featured over a dozen times in the article. As he reached the end of the story, he was relieved to discover that whoever was responsible for providing the information to the press had seen fit to omit Jack's name.

Who knew how long that would last? Any self-respecting journalist would love to find out who this mysterious Australian was. But if he kept a low profile and no one at the Polícia Judiciária leaked, he wouldn't be disturbed.

Music back on. *Destructors*. "Meaningless Names."

He made another strong coffee, sat down to study a map of the neighbourhood. A leisurely stroll to clear his mind of drama was in order. Another one of those custard tarts would go down a treat. Where was that bakery again?

Just then the ringtone "Down Under" cut through the belting punk song. *Not Skye having a meltdown, please not that.*

Music off.

The call was from an unknown number, a local one with the prefix +351. Curiosity won out. 'Hello?'

'Jack. Good morning, It's Zé Da Silva.'

His hand shot to his head. *What does he want now?* 'Yes?'

'Have you had a chance to look at those documents I gave you last night?'

*There's no beating about the bush with this bloke.*

'To be honest, no. I figure you and your team are more than capable of tracking down the killer without me getting under your feet.'

'You won't be getting under our feet, as you put it. I'd just like your personal views on the material. If you have the time. If not, I will completely understand.'

Jack sighed. The man had rubbed a nerve that connected with Jack's professional pride. *What if I can solve a crime on foreign soil?* 'OK, but I ain't spending too much time on it. My daughter's been traumatised and needs me.'

'Understood. Save this number and call me back if you have any, what do you call them, hunches?'

'Hunches is right, sport. I'm more famous for mine than Quasimodo.'

Silence hung in the air as the joke fell flat.

'Just to let you know. We've already identified one person as a potential suspect.' Da Silva described what he and Rebelo had discovered at the victim's apartment, in particular the warning left on the answering machine.

'She sounds like one disgruntled woman. I'd be putting a big red circle around her name.'

'Our thoughts exactly. We traced the number first thing this morning. Raquel Quintal is about to drop by her address unexpectedly.'

'On her own?'

'Don't underestimate Raquel. She's a force of nature and can handle herself in dangerous situations. A black belt in karate comes in handy for lady cops.'

Jack quietly agreed. He'd be pushing DC Taylor to undertake some martial arts training when he got home. Violent crime was on the rise and he wanted her better prepared. Which was a nice mental segue into his next observation. 'I saw the murder has made the Australian news. I'm guessing it's all over the local media?'

'Correct. Wall-to-wall coverage on TV, radio, Internet. We issued a statement very early this morning and the phones have been running hot ever since.' A pause. 'Unfortunately, no tips from the public, just requests for more information from the media.'

The two detectives bade each other farewell, Jack trudged upstairs, brought the file of documents downstairs and sat cross-legged on the couch. Full attention for a spot of light reading.

Music on. Chopin. Nocturne op.9 No.2.

## Chapter Eight

PINS AND NEEDLES fizzed in his feet. Sitting like Buddha doing yoga on the couch wasn't going to cut it. Only the discipline of a straight spine behind a solid desk would do. Jack found Mirabella's home office on the ground floor and decided to do his digging in there.

Before attacking Da Silva's documents, he couldn't resist a quick browse through his work emails – which he'd promised himself he wasn't going to do while abroad. *Married to the job, Lisbon?*

The first email was a thank you from Inspector Joe Batista to all staff. The last case Jack had worked on concluded yesterday in the Yorkville Magistrates Court with a big win for the local CIB. The accused, Mitchell Morris, who slaughtered a man on a golf course by means of an armoured drone, was sentenced to life in Copperhead Prison with no parole. The perpetrator had threatened to withdraw his confession, but in the end saw the folly of such a move and relented. Jack gave a small fist pump.

A third coffee was required before re-addressing Da

Silva's pile of papers. It was only a couple of centimetres thick. He could polish off a Stephen King novel in no time, so this presented but a minor challenge. Two glugs of espresso inside him and he started reading.

First up, a rundown on the victim's recent articles. Dry-as-chaff material about international relations, not much in addition to what Da Silva spoke about last night. Three hours in and he flipped over the last page. Nothing in these printouts gave Jack time to pause and wonder. It was simply a shopping list of her family situation, education and work history. Boring.

He stood, stretched, made a cup of herbal tea on account of caffein overload.

Perhaps if he read an article or two written by the victim herself, got a feel for the meat and potatoes of the subject matter, he might intuit a lead or two.

A quick Internet search found ten articles written by Salma Farooq in the last year and a half. All translated into English, or perhaps composed in English. Who knew? Some had been written in conjunction with other people, but most were posted under her own byline. Not bad for someone of her youth and, one would expect, inexperience of the world. But then again, maybe Jack was being a touch paternalistic in his thinking.

For no good reason, he decided to work backwards chronologically. The most recent article, a solo effort published in *Euro Politics Today*, was dedicated to trade relations between Northern African and European nations in general, Morocco and Portugal in particular. No huge surprise there, given her heritage and allegiance to both countries. Deep into the article Jack caught his breath. Farooq asked a couple of tantalizing questions without offering answers. *What are the dangers of jumping into bed with companies when we don't know their entire history – or if we are aware of that history but choose to ignore it? For among the big players in our region, there are those with dark and shameful, some might say sinister, histories. Should these companies be precluded from trading today, given what they have done in years gone by?*

Jack glanced out of the long double-glazed window across from Mirabella's desk. Outside, a garden resplendent with orchids, birds of paradise, sago palms. A tranquil environment that belied last night's brutal assassination. He thought of the numerous companies he had heard of with dodgy pasts, to say the least. Ties to dictatorial regimes, the imposition of inhumane working conditions, yet they still conducted their business today as if nothing happened. He turned his attention back to Farooq's piece.

*In a follow-up article, this magazine plans to expose a very prominent Portuguese company that has profited from horrific practices, in particular human rights abuses across North Africa. What's worse, it is still turning a blind eye to these practices today. The company in question has done a wonderful job keeping their dark past a secret. Until now.*

Jack turned off his laptop, grabbed his phone and headed out onto the terrace by the swimming pool.

He reclined in a banana lounge and dialled Da Silva's number.

'Yes, Jack?'

'You need to speak with the editor of *Euro Politics Today*.'

'Because?'

Jack described the article he'd read. 'And I haven't even begun to dig.'

'We're on top of that article already. And I think you're right. The editor needs to be a priority.' Da Silva mentioned the letters from the Entrega Rápida company in Farooq's apartment.

'Why do you think the CEO declined to be interviewed by Farooq?' said Jack. He sipped his chamomile tea before adding: 'You think this Alvarenga character might be heading up the very company Farooq was set to expose?'

'Without seeing the follow-up article, it's impossible to say. Perhaps it's on her laptop?'

'You have it, I assume?'

'Yes, I found it in her apartment last night. It's in our evidence room, along with her phone, original copies of letters and a bunch of other stuff.' Da Silva paused. Jack heard the sound of a match sparking, the inhalation and exhalation of cigarette smoke. 'Our IT guys will crack it open later today, I imagine.'

'If the article's not on her computer, there could be emails between her and the editor that contain clues or draft versions. Or stored "in the cloud" as they say these days.'

'We'll get a warrant to gain access to the magazine's electronic correspondence if the editor refuses to play ball.'

'Have you looked into this editor?' said Jack.

'She's a woman by the name of Marina Ventura. She's a veteran, been at the helm of the magazine for ten years. But there's one problem.'

'What's that?'

'Farooq was a freelancer, not a permanent employee of the company. Which means…'

'Which means Ventura might not have a lot of the details a normal employer would have,' said Jack. 'Plus their relationship would have been more arms-length than in a fulltime job situation.'

'Exactly. Still, they may have had a close working relationship. We've had a quick look into the woman and it seems she is rather...how do you say...intransigent. Interviewing her isn't going to be easy.'

Jack was sensing a major hint. 'You want me to assist you, is that what you're driving at?'

'Ah! It was a hope of mine, but since you and your daughter are heading to the Algarve. Oh... you have probably already arrived there? How's the weather?'

'Due to circumstances beyond my control, Skye and I are stuck in your lovely city for another three days, so...I guess I can offer my services. As long as I'm not treading on anyone's toes.'

'Not at all,' assured Da Silva.

'When did you want to speak with this editor?'

'How does right now sound?'

'Give me five minutes,' said Jack. 'I'll be waiting at the front gate.'

## Chapter Nine

DETECTIVE QUINTAL BANGED the heel of her fist on the door of the apartment. The suspect lived in a three-bedder in the fashionable Avenidas Novas district. Recently renovated, the block in the expensive precinct in the north of Lisbon smelled strongly of fresh paint and money.

After three rounds of insistent knocking, the door opened a couple of millimetres. A timorous voice said. 'Yes?'

'Police,' barked Quintal.

A sharp-featured face crowned with a dyed-blonde curly hairdo tentatively poked around the side of the door. '*Bom dia*. Can I see some identification?'

Quintal obliged before asking directly, 'Are you Anita Oliveira?'

'Y-e-e-e-s.' She tucked a ringlet of damp hair behind her ear. 'What do you want?'

'To speak to you about a serious matter.'

The woman's spider-veined eyes shifted left and right,

then focused on the detective. She made no movement to admit the officer. Just stood there, doing her eye dance.

'If you don't let me in, I'm going to arrest you and drag you down to the police department for questioning. Which way is it going to be?'

'Oh...' Oliveira seemed to snap out of a trance. 'Please, come in. I guess I know what this is about.'

The resident, dressed in a gossamer nightie that barely reached the top of her pale thighs, stood aside for the officer to pass. She closed the door with a thunk and leaned her back against it. Quintal turned her head around and said, 'You seriously want to chat here standing in the corridor?'

A quick nod. 'Uh-huh. If you don't mind. The place is a mess and I'm rather embarrassed to have guests in my—'

'I'm not a guest. I'm here to find out if you are in any way responsible for a horrific crime committed yesterday. The message you left on the victim's answering machine would seem to suggest you might be.'

Oliveira's shoulders straightened, the beginnings of clarity returned to her darkly ringed eyes. The detective sniffed out a sense of relief. 'So you're not here about me not fronting up to court over the drugs charge?' A sigh followed the rhetorical question.

'No chance,' Oliveira scoffed. 'The amount you were charged with possessing wouldn't get my canary high. That's not my area. My area is homicide.'

Fingers sporting long, carefully manicured nails decorated with alternating green and blue polish waved about Oliveira's face. 'Wait, wait, wait...what's going on here?'

Quintal said over her shoulder as she marched down the corridor, footsteps thumping, 'I refuse to conduct this conversation standing in a hallway. I'm sure you have a table and chairs in this ritzy pad. Follow me or I really will arrest you. I'm in a foul enough mood as it is.'

A minute later, a slouching Oliveira sat opposite the detective, her face a knot of confusion.

'I'm not going to waste everybody's time.' Quintal pulled a small notebook from her handbag. 'Did you or did you not leave a message on Salma Farooq's answering machine with the following content: *Leave my man alone, bitch. I've told you before, I won't tell you again*'? Since she was murdered last night, I'd be answering candidly if I were you.'

'Wh-wh-what? Salma is *dead*?'

'As a doornail. Now, please answer my question. Did you leave that threatening message yesterday?'

'I don't recall.' Oliveira pointed at an empty bottle of Tanqueray gin on the kitchen sink. 'I was drowning my sorrows last night.' She shrugged her thin shoulders. Quintal couldn't help thinking the woman, attractive by most standards, was a couple of kilos off being officially anorexic. The drugs charge Oliveira mentioned was for cocaine possession, and she certainly had the physique and mannerisms of a chronic abuser. 'I honestly can't remember a thing.'

Quintal nestled into the chair, the most comfortable kitchen chair she'd ever sat in. And it didn't even have any padding or cushions – just wood. Must have been designed by one of those Danish geniuses, she thought. A sweeping gaze about the open-plan apartment told her Oliveira was a spoiled brat. Condos in this part of town can sell for two million plus euros. Her gut told her this place was at the top end of the price scale. 'Listen to this.' Quintal's iPhone plonked onto the table, she pressed a button and the sound of the suspect's angry voice saying the exact words the detective had recited filled the air.

Oliveira cradled her head in her hands, her body trembling. 'Oh shit. That *is* me. But...' she glanced up, eyes even redder than before, 'I honestly can't remember saying it.' She pointed at the bottle again. 'I was drunker than a sailor.'

'I've only got your word for that. Besides,' Quintal leaned back, rolled her shoulders, 'You could have made the recording before you got tanked.'

'Come on! You can hear it in my voice how intoxicated I am. Play it again, you'll hear it.'

A shake of the head from Quintal. 'Whether you were sober or drunk, makes no difference. You aren't excused, just like the law doesn't excuse a drunk driver who gets behind the wheel of his car and kills an innocent pedestrian.'

'But I didn't kill anyone!'

This skinny princess needed a wake-up call. The detective raised her voice. 'Are you aware that Ms Farooq, *that bitch*, as you put it, was the victim of a shooting assassination on the number 15 tram to Belém last night? Executed in cold blood.'

'No!'

'On her way home after chatting with her editor. Probably contemplating having a quiet night in, maybe doing some research for her Master's thesis.'

'Jesus,' whispered Oliveira. 'I can't get my head around this.'

The woman had been softened up sufficiently to put the obvious question Quintal had kept up her sleeve. 'Why did you threaten Ms Farooq?'

'Because...she stole my man from me.'

The detective let out a sharp puff of breath. Jealousy was a strong motive. But the MO didn't tally. Witnesses at the scene described a man of average build in dark clothing fleeing the scene. Of course, Oliveira could have ordered a hit, she certainly seemed to have the financial wherewithal to pay for it. 'What man?'

'A journalist.'

*Now we're getting somewhere.* 'Does this journalist have a name?'

'Caspar.'

'Doesn't sound Portuguese. Is he a foreigner?'

'American. He's a correspondent for the *New York Times*, based in Lisbon.'

'Last name?'

'Phillipson.'

'Spell both names, please.'

Quintal jotted them down. 'His phone number please.'

'I...ah...'

'I can easily get it by ringing the newspaper's office. It'll look a lot better for you if I don't have to go to all that trouble.' She looked up from the notebook. 'I'm going to make us both a coffee while you get your story together. Agreed?'

Oliveira nodded slowly. 'Sure.'

Five minutes later, Detective Quintal had learned how the suspect had met the American on a dating app not long after he arrived in the country. They had, in Oliveira's words, a hot and steamy romance, and she was certain she and Phillipson were going to get married at some point. Mid last year, he met Salma Farooq at a press conference at the Portuguese parliament and was instantly besotted with her.

Quintal said nothing during the narration, kept her gaze fixed on the pathetic woman. *Prolonged silence makes them squirm.* On a different tangent, she said, switching to good cop after the bad cop act, 'Nice place you got here. You own it?'

'I inherited the property from my parents. They were killed in a plane crash in Switzerland.'

'My condolences.'

Oliveira waved away the concern. 'It happened when I was ten years old.'

'How old are you now?'

'Thirty-four.' She toyed with the coffee cup, rolled the bottom edge around the saucer. Without looking up she said, 'Yes, I know what you're thinking. Salma was a lot younger than me. More attractive too, I admit it. But she didn't *love* him. Not like I do. You have to believe me, I would never have killed her. Even if I said horrible things to her on the phone. No way in the world!'

'Did they…you know…form a relationship?'

'They went on a couple of dates, then I think she lost interest. She's a Muslim, you know. They're not supposed to have sex before marriage, so I don't even know why she was leading Caspar on.'

'Maybe they did have sex? This is Portugal, after all, not Morocco. No one is going to make a big deal about it here.' Quintal put a finger to her chin. 'Except for a jilted lover, perhaps.'

'No, no, no!'

'I'm afraid I'm going to have to ask you to accompany me to the station.'

'What? Surely you're not arresting me. I didn't DO ANYTHING!'

'I'm sorry, but your word isn't good enough. You must provide an official statement regarding your whereabouts at the time of the murder. You will also be fingerprinted, and you will be required to provide a DNA sample. Right this minute, you are our number one suspect.'

Oliveira started to hyperventilate. 'Holy shit…please…I need to lie down.'

Quintal wondered if she'd gone too far. She decided to push just a little bit harder, then take her foot off the gas. 'Come on, I'll help you to the couch.'

Lying horizontal with the cop hovering over her like a hawk watching a fieldmouse, Oliveira cracked. 'I'm not capable of murdering a fly.' She adjusted a cushion under her head. 'But Caspar is.'

'Why do you say that? I thought you loved him.'

'I do. But I love my freedom more.'

Quintal took a seat in a sumptuous leather armchair ten metres from where Oliveira lay, her bony chest rising and falling with heavy breathing. 'Tell me exactly why you think your ex-boyfriend would murder someone he was infatuated with.'

'Because he stalked her. She wasn't responding to him and he was starting to lose his mind.'

'How do you know?'

She burst out laughing, which morphed into a coughing fit. 'Because I stalked *him*. I watched from a distance as he mumbled to himself, swore at strangers.'

Despite her turncoat act, it didn't save Oliveira from being driven to police headquarters. The clinching argument to gaining the woman's co-operation was Quintal's hypothetical comment. 'It would be a shame if your rich neighbours caught a glimpse of you being led away in a pair of handcuffs.' The mere mention of such a possibility brought on a cascade of tears.

'All right, I'm coming, don't keep hassling me.'

'Grow up. You're not a child.'

'Can I call my lawyer? I'd like someone to be there to look out for me.'

'Sure you can have a lawyer present. Don't you have any friends?'

More tears, a river this time. 'No. Everyone abandoned me when I hooked up with Caspar. Even my best friend, Carla.'

'Why would she do that?'

'She hated Caspar. Said he was an egotist, that he was only with me because of my money. Now, I'm starting to think maybe she was right.' She scrambled to a sitting position. 'Before we go, I want a cigarette. Is that allowed?'

Quintal nodded, followed the suspect onto the huge balcony where they both lit up. 'Are you telling me the whole truth, Anita? Something tells me you're holding back on me.'

A fierce denial was followed by a huge inhalation of smoke that almost burned the cigarette down to the butt. 'I've got no reason to lie. Can we get this ordeal over with? I've got another bottle of Tanqueray I'd like to get stuck into.'

As Quintal opened the door for the sobbing woman, who had changed into a sleek outfit of designer jeans and a blouse that would have cost two months of a detective's salary, her instincts weren't leaning one way or the other.

Either Oliveira was guilty as sin or she was a consummate actress.

## Chapter Ten

THE STARK WHITE interview room was silent apart from the soft hum of the ducted air-conditioning and the breathing of the three people present. Quintal the interrogator, the human train-wreck of a suspect Oliveira, and her elderly lawyer Diogo Miglietti, an advocate whose reputation of stubbornness preceded him. Jack Lisbon would have been a handy partner for this interaction, the detective mused. Most of her own colleagues were way too soft when it came to grilling suspects and putting lawyers in their place.

Miglietti was a shambolically attired and heavily wrinkled man who looked like he should have quit his job ten years ago. This was already a bad sign in the detective's mind: he had probably kept on working because he was driven by a passion for his job, a dogged determination. Why else not close his practice and enjoy a quiet life on the pension? That was certainly her intention once the clock struck retirement.

'I'd normally have another person present from our

side,' said Quintal, smoothing down her trousers under the steel table. 'But this shocking case is consuming most of our investigative resources, as you can imagine. The prosecutor's office wants us to nail the perpetrator ASAP. The city administration is pressuring us, too. A murder like this one is bad publicity. Which means most of the detectives are out on the road, chasing up other leads.'

'That's all well and good,' said Miglietti, wiping his glasses with a square piece of cloth. 'Admirable, in fact. But those concerns have nothing to do with my client. If the national force is under-resourced, how is it her fault?'

Quintal observed a smile creeping across Oliveira's face.

The lawyer continued, 'I demand a second officer be present.' He locked his rheumy eyes with Quintal's wide-open ones. 'To make sure you don't try any funny business. I'm already getting a bad vibe from you.'

'I don't think I appreciate your tone and attitude.' She took a deep breath. 'I'm just doing my job.'

'And I mine.' Miglietti shrugged. 'I'll be blunt. If you cannot arrange for a second person, then I respectfully request you let my client go about her business and leave her alone until you get a warrant. I needn't remind you, she is here voluntarily.'

Quintal felt her blood pressure rise as she resisted the urge to grab the old fart by the collar and drag him across the table. 'Very well. Wait here.'

Ten minutes later, Quintal was back with a pudgy filing clerk from the admin and records section in tow. She'd just missed Catarina Rebelo, who, Quintal was informed by one of the duty officers, was taking an important call from a key witness.

'Who is this?' said Miglietti, scratching a nest of concentric circles on a notepad. 'He doesn't look much like a detective to me.'

'My name is Abel Machado,' volunteered the clerk with a slight stutter. 'Assisting–'

'He's a full-time employee of the Polícia Judiciária,' cut in Quintal. 'That's all you need to know about him. I'm not playing anymore games, sir. We are investigating one of the most serious crimes our city has ever seen. Be assured, if we weren't short-handed there would be another senior detective here and they wouldn't be as nice as me.' She shifted her gaze from Miglietti to Oliveira, then back again. 'Your cooperation in good faith would go a long way towards convincing me your client had nothing to do with this murder. Right now, she's got a lot of motive.'

'Fair enough.' The man's voice wavered, the initial burst of arrogance tucked away for the moment. 'Of course my client wants to see the murderer caught and punished. Please proceed.'

Quintal briefly glanced at the clerk, who couldn't stop blinking and fidgeting with his chubby hands. When she had marched him to the interview room, she warned him to keep his participation under his hat, and not to speak during the interview unless she told him to. He had already broken that rule by introducing himself. She was under no illusions he would keep it to himself forever, of course. Either way, it would all be captured on the official video. Abel would certainly have a helluva story to tell his friends and family later. She was unsure of Da Silva's reaction, though. He might laugh his head off, or he could just as easily tear her a new one for thrusting the kid into his one-off role. Yes, she could have waited for Rebelo to show up, maybe rescheduled the interview, but patience was never one of Quintal's virtues.

After a couple of introductory formal remarks for the tape, Quintal cut to the chase. 'Where were you at the time Salma Farooq was murdered, Wednesday, 5$^{th}$ of May, at 17:20?'

'At home.'

'Not riding the No. 15 tram to Belém?'

'Of course not! I take Ubers everywhere, never use public transport.'

'What were you doing at the time I mentioned?'

'Drinking Tanqueray and listening to music. Katy Perry or something mindless like that.'

'Can someone verify that?'

'No. I told you before, I have no friends. I spend a lot of time alone with my computer and stereo for company. This was one of those occasions.'

Quintal scribbled down the answers. 'I forgot to ask you before, Ms Oliveira. What do you do for a living?'

'I'm an influencer on social media. Mainly Instagram.'

Quintal raised both eyebrows and tilted her head slightly to one side. 'Impressive. I don't think I've ever met one of those before.'

Oliveira shrugged. 'Well, now you have. I don't spend as much time on it as a lot of other influencers. I don't need to earn a lot of money because my late parents made sure I'd be all right.'

'What or whom do you influence? Public opinion?'

'I…ah…do reviews on different types of gin. It's a very popular drink these days. In English it sounds pretty cool – ginfluencer.'

The clerk burst out laughing, the others remained quiet for a moment.

'Hmmm.' Quintal broke the silence. 'Yes, I seem to remember seeing lots of empty bottles at your flat.'

'Please stick to relevant questions, Detective,' said Miglietti, doing nothing to hide the tetchiness in his voice. 'None of this is at all appropriate.'

'Is that how you met the American journalist Mr Caspar Phillipson? The man you suggest may have had enough motivation to murder the victim? Through your...gin reviews?'

'No.' She blushed. 'We met on a dating app.'

'How very modern.' She pretended to read important notes, furrowing her brow. 'Aha. The weapon. Let's go over that.'

'What are you talking about? I know nothing about the weapon.'

'The pistol used to...assassinate...Ms Salma Farooq. Americans are famous for their love of guns. Did Mr Phillipson share this passion?'

Oliveira shook her head. 'No.' She then pressed a finger to her lips, made a face like she wanted to rectify a misspoken word. 'But now that I think about it, he really enjoyed watching violent movies. Stuff with lots of shooting.'

'What is one example of such a movie?'

'Um...I can't remember.'

Quintal tsk-tsked. 'I think you are making things up to make the man look bad and deflect suspicion from yourself.'

'No! I'm not. The movie was...ah...Kill Bill.'

'Right,' said Quintal. 'It sounds to me like you just plucked the name out of the air.'

'No, it's true. We watched it on Netflix at his apartment. I can prove it...it'll be on his account history. Check it, you'll see!'

'Don't worry, we'll absolutely do that.' She was confident the police would not waste a minute of their time on such a triviality, which would prove absolutely nothing in any case. 'Now, for the record, I'm going to play the message we retrieved from the victim's answering machine.' She pressed the button on a digital recorder to play the hysterical message. Miglietti winced and squirmed a little in his seat. 'Ms Oliveira, can you please tell me why you made that threatening statement?'

Head cradled in her shaking hands, she mumbled something inaudible.

'Please speak louder for the tape, Ms Oliveira.'

The hands left her cheeks. 'I told you already! It was the alcohol talking. I'm not a violent person. Never have been.'

'*In vino veritas*, as the Romans used to say.' Quintal folded her hands across her bosomy chest.

'What the…?' said Oliveira.

'Is that a question, Detective?' said Miglietti. 'Because it didn't sound like one. Or perhaps you're trying to show us what an erudite person you are with your knowledge of Latin.'

'I apologise. It's a common enough phrase. We all know people often speak the truth when they're drunk; they say things that they harbour deep within their souls; dark things, things they would never dare say aloud when they're sober. I guess what I'm trying to say is those words – *Leave my man alone, bitch. I've told you before, I won't tell you again* – reflect Ms Oliveira's real feelings. Her murderous intent.'

'OK, I'll admit it,' Oliveira threw her hands up in the air. 'I hated Salma's guts. She stole my man from me. But… I…'

'There is no direct threat in those words,' interrupted a flush-faced Miglietti, fountain-pen raised in the air. 'There is no elaboration of consequences should the person the words were addressed to–'

'The victim,' corrected Quintal.

'As you prefer. Should *the victim* fail to do as my client asked. In other words, Ms Oliveira doesn't say *if you don't do x, y will happen to you*. In my opinion, it's a fairly innocuous warning.'

'Semantics,' countered Quintal. 'Any right-thinking jury would logically conclude there was an implicit threat of consequences, even if it wasn't explicitly stated. The hostile tone is enough. I mean, she sounds completely unhinged!'

'That's an assumption that could only be tested in court. And for that, you will have to charge my client with a crime. Are you going to do that?'

'At this stage, no.'

'Then perhaps you could try another line of questioning? Badgering Ms Oliveira in this fashion is most unproductive.'

The lawyer was clearly no dummy. No wonder he'd survived so long in the system. Quintal moved some non-relevant papers about on the table for visual effect alone, glanced at the clerk, who sat open-mouthed at the unfolding drama, as he had since it began. 'OK. You told us earlier that the man you claim was stolen away from you by the victim, like you, has a very strong motive for this crime.'

'You mean Caspar Phillipson?' Tiny tears started to form in the corners of Oliveira's eyes.

'Of course I mean him!' Quintal thundered, making the clerk beside her jump a centimetre or two in his seat. 'We were speaking about him barely minutes ago.'

'Hey,' said Miglietti. 'No need for that.'

'I apologise,' said Quintal, shaking her shoulders. This suspect was going to try her patience like nothing else. The anger needed to be kept in check, though, or she and her brief would walk away mid-interview. 'At your flat, you said he was losing his mind because Salma dumped him.'

'Yes.'

'And you know this how?'

'Like I told you. I...stalked him. Watched from a distance. Saw the way he was talking to himself like one of those homeless people with voices in their heads. No offense to them.' She turned her neck, stared at a random spot on the wall. Without looking back she said, 'I felt bad for spying on him, but it confirmed that he was even more besotted with her than I was with him.'

'Was?' said Quintal. 'The message you left on Ms Farooq's answering machine was...let me see...' She consulted her notes. 'Only two days before the murder. I'd say you're still besotted with him.'

'Not true.' Oliveira's words lacked even a modicum of conviction.

'Any more questions?' said Miglietti. 'Unless you have something more than a jilted lover's understandable anguish and some angry words left on a phone message, I suggest we are done for today.'

'OK,' said Quintal. 'Let's assume Caspar Phillipson was as upset as you suggest he is. Did he ever lose his temper with you?'

'No.' Oliveira turned her lips into a rose-knot. 'He was always the gentleman with me.'

'Did he ever mention the victim to you when you were together?'

'Yes. The day after the press conference where he met her. He went on and on about how interesting this woman was, and what a difference she was going to make to the world with her ground-breaking journalism. Blah, blah, blah. It was sickening, to be honest.'

'Did he discuss with you the nature of her journalism? What stories she was working on?'

'No. He knew I wasn't interested in that kind of thing.'

'From what I understand, journalists are pretty obsessive about their jobs, the stories they're working on at any given time.'

'Yeah. He was a bit like that. But he never talked about that stuff with me.'

'Then what were you and he interested in?'

'Sex, Detective. Hot, steamy sex. Want to know all the… ins and outs?'

Quintal coughed into her fist. *Don't take the bait.* 'And how long after Phillipson met Salma Farooq did you and he end your relationship?'

'About a week later. And it wasn't mutual, by the way. He ended it, the prick. In a cowardly fashion – via text.'

'And I am ending this,' said Miglietti, picking his briefcase up off the floor. 'My client has provided you with a lead. Now, go and chase it up!'

## Chapter Eleven

ON THE SHORT drive to the office of *Euro Politics Today* in Rua Tomás da Fonseca, Da Silva filled in Jack on the latest developments in the investigation. He began with Mrs Farooq's reaction to the news of her daughter's death. 'Horta and Costa had to call an ambulance for the poor woman. She couldn't speak for over an hour. When she finally managed to pull herself together, we got some fascinating information out of her.'

Jack chewed a fingernail as the Škoda Octavia slowed to squeeze between two other vehicles in the narrow street. 'I guess she didn't request a viewing of the body?'

Da Silva cursed under his breath as a deafening tuk-tuk, right rear wheel off the ground, cut across in front of him. He leaned on the horn but the driver and his two passengers were laughing too hard to care. 'These damned things should be banned.'

'I agree,' said Jack, despite having every intention of trying one out with Skye at the first opportunity. Maybe tomorrow.

'Sorry,' Da Silva resumed. 'Where was I? Oh yes. The victim's mother. She said she *does* want to see the body, couldn't say good-bye to her beloved daughter without seeing her.'

'You sure that's a good idea?'

Da Silva somehow managed to shrug while keeping his hands at ten-to-two on the steering wheel. 'Not for me to say. The autopsy was a formality in this case. Not too much disfigurement from the bullets; you saw that yourself.'

'Yeah. I've seen a lot worse from gun blasts. Heads half missing, eyes on the floor, brains all over the—'

'I'm sure you have. Anyway, Salma will be released to a funeral director tomorrow. The body is then out of our hands.'

'Did your officers ask the mother who might have had it in for Salma?'

'Of course.' He sounded slightly offended Jack would even ask the question. 'And she gave us an interesting lead.'

'Don't leave me hanging.'

'Because the two were so close, Salma shared everything with her mother. At least as far as her personal life went. She knows nothing of the research her daughter was doing. She wouldn't even begin to understand the economic stuff Salma was investigating. Horta and Costa described Suzana Farooq as a simple woman. Apparently she moved to the city from central Portugal in—'

'All very interesting,' Jack interrupted, digging around in his pocket for chewing gum. 'But what's the lead?'

'A jilted boyfriend who's been, what's the English word, stalking Salma for months. She broke off with him and he didn't like it. Her mother was very worried about this guy and reckons we should be looking at him.'

Just then the police chief's phone rang, connected through Bluetooth to the Škoda's speakers. 'Excuse me, Jack. It's Catarina Rebelo.' He pushed a button. 'Olá, Catarina. Detective Lisbon's with me, so speak in English please.'

'Oh, sure.' She didn't exactly sound elated, Jack thought. 'Remember that guy with the shopping bags who let us into Salma's apartment building?'

'Yes.'

'His name is Andre Ferreira, works at the local supermarket as a cashier and shelf stocker. He rang the main number and the call was put through to me. He told me he remembered a guy hanging around the building a couple of days ago, acting weird. He was walking around in circles, talking to himself like he was on drugs. The man approached our informant and asked him for a cigarette.'

'Not unusual in itself. Plenty of eccentric people in that neighbourhood.'

'Yes, but he was speaking English in what the witness thought was an American accent. But, here's the best bit, the physical description he gave me fits that given by Salma's mother of her American ex-boyfriend, Caspar Phillipson. I'm heading to the *New York Times* where he works.'

'Good thinking. Where's Quintal? I'd like her to go with you.'

'I'm told she's in the interview room grilling that woman who left the threatening message on Farooq's voice mail. Apparently her lawyer demanded she have another officer present so she grabbed a random guy from the admin and records section because she couldn't find a spare detective anywhere.'

'But you were there! You still are.'

'I know, but I was getting information out of Ferreira. He's one of those people who doesn't shut up once they get started. And I guess Quintal didn't want to wait.'

'I hope Quintal's impatience doesn't backfire on us.'

'I'm sure it won't, sir.'

Da Silva braked to a slow stop at a set of traffic lights. 'When she's finished, assuming she doesn't get a confession out of Oliveira, tell Detective Quintal that Jack and I are heading to the offices of *Euro Politics Today* to talk to Farooq's editor. We've also got a company called Entrega Rápida in our sights. It's the company that Farooq was set to expose in her article. The place is bound to be crawling with suspects.'

*Not too many I hope, thought Jack. The optimal number of suspects is one.*

'Call me when you're finished with the American journalist,' said Da Silva. 'I want to know everything about this man, down to what colour tie he wears and what he smells like.'

'Uh…OK.'

'Quintal won't let him off the hook. Your job on this assignment is to watch and learn as much from her as you can. Understood?'

'Yes, sir.'

'Another thing. If you two finish with Caspar Phillipson before we're done at the magazine, head over to Entrega Rápida and get a start on grilling the management. Ask for a man called Gorge Alvarenga. He's the CEO. No warning calls. Just show up.'

'Um, I don't want to sound disrespectful,' said Rebelo, who sounded to Jack like she was walking on figurative eggshells, 'but if you're planning to go there anyway, couldn't Detective Quintal and I take a look at the university professor? As far as I remember, he rounds off the short-list of priority figures we came up with at the first briefing.'

The woman was smart as a whip and had an excellent point. Jack decided to back her up. 'I think she's right, Zé. It's only just gone 12:30. How long can it take to interview the editor? An hour, tops. Still gives us plenty of time to talk to Alvarenga. The Entrega Rápida angle deserves your attention as the highest ranking detective on the case. Catarina and Quintal *would* be better deployed elsewhere at this early stage.' He busted out his best apologetic smile. 'But it's your call at the end of the day.'

Da Silva massaged the back of his own neck, a sheen of sweat coating the skin. The man's face had acquired a reddish tinge, little veins popping out all over his eyeballs. Here and there shaving nicks on the chin, the moustache not as tidy as yesterday. He was under plenty of stress, that much was clear. Da Silva was immensely likeable as a person. Jack would later gently probe the guy to find out what was bothering him. He'd lay even money it was trouble on the home front.

'Of course,' relented Da Silva. 'You're both right. Hit up the professor once you've finished with Phillipson.'

'Yes, sir.'

Jack had a question for Rebelo. 'Did you happen to catch a glimpse of the suspect Oliveira at the station?'

'No, I was busy talking to the witness who called in, Ferreira, when…actually, Detective Quintal is just coming now. She's escorting a woman through the foyer with someone I'm guessing is her lawyer.'

'How's the body language?' said Da Silva.

'To be honest, the suspect and her legal representative

have more spring in their step than the detective does. So, no confession obtained, I'd say.'

'Indeed,' said Da Silva. 'Best of luck with Phillipson.'

'I can't wait to hear what Oliveira had to say for herself,' said Jack when Da Silva terminated the call.

'Quintal filled me in on the results of her initial conversation with Anita Oliveira. A rich orphan who fell in love with this American journalist who in turn fell in love with our victim. Of course, Oliveira denied she had anything to do with the murder, said she was drunk when she made the threatening call. She believes Farooq *stole* Phillipson away from her, but Farooq didn't return the love and then Phillipson started to stalk her.'

'Stalkers grow up to be killers,' Jack mused out loud. 'We know that's quite a common phenomenon. I'd be ranking him and this Oliveira as equal top suspects at this stage.' He chewed pensively on his gum as Da Silva nosed the Škoda into the steep driveway of an underground garage.

'There's another thing that carries a lot of weight against Phillipson.' Da Silva recounted that three witnesses – Farooq's mother, Anita Oliveira, and now the resident at the victim's apartment building, Andre Ferriera – had all pointed the finger at Caspar Phillipson. 'The most surprising thing is that our first prime suspect, the one who was supposed to be in love with him, was so quick to, as you say in English, throw him under the bus.'

'Self-preservation is the strongest motivating force there is.' Jack popped a fresh stick of spearmint gum into his mouth, gave it a good mashing. 'Don't matter how much you love someone, freedom's gonna look a much better option for a big chunk of the population. Sounds like Oliveira fits right into that category.'

Da Silva nodded his agreement, then flicked on the headlights in the dark underground lot. He eventually found a guest parking spot that he was just able to squeeze the car into and killed the engine. 'Right, we're here,' he said. 'Let's see what this editor can tell us.'

## Chapter Twelve

MAGAZINE EDITOR MARINA VENTURA was a pocket rocket. Barely 5'2" and fingers tangerine with nicotine stains, she spoke at a rapid rate of knots. Her physical movements were robotic, almost jerky, her manner assertive, bordering on rude. Jack knew the type: he'd been dealing with media people for years. Yes, this was an "intellectual" publication, but a common thread ran through them all. Big egos, always in a hurry, trying to sniff out the next big story, score an exclusive to get one over on the competition. This lady was no exception.

'You don't seem too upset that one of your star writers has been killed?' said Da Silva.

'Nonsense.' Her eyes glared through her rimless glasses. 'I am totally devastated.'

'Is it because she didn't get the chance to expose the company that's been flaunting human rights?' said Jack. ' I know she was one article away from the big reveal.'

Ventura's viciously plucked eyebrows elevated. 'How dare you! Of course that's not why I'm upset. How heartless do you think I am?' She turned her attention to Da Silva, sitting in a chair next to Jack behind the editor's huge desk, spat out a sentence in Portuguese that Jack didn't understand yet understood pretty well.

'English please, Ms Ventura.' Da Silva clasped his hands in his lap.

'For heaven's sake,' she said, in English. 'Look, I'm not used to being harassed by the police. I mean, what do you honestly think I can contribute to your investigation?'

'I think you can contribute a lot,' said Da Silva.

'I understand your reluctance to open up with me here,' said Jack. 'But I can assure you, I'm with Detective Da Silva in an advisory capacity only.'

'Very well.' She buzzed the secretary in the reception just outside the door, asked her to bring in refreshments.

'What do you know about a company called Entrega Rápida?' said Jack.

'I thought you just said you were here as an advisor?'

'I am. And my advice to my respected colleague here is to let me ask a few questions.'

Da Silva grinned and shook his head appreciatively before letting out a chuckle.

Ventura leaned back in her seat. 'My word, you've got plenty of chutzpah.' The harsh lines around her eyes softened suddenly. It was like she admired people who stood up to her.

'Let's get back to Jack's question,' said Da Silva. 'What do you know about this particular company?'

A knock on the door interrupted the flow. A young woman delivered a pot of percolated coffee and a selection of pastries, served the men but not her boss who went to a small bar fridge and plucked out a glass bottle of something green that resembled algae.

'What do I know about the company?' said Ventura resuming her seat. 'Not much. Like many of our readers, I was waiting impatiently for Salma's final instalment, but now…up in smoke, as they say.'

'So she hadn't emailed you any drafts?' said Da Silva, taking his time before choosing an éclair.

'No. That's not how we worked. She always sent me the final version, which we would edit to conform with our style standards if necessary, but doing nothing to change her voice. Salma had a raw natural writing talent. She provided clean copy that required virtually no polishing. She had a big future ahead of her.'

'The article probably isn't "up in smoke", as you put it,' said Jack reassuringly. 'The police have her laptop and there's every chance the final piece of the puzzle is on it.'

'Publishing it would be a fitting testament to her career, tragically cut short,' said Ventura. Jack marvelled at the lack of empathy in the woman's tone despite the words.

'At her apartment I found two letters addressed to her from this company she was looking into,' said Da Silva, spooning a second sugar into a small china cup. 'One confirming there was a big deal going ahead with a Moroccan company, and a second in which a request to interview CEO Gorge Alvarenga was denied. This tells me straight away they have something to hide.'

'Just one moment, I'll pull up the file.' Ventura flipped open a silver laptop and clicked a few buttons. She took a glug of her green goop then said, 'I really liked Salma, but we didn't interact very often. Socially, never. Most of our interactions were about work, via email and phone conversations and…Oh, here it is. Some background on the company she sent me when she first went sniffing them out.' Ventura quickly summarised what she was reading from the screen. Entrega Rápida was founded from nothing in 1920 by a couple of Lisbon entrepreneurs. It began as a courier service that transported goods across Portugal and parts of Spain. The company flourished after World War I, expanding operations to other parts of Europe: France, Belgium, the Netherlands and Germany. They traded under the name of the founders as the Carvalho and Villela Courier Company. By the late 1930s and having survived the Depression better than most, Senhores Carvalho and Villela were multimillionaires. And they were able to do so well, according to what Salma told me, because they were prepared to put ethics to one side in their relentless pursuit of profit.'

'What put her onto this company?' said Jack. He was already connecting the dots. A powerful company like Entrega Rápida that flaunted human rights abroad wouldn't blink when it came to offing a nuisance journalist on home soil.

Ventura chewed her lip for a second. 'From what I recall from an early phone conversation when she floated the idea, it was a source in the Department of Foreign Affairs. Salma told me Entrega Rápida often negotiated at such a high level that government representatives from Portugal, and other countries too, were involved in getting contracts over the line.'

'Useful information,' muttered Da Silva. 'And the name of that source?'

A head shake accompanied by a crescent smile. 'You know the journalists' creed: protect your sources.'

'It's frustrating for police investigations, but perfectly understandable at times.' Jack interlaced his fingers, pushed his palms out and cracked the knuckles. 'However, since Salma is, you know, dead 'n all, there's not much point in keeping it a secret is there? The person's name will not be revealed in any news stories, so protecting their identity isn't an issue now. On the other hand, this person most certainly has information that could progress enquiries. Perhaps even point to the killer.'

Ventura sighed and rolled her eyes. 'Very well. The contact is a woman called Rosa Braga, or something like that. I'm sure you can find her.'

'Many thanks,' Jack offered a watery smile.

'Just a couple more questions for you before we go,' said Da Silva.

'Sure.'

'When was the last time you saw Salma?'

'Yesterday, around 3:00pm. She came in all excited about the second part of the article. It was just about ready, a couple of reference checks and edits left to do and then she was going to email me the finished product later in the evening.'

'Anything else she mention to you?'

'Um. She said she was staying with her best friend instead of going home.'

'Do you know the name of this best friend?'

Ventura offered a lopsided look of apology. 'No, but they'd been friends since school days, so perhaps you could ask her mother.'

'Will do.' Da Silva scribbled himself a note. 'Do you think Salma was afraid?'

'I thought she was apprehensive more so than afraid. But perhaps she *was* scared, now that you mention it.'

'What would she be scared of?' Da Silva had his pen raised, ready to jot the answer down.

'What do you think?' She glared at the detective like he was a fool. Yes, the question was obvious after what they'd been discussing, but Jack knew getting a direct answer to a direct question made the most sense from an investigative point of view. 'Reprisals from Entrega Rápida, of course. She wasn't going to hold back on the detail.'

'But the article hadn't yet come out that named the company?' Da Silva was good, Jack thought. Thorough. 'So why would they make what you might call a pre-emptive strike and kill her on the off chance it *was* Entrega Rápida?'

Ventura swirled the remains of the green goop. 'They *had* to know. She was trying to interview the CEO and the first article made it plain she was about to expose a big company.' She paused, then said, 'Or, how's this for a scenario, detectives? The informant who was feeding her information had a change of heart, then went to the company's management and confessed she was ratting them out via Salma?'

Jack scratched his jaw, leaned forward in his seat. 'Very perceptive.'

'One more line of enquiry before we leave you alone, Ms Ventura,' said Da Silva in a cordial tone. 'Did she ever mention a jilted lover who was stalking her? Or that man's ex-lover who was so jealous she left a threatening message on Salma's answering machine?'

Ventura's lips formed a tight circle. 'Nope. Like I said, our relationship was strictly business.'

The detectives thanked Ventura for her time and each shook her hand. As a departing word Ventura assured them that, despite her cold and clinical answers, she was devastated by what happened yesterday. By nature she was bad at showing her feelings, perhaps it was a mild form of autism; she didn't know if she had it because she was too afraid to seek a diagnosis in case she did.

Back in the car Jack buckled up then said, 'What did

you think about the theory of the informant being a double agent?'

'I think Ventura wouldn't be wasted in the police force. Even if she is autistic.'

Jack nodded. 'My thoughts exactly. They reckon Sherlock Holmes had it.'

'Really? But he wasn't a real detective.'

'Don't shatter my dreams, Zé!'

Both men chuckled grimly as the car eased out of the parking garage into the bright summer sunshine. Calls by Da Silva to Quintal and Rebelo went to message bank. 'They must be talking to our suspect,' said Da Silva.

'I'd say so. How far away is this company?'

'Fifteen minutes. Not far from the aquarium.'

Jack looked at the passing buildings, a blend of old and new, as Da Silva put through a call to Salma Farooq's mother. Not a word of the conversation made sense to Jack, although the grieving woman's aching sobs certainly did. Da Silva pulled over to the side of the road, jotted down three lines of information, said the "thank you" word Jack understood – *obrigado* – and hung up.

'What was that about?' said Jack, his curiosity piqued by the raw emotion in the mother's voice. 'All I got was "hello" at the start and "thank you" at the end.'

'Getting the details of the friend Salma stayed with the night before she was killed. She had also planned to stay for another night or two to avoid Phillipson's stalking.' He picked up his phone, barked a few words down the line. 'I've redirected a couple of junior detectives, Bernardo Horta and Joana Costa, from other cases to have a chat with the woman Salma stayed with.' He smiled broadly. 'They're a couple of juniors, but I've taken a leaf out of your book. So much ground to cover, and we haven't even got proper forensics and ballistics reports back.' He wiped sweat from his brow. 'I've been called upon to address the media tomorrow.' He glanced at Jack. 'I'm not very good at this stuff. Got any tips?'

'Back it up a sec. What book were you talking about?'

'The prioritisation book.'

Jack nodded. 'Yeah, it's tough knowing where to hit first and hardest. And now that you mention it, there's something I need to prioritise.'

'What's that?' said Da Silva, easing the vehicle onto the main road. A flick of the indicator and he executed a risky U-turn in heavy traffic.

'My daughter, innit.'

'Of course.' He flashed Jack a look of contrite apology. 'I've been monopolising you for too long. I can take you back to your accommodation in Belém now if you like.'

Jack checked his wristwatch. 'Mirabella and Skye won't be back for another couple of hours. Drive on, sunshine.'

'Pleased to hear it.' The car accelerated faster as Da Silva zig-zagged between slower cars.

'Once we're done with this company whose name I can't even pronounce, you can take me back to Mirabella's. I've got a trip to the Algarve to prepare for.'

'No problem.'

## Chapter Thirteen

RAQUEL QUINTAL almost felt sorry for the American journalist. His eyes were bloodshot, complexion flushed. The man had clearly been crying bucketloads. Whether out of grief or guilt remained to be seen. She wouldn't let him off the hook simply because the victim's death caused him sadness. Criminal psychologists will tell you, even the cruellest of killers are capable of feeling sorrow.

'Please, come into my office. I've been waiting for a call or a visit from the police.' He almost looked relieved to see the cops as he unbuttoned the cuffs of his designer business shirt and pushed the sleeves up to the elbows. 'I wasn't going to come into work today, as you can imagine after the...' he choked back a sob '...oh dear, sorry.' He took a drink from a red mug bearing the logo of Lisbon's Benfica football club. 'If you were to ask me where to start looking for Salma's killer, I'd recommend the commercial world. If you read the first part of her exposé...oh dear, excuse me...' He reached for a tissue from a box on his desk. He dabbed at his eyes, which were damp at the edges, then blew his nose loudly. 'I'm sorry about that. Anyway, dig into her writing. I'm sure the perpetrator wanted to silence her before she—'

Quintal held up a hand. 'We'll come back to your theories in a moment. I apologise, but I'm obliged to put this question to all persons of interest. Do you have an alibi for the time of the murder?'

'You must be joking, right?!' His eyes expanded like invisible strings were tugging at the lids.

'Not at all. Standard procedure.'

'Remind me when that was exactly. All I know is it happened…oh my God…yesterday afternoon.' He buried his face in his hands for a few seconds before looking back at the detectives, eyes moist and nose pink.

Quintal checked her watch. 'Almost twenty-three hours ago. Time of death was established as 17:20.'

He sucked in a long, rattling breath. 'I was on my way home at that time. Stuck in peak-hour traffic on the 25 de Abril Bridge.'

'Convenient,' she muttered softly. Then louder, 'Where do you live, Mr Phillipson?'

'Sobreda.' He gave the exact address as Rebelo wrote it down, pen flashing across the page.

'Look, if you don't believe me about my whereabouts, you can have my phone records. Data will show my movements. None of which include the No.15 tram to Belém.'

'Will checking your Netflix account records show us that you watched the movie Kill Bill in the company of Ms Anita Oliveira some weeks ago?'

Utter confusion knitted Phillipson's thin eyebrows. 'What…no…I mean yes. I think I did watch it with her.' He laughed awkwardly. 'Who doesn't love a good Tarantino flick, right?'

Rebelo smiled and nodded. 'I certainly do.'

'Hmmm. Me too,' agreed Quintal. 'Although they are very brutal aren't they? Lots of shooting, dead bodies all over the place.'

'What are you insinuating? That because I watched a violent movie I'm going to go bat-shit crazy with a gun on a tram?' His beseeching eyes drilled into the two women. 'Are you both insane?'

'I'm just trying to establish what type of person you are. Nothing more. And,' Quintal pointed a forefinger at nothing in particular on the wall behind Phillipson, 'the reason for my intense interest in you is because three separate people have suggested that you were angry at Salma Farooq for dumping you. That you could have murdered her.' She looked him square in the eyes. 'It's not often you find such a level of agreement among witnesses. Which makes me think there might be something to the theory.'

He pushed back from his desk, the swivel chair careening across the wooden floor on its casters. 'No way in the world! I loved Salma with all my heart. I would never have done anything to hurt her.' His chest heaved as he regained his composure. 'Yes, it hurt like hell that she didn't feel the same way about me. And maybe I behaved a little… erratically at times. But I came to terms with it. Here, look at this.' He scrabbled around on his desk for his mobile phone, swamped under a pile of papers. He pushed a few buttons and turned the device around. Quintal picked it up. On the screen, an attractive, toothy, dark-haired woman in a revealing fluoro orange bikini. 'I met Keira on a dating app.'

'The same one you met Anita Oliveira on?'

A head shake. 'No. A different one. For ex-pats. Keira's a Kiwi.'

'A piece of fruit?' said Rebelo, screwing up her eyes.

'Ha ha, no. It's what they call people from New Zealand. A kiwi is a rare flightless bird native to...' His voice trailed off as he looked at the back of his hands. 'Anyway, I had a date lined up with that lovely lady for tonight, but of course I've cancelled.'

'Why?' said Quintal.

'Out of respect for Salma, what do you think!'

A knock came at the open door. 'Caspar?' said a middle-aged man holding a clipboard and peering over a pair of rimless glasses. 'Oh, I'm sorry. I didn't realise you had company.' He coughed nervously. 'Will you be long? Only we've got a planning meeting in ten minutes and–'

Quintal side-eyed the man standing in the threshold. 'Cancel it.' She held out her ID. 'Mr Phillipson will be answering my questions until I'm done with him.'

'Well,' ventured Phillipson. 'That won't take long at all. Jeff, postpone for a couple of hours, can you?'

'I dunno.' He chewed a fingernail for a second. 'We may have to start without you. The boss is keen to go over the European Parliament's latest–'

'Then start the fucking meeting without me!' Phillipson bellowed. 'I'm not involved with that story anyway.'

'Covering the latest murder instead, are you?' said Rebelo. Quintal turned to her and gave an approving nod. *Nice way to wind up the suspect.*

'How dare you!' thundered Phillipson as clipboard man beat a hasty retreat. 'Embarrassing me like that in front of my coworker. That's the most insensitive thing I've ever heard from a police officer. Even back in the States they're not as rude as you.'

'I'm sorry you took my colleague's question that way,' said Quintal. 'But please remember, English isn't our first language, so perhaps there was a bit of a misunderstanding there.'

'Bullshit. She knew exactly what she was saying.' Phillipson ran manicured fingers through his wavy dark locks. 'You Portuguese have a better grip on English than half the people in this newspaper office.' Quintal had to admit to herself, the young man was a devilishly handsome specimen, even with a cry-face on. The type who could melt the hearts of many a fickle female if their main priority was looks. Luckily for her, handsome men didn't impress in the slightest.

An uncomfortable silence hung in the air for a moment before Quintal made an inquisitive eye gesture towards the visitors' seating arrangements. Phillipson had yet to ask his uninvited guests to take a seat, despite there being two free leather chairs on the opposite side of his desk. He blinked as if realising his social faux pas then returned Quintal's gesture with one of his own and said, 'Yeah, of course.'

'I'm sure you understand the gravity of the situation,' said Quintal, tucking her small handbag under the seat. 'And yes, you may have been nowhere near the scene of the crime. We *will* check that, by the way. However, in my opinion this case bears all the hallmarks of a hit job.'

'Now it sounds like you're the one who's been bingeing on Tarantino films. Are you seriously suggesting I paid someone to…shoot Salma on a tram? You are off your rocker.' He pulled his seat closer to the edge of the desk, drained what was left in his mug.

'What about the stalking?' said Rebelo.

'I beg your pardon?'

'Salma's mother said you were harassing her.' Quintal's gaze never left Phillipson's highly animated face.

'Her mother is very protective and prone to exaggeration,' countered Phillipson. 'I've only met with the woman on two occasions. I got the feeling she didn't like me. Both times she barely spoke to me.'

'She doesn't speak English, so that's no surprise. Do you speak Portuguese?'

'Barely. I was attached to the Spanish office before they sent me here. I guess the paper thought since I could handle Spanish, Portuguese would be no problem. Bah! I can't understand any of it.'

Quintal agreed it was a tough language to learn then said, 'You rang Salma's number many times and left no message. To many that can feel intimidating.'

'It's my standard practice not to leave messages, no matter who I'm calling. I find it to be a pointless exercise.'

'You rang her on…let me check.' She flipped open a small notepad. 'Monday. True to form, you left no message, just five seconds of silence.' She tapped her finger on the desktop. 'And you were already planning a date with this new woman. What's going on?'

'I…ah…wanted to return something to her. A USB drive with some of her favourite songs on it, other personal stuff. She left it in my car and I wanted to give it back.'

Rebelo shook her head. 'You could have sent it by normal mail. Registered post if you were concerned about the personal files.'

'Yeah, well, I didn't want to.'

'Do you still have that flash drive?' said Quintal.

He wordlessly slid open a drawer by his side, tossed a small olive-green rectangle across the desk. 'Yep. All yours.'

'Appreciated,' she said through tightly pressed lips.

'Look, I'm not feeling very well and I'd like you both to go now. I know my rights, even in this country. Charge me, get a warrant to search, either this office or my home – shit, look through my car for all I care. Either that or leave me alone.'

'May I see your passport, please?' said Quintal.

'No you may not. It's at home.'

She reached under the seat and retrieved her bag, stood, and beckoned to Rebelo with a we're-done-here nod. At the door she turned and said, 'Don't even think about leaving the country until you've been given the all clear. You'll be on a watch list. I'm formally advising you that you are a suspect in the murder of Salma Farooq. You may be called upon to give an official statement. You may also be asked to surrender electronic devices and give DNA samples. If you don't have legal representation, perhaps have a think about organising that. Good day to you.'

'Anita's the one you should be looking at, not me,' he called out, a hint of desperation constricting his voice box.

'Don't worry, Mr Phillipson. We are.' She paused. 'But, to be totally honest, you seem the more likely candidate.'

In the squad car heading back to the station Rebelo said, 'Does he really seem the more likely to you?'

Quintal grinned. 'Is his handsome face having an effect on you?'

'No!' Rebelo blushed. 'I was being serious.'

'If I had to pick between him and Oliveira, he's the more plausible of the two.' She checked the rearview mirror as the afternoon traffic started to build. 'But I think we need to be looking elsewhere. My gut tells me neither of them had anything to do with it.'

'What makes you say that?'

'The MO. A jilted pretty-boy journalist and a ditched, alcoholic heiress would choose something a lot more subtle than an assassination in broad daylight. Phillipson was right about looking into the commercial world. If I were to bet money, I'd say Da Silva and the Englishman will find Farooq's killer, or whoever hired the killer, among the employees of Entrega Rápida.'

'How much would you bet?' said Rebelo, rolling the USB drive in her fingers.

'A hundred euros,' she laughed. Then added, 'out of your wages.'

## Chapter Fourteen

AS THEY ENTERED the cavernous lobby of the glass-steel-and-chrome building owned by the Entrega Rápida company, Da Silva's mobile rang raucously in his pocket. No loud speaker for Jack's benefit this time; the short conversation was conducted in machine-gun Portuguese. Pocketing the Samsung, Da Silva told Jack the interview with Phillipson was over and he'd ordered Quintal to track down the Foreign Affairs informant Rosa Braga. And preferably interview the woman before close of business.

'What was Quintal's impression of Phillipson?'

'I'm sure she'll tell us at the general briefing tonight.'

'What, she didn't have a feel for the guy?' Jack asked incredulously. He couldn't fathom the lack of the lead detective's curiosity. Places reversed, he'd want to know all about what went down. Immediately.

Da Silva sighed. 'I'm sure she did, but she didn't share it with me. And I didn't ask.' He inclined his head towards the two head-set wearing receptionists typing away behind a gleaming granite divider. 'I want to get stuck into this company's directors first.'

'Of course, you're right.' Jack thrust his hands in his pockets, rummaged about among gum wrappers he'd meant to toss but hadn't gotten around to. He arched his neck to survey the splendour of the firm's headquarters. A vaulted atrium criss-crossed with a honeycomb of metal struts let in abundant sunlight, the perfect warm and bright environment for the masses of deep-green indoor plants. A fountain in the centre of the foyer boasted golden angels and dolphins spitting water out of mouths, trumpets and blowholes. A more ostentatious display of wealth and success you couldn't hope for. He made the observation to Da Silva, 'They don't like to hide their light under an effin' bushel, innit?'

'And I thought I understood English well.' The detective shook his head and made for the reception, Jack on his heels. On the way Jack liberated the annoying gum wrappers and dropped them into a shiny rubbish bin that looked like an expensive engineering and design masterpiece in itself. Da Silva politely showed one of the women his police ID and asked a couple of questions, the content of which, naturally, escaped Jack. However, the receptionist's engaging smile and extended index finger pointing to the bank of elevators, accompanied by Da Silva's grateful bow, was enough to tell him they were on their way to see someone important.

The lift sped its way to the top floor and they arrived in what seemed like seconds. The doors opened with an echoey ping, revealing a scaled-down version of the downstairs reception. Jack sat in a plush chesterfield armchair while Da Silva did the talking again. A repeat performance, but with a slight difference. The receptionist at this level did not smile. Her face was immobile, save for minute movements of her lips and a slow head shake. Da Silva's voice rose a fraction before he marched back towards Jack and plonked his backside into an identical chair.

'He's refusing to talk to us?' Jack ventured.

'Yes. Too busy conquering the world, apparently. But we'll wait him out!'

*Bravo, sir.*

The clock ticked along until 16:30. Still no sign of anyone emerging from the CEO's office.

'Maybe you should go and apply for a warrant, sunshine? He's probably monitoring us on CCTV.' Jack pointed to a dark blue hemisphere clinging to the ceiling. 'Waiting for us to give up and leave.'

'Five more minutes,' huffed Da Silva.

Jack crossed his arms. 'OK, but I'm timing it. You can stay here all bleedin' night if you want, but I'm off if he doesn't show in five.'

Finally, exactly four minutes and fifty-five seconds later, the heavy oak panelled door opened and two men emerged. A prior internet search had already enabled the detectives to identify which of them was the big boss. Perhaps ironically, it was the less physically imposing man. It was impossible to gauge his height, since he was wheelchair bound, having lost his legs after contracting a rare flesh-eating disease while on safari in Africa in his early twenties. His lap covered in a thick black blanket, Gorge Alvarenga smiled affably as he and the man pushing him approached. His small eyes, peering out from under a hedge of bushy eyebrows, glowed with a fierce life-force. At sixty-seven years of age, he exuded the energy of a man with a lot left to achieve in his lifetime.

He snapped out a command in nasally Portuguese to the

lanky man, who appeared to be ten years older than Alvarenga. The man nodded and wheeled the CEO alongside the two detectives like a cruise ship docking at port. Da Silva made to stand up, but Alvarenga waved him back into his seat. His gaze shifted to Jack and those bushy eyebrows lifted in a flash of recognition. 'It cannot be true! Is it Detective Jack Lisbon?'

'Ah, yes indeed.' Jack felt prickles of heat creeping up his neck. 'Don't tell me you've read the—'

'*Sim.* Yes. The blog post. Of course. I know a lot about you, Mr Lisbon.'

Da Silva said brusquely, 'Perhaps you don't know this about him. He's on rather a tight schedule.'

'Oh?'

'Yes,' said Jack. 'I've got a lot on my to-do list before I return to Australia.'

'A shame,' said Alvarenga. 'I've been following your career – off and on – with some interest. I would have enjoyed having a chat about your exploits.'

'Maybe some other time,' said Jack.

Da Silva cleared his throat. 'Time is of the essence, Senhor Alvarenga. I suggest we get straight down to business. Detective Lisbon is here to assist me in investigating the murder of the journalist Salma Farooq. He is lending a hand to the Polícia Judiciária out of the goodness of his heart, so I'd appreciate your full cooperation.'

A smile crept across Alvarenga's face, creasing the skin around his hooded eyebrows. 'Wonderful. You will have the crime solved in no time at all.'

'As part of our investigation, we would like to put a number of questions to you that we believe you can help us answer.'

'Of course.' Alvarenga patted his devoted carer on the

wrist. 'Marco. Take me back into the office and then you can take a break. I'll call you when it's time to take me home.'

'*Sim*, Senhor Alvarenga.'

Jack smiled to himself as he and Da Silva tucked in behind the wheelchair and followed its wake into the CEO's lair. The fact Alvarenga addressed Marco in English was impressive. *Inclusive*, to use a current buzz word.

Inside, Jack observed a distinct contrast. Not in-your-face opulence – this space was striking by its lack of ostentation. Bare almost to the point of austere. Yes, there was a large conference table, capable of seating twelve comfortably. Other than that, there was just a plain pine desk for the boss and a nondescript closet in the corner.

Marco removed a chair at the head of the table and Alvarenga slotted in. Jack and Da Silva sat opposite each other a metre from the CEO. As he retreated, Marco received a final instruction: send up refreshments for the honoured guests. Jack had a premonition Alvarenga's genial attitude – which came across as a hundred percent fake – wouldn't last too much longer.

'Before you start asking questions,' said Alvarenga, both hands on the desk. 'Let me say for the record that Entrega Rápida and all its employees are devastated by what happened yesterday.'

Da Silva placed a recording device on the table. 'Do you mind if we record this conversation?'

'Not at all. Actually. I might do the same thing. One moment.' He placed a call on his mobile and the woman from the reception appeared in seconds with an iPad. She placed it on the table, pressed a button and disappeared without saying a word.

Jack leaned back in his wire mesh chair, its basic design

belying the comfort it afforded. If the beanpole Marco didn't arrive with coffee soon, there was a risk he'd fall asleep. As if on cue the man returned, pushing a trolley laden with a jug of water and glasses, a large coffee pot, cups, saucers and an assortment of dry crackers, cheese and dried fruit. Neither Da Silva nor Alvarenga stopped their recordings while each served himself a hot drink. Jack was the only one to reach for the food. He nibbled a dried apricot, washed it down with ice-cold water. The coffee was subpar for a company like this, but a welcome hit of caffeine nevertheless. To his surprise, Alvarenga placed a packet of Rothmans cigarettes and a portable ashtray on the table.

'Either of you mind if I smoke?'

'Not unless Jack objects,' said Da Silva.

Jack hadn't smoked for a couple of years and would never take it up again, however inhaling some sneaky second-hand stuff sometimes felt like a naughty indulgence. 'Knock yourself out.' He immediately regretted his answer when Da Silva produced a silver cigarette case. Soon the two were puffing away like old friends about to break open a chess set. Luckily, the air-conditioner sucked the carcinogenic cloud away, leaving only the scent of tobacco.

'OK,' said Da Silva, producing a copy of the letter he'd retrieved from the victim's apartment. He turned it around for Alvarenga. 'Recognise your signature?'

'Of course,' he said, pulling the letter closer and holding it inches from his eyes. 'Ah yes, I remember. I refused her request for an interview.'

'And why would you do that? Were you afraid she would put some rather uncomfortable questions to you? Ones you'd prefer were never asked?'

'Not at all. I simply had no time available in my crowded schedule.'

'Funny,' said Da Silva, taking the letter back and reading it silently. 'I can't seem to see a specific time in the letter.'

'It's irrelevant. If I were to speak to a journalist on the record, it would only be an accredited one from a major newspaper, not some niche magazine with a tiny readership.'

'Not true,' said Jack.

'I beg your pardon?' said Alvarenga in a sharpish tone.

Da Silva elevated half of his eyebrow hedge. Jack sensed the CEO wasn't at all thrilled about being challenged.

'It may be niche, as you say, however the readership is huge.' Jack dragged out the last word. 'It's published in several languages and has a circulation of several hundred thousand. It's quite an influential publication.'

Alvarenga crushed out his cigarette and immediately lit another one. 'Really? I had no idea. Perhaps I based my decision on the fact I'm not overly familiar with that title. I'm a busy man, Detective Lisbon.'

'Were you aware that Ms Farooq was about to expose your company?'

'Expose?'

'For human rights abuses, among other things.' Jack kept his expression as neutral as possible.

'I might like to call on my legal advisor, if you don't mind.'

'We're not charging you with anything,' assured Da Silva, tapping ash from the end of his cigarette.

'I'm fully aware of that,' said Alvarenga with unbridled confidence. 'I just want to make sure you don't try and, as the English say in their TV cop shows, fit me up.'

The detectives agreed it would be a good idea for the company's legal man to observe the interview. Five minutes later, a jaunty athletic man called Carlos Ahmad joined them in the boardroom. He put down the takeaway coffee cup he'd brought with him, shook the guests' hands and flashed them an engaging smile. Jack knew it was best to view lawyers' smiles with the same amount of caution as you would a snarling pit bull.

'You'll be pleased the smoking will now stop, Detective Lisbon. Carlos cannot abide my habit.'

'I thought you were the boss?' said Jack.

'Ha ha. Good one. Yes, I am, but Carlos here is an absolute marvel. I accede to his wishes because losing him would be a terrible loss for the company.' The lawyer proudly thrust out his long chin as the CEO sang his praises. 'We recruited him from the Ministry of Foreign Affairs, you know?'

Jack sat back in his seat, then leaned forward again, intrigued by this revelation.

Da Silva looked from Alvarenga to Ahmad and said, 'Salma Farooq was interning for the Ministry. Were either of you aware of that?'

'I left there, how long was it, eight months ago.' Ahmad rubbed his cheek. 'I'm sure we never crossed paths.'

'I see.' Da Silva gnawed a fingernail for a couple of seconds. Jack knew why – the victim had started at the Ministry around six months ago, so Ahmad was telling the truth and a different approach was needed. 'Ahmad...' said Da Silva. 'Is that a Moroccan name?'

'My heritage is half Egyptian, actually. I am very proud of it. But your question seems a little, and I don't want to sound hysterical, xenophobic.'

'For goodness sake!' Da Silva produced the second letter

he'd found at Farooq's apartment. 'This letter,' he tapped it with his fingernail, 'signed by the CEO, confirmed to the victim that a trade deal was going ahead with a Moroccan textile company. Farooq has a Moroccan father and dual nationality with that country. I thought perhaps you may have had a hand in stitching this contract together based on a possible shared background. That is the only reason I asked.'

Ahmad stapled his fingers together. 'Hmmm. Interesting you make the connection simply because I have an Arabic surname.'

Jack had to leap to Da Silva's defence before he was unjustly accused of being an out-and-out racist. 'My friend Zé here is asking a question any police officer would ask. Me included. There's no need for you to get all offended about it.'

Alvarenga held up a hand. 'Of course. No one is suggesting anything improper.'

'On the contrary,' said Jack, warming to the chase. 'Salma Farooq was suggesting a company was engaged in some highly improper activities.'

'Do you have evidence it was my company?'

'We're confident the second part of Ms Farooq's article will be found on her laptop computer,' said Da Silva. 'And that it will name Entrega Rápida.'

'So,' said Ahmad. 'You have her laptop in your possession, yet still haven't been able to access its files? I would have expected better from the Polícia Judiciária.'

Jack sensed Da Silva squirming beside him. Time to stick it to the head honcho. 'There's one thing I don't understand, Senhor Alvarenga. You say you were far too busy to grant Ms Farooq an interview, yet not too busy to draft rather lengthy letters to her.'

'It took no time at all to "draft" them, as you put it, because they are based on templates.' He buzzed the receptionist, spoke no more than half a dozen words. She brought in an opened laptop. Within minutes, Alvarenga had demonstrated that, indeed, both letters sent to Salma Farooq would have only required minor tweaking to personalise them; otherwise, the content of the templates was identical to the letters she had received from the company. 'Again, let me state that I, Carlos here, the entire Entrega Rápida company, offer our sincerest condolences to the victim's family. However, unless you have concrete proof of any involvement, I suggest you focus your attention on other suspects.'

'That's assuming you've found any,' added Ahmad, with, Jack thought, a touch too much smugness.

'Once we crack the laptop, we'll be back.' Da Silva gathered his cigarettes and lighter.

'Even if you do,' said Alvarenga, rolling his shoulders, broad from years of using them for propulsion, 'and it is our company that she had it in for, it will only be one woman's opinion. We've been accused of all kinds of nonsense over the years. And I've never found it necessary to liquidate someone for making those accusations.'

Da Silva stood, thanked Alvarenga for giving of his time. He turned to Jack. 'Let's go.' And added, loud enough for the CEO and his lawyer to hear. 'Let's see if they change their tune after Quintal has spoken with the informant from the Ministry of Foreign Affairs.'

'What informant?' said Ahmad, his voice squeaking a little on the last syllable.

But Da Silva and Jack were already out the door.

## Chapter Fifteen

JACK'S MOBILE buzzed in his pocket. He fished it out, read the text, pocketed the phone. 'Can I ask you something, Zé?'

'Sure,' said Da Silva, his eyes narrowed as he concentrated on negotiating the late afternoon traffic.

'Mirabella tells me she's taken Skye for a drive to Cascais. Where's that?'

'A seaside resort town, about thirty minutes' drive from Lisbon.'

'She says they'll be there for another couple of hours. Which means...' He fumbled for a stick of gum to rid his throat of the clinging taste of tobacco.

'You've got time to attend the briefing?' came the hopeful prompt.

'*Exatamente*, sunshine.'

THE SITUATION ROOM, or whatever they called it here in Portugal, reminded Jack of the larger get-togethers he'd experienced in London and Brisbane. Shoulder to shoulder cops eager to contribute to a big case. He'd gotten unused to them over the last few years, with the Yorkville CIB's debriefs numbering fewer people than you can fit into a phone booth. Yes, Da Silva was leading a small team of senior detectives at the pointy end of this investigation, but there were dozens of others, plain clothes and uniformed officers, beavering away in the background, doing the boring desk work, monitoring social media chatter, knocking on doors. At a guess, there were between thirty and forty bodies on deck tonight. A quarter were sitting, the rest standing around the edges and at the rear of the room.

Da Silva, hands behind his back, addressed the team in Portuguese; by the tone Jack assumed he was asking a question. A resounding *sim* with no audible dissenters echoed around the room, and the man switched to English. Just for his benefit. Jack shook his head slowly in disbelief at the display of courtesy.

The state of play, as summarised by the boss, was as follows. Physical evidence so far was not providing clear answers. The tram was still impounded, although forensics were nearly finished with it and the vehicle would be back on the streets tomorrow, much to the relief of the head of the transport department. No murder weapon had been found. The autopsy was cut and dried and offered no further clues as to the identity of the killer.

Next up: the human factor. There were two clear suspects identified, each with solid motives for murdering Salma Farooq, and each pointing a finger at the other party. And a "collective" suspect in the Entrega Rápida company.

After detailing what he and Rebelo discovered at the victim's apartment, and the inconclusive interview just completed with Alvarenga and his lawyer, Da Silva called upon detectives to report on their findings, starting with Raquel Quintal.

'As per Detective Da Silva's orders, Catarina Rebelo and I spoke to the informant inside the Ministry of Foreign Affairs, Rosa Braga, at her place of work. She was most reluctant to speak, at first denying she was the mole at all. A flash of our ID and the alternative option of us approaching her superiors with a warrant helped to change her mind.' Murmurs and soft chuckles ensued before Quintal added, 'She took us to a nearby café where we put a number of questions to her. Wary from the start, Braga did eventually confirm that she had been feeding Salma Farooq information about secret negotiations between Entrega Rápida and a Moroccan textile company, Vital Fashions. She also shared her suspicions about gross human rights violations in Morocco that Entrega Rápida was turning a blind eye to.'

'Did Braga say why she was giving information to a journalist?' said Da Silva.

'Yes, sir. But I had to coax it out of her. She said she became friends with Farooq, who convinced her the human rights abuses Entrega Rápida was profiting from were so bad they warranted the company being exposed.'

'Did Braga say how she happened to have access to this information?'

'No, sir. She's like a frightened rabbit. I recommend we go carefully with this witness.'

*Not if I was handling it, thought Jack. Go hard or go home.*

'Did she mention a man called Carlos Ahmad?'

'No, sir. Should she have?'

'Not necessarily. But it is interesting that he used to work at the Ministry of Foreign Affairs until, how long ago was it Jack?'

'Eight months.'

'Yes. And Farooq started her internship there six months ago. Technically, they would not have crossed paths at the Ministry. However the window of two months separating the two events – him leaving and her starting – is so small it raises questions in my mind. Questions we ought to follow up on with Senhorita Braga.'

'Yes, sir,' nodded Quintal.

'What was the Portuguese company's role in the deal?' the question came from a tall female at the back with a blue-tinged buzzcut.

'Good question, Beatriz,' said Quintal. 'Exclusive rights to ship cheap garments all over Europe. But here's the interesting part. Braga believes the deal wasn't a very lucrative one in terms of the money to be made by each company.'

'Then why were these negotiations "secret", as you described them, Raquel?' said Da Silva.

'Braga wasn't sure, but she believes there was some personal transfer of wealth involved at the top level.'

'Quo bono? Who stood to gain?' said Jack, who sat in the second row directly behind Rebelo.

Quintal pursed her lips. 'Braga claims she doesn't know. However, I believe she's lying. She was reluctant to speak at all.'

'If Braga did divulge that information to the victim, there's a good chance it's on Farooq's laptop.' Da Silva called on a representative of the digital forensics unit. 'Estêvão. Any progress with the victim's computer?'

'It's proving a difficult task, sir. The device, a MacBook Pro, is protected like nothing I've ever seen before. We are hopeful tomorrow we can unlock the hard drive.' He paused, then added with a touch more confidence. 'However, the mobile phone was not so tough. I mean, the provider has given us the logs of all her calls, texts and even emails she sent from the phone. You will have a printed report on your desk, and all detectives will receive copies in their inboxes.'

'Well, that's something I guess.' Da Silva tapped a whiteboard with the names of the three suspects written in black marker pen, the third one generically referred to by the company's name followed by "Alvarenga/Ahmad" and a question mark. 'There were three more persons we identified initially who had the most contact with the victim.' On the board he wrote Rafael Xenos AKA "The Porcupine", best friend Fernanda Brito and Professor João Grosso.

Rebelo said from the front row 'Xenos should be eliminated from inquiries. As suspected, he's a troll who spends all day attacking hundreds of social network users, not just Farooq. We've contacted the platforms he cruises with requests for account information. We should have that tomorrow, but in my opinion he doesn't figure as a serious suspect.'

'Excellent, Catarina.' He pointed at the Professor's name. 'What about this guy?'

Quintal, hands thrust deep in her pants pockets, said, 'We arrived unannounced at the university. He wasn't there, so we drove to his home. A rather modest bungalow on the south side of the river. He wasn't keen to talk, wouldn't let us in the door. He appeared to have done a lot of crying and, by the smell on his breath, drinking. He said he couldn't face going to work and was taking the rest of the week off. He did agree to talk to us at his home tomorrow. He seemed kosher.'

'Catarina?' said Da Silva.

'I agree. A couple of random people at his university department we spoke to said he was a great teacher and devoted to his students. No favourites, he loves them all the same.'

*How touching, thought Jack. Of course he has favourites. Everyone has favourites. However, he kept his mouth shut.*

'Before I wind this up for tonight, could Detectives Horta and Costa tell us what they got out of Farooq's best friend, Fernanda Brito?' said Da Silva. Jack could sense the shared relief as the assembled officers realised they could go home soon, unless they were on night shift.

Jack rested his arm on the back of his chair as he twisted his body around to see better.

'We managed to verify that Salma Farooq stayed with Brito at her home the night prior to the murder.' Junior Detective Bernardo Horta looked up from his notes. 'Before I get into the results of the interview, I have to say, like others have reported, this witness was devastated by what happened.' A glance back at the notes. 'Detective Joana Costa and I met the witness at her apartment where she lives alone. She said she and the victim stayed up late on the Wednesday night, Brito watching TV reality shows, Farooq working away on her article.'

'They didn't interact during the evening?' said Da Silva.

'They did,' confirmed Costa. 'Farooq took a couple of breaks before Brito went to bed. She confided to Brito she was stressing about the article, wanted to make sure everything was accurate. She had an appointment with her editor tomorrow, and she believed everything would work out fine, even though someone from Entrega Rápida was threatening her.'

The room sucked in its collective breath.

'Who?' yelled out Da Silva.

'A man you mentioned already. A Senhor Carlos Ahmad.'

## Chapter Sixteen

'ZÉ.' Jack massaged his jaw as an idea occurred to him. 'Tell me why the IT guys still haven't gotten inside Farooq's laptop.'

'I can't answer for them. But they are doing their best, I can assure you.' Da Silva's voice contained a smidge of shame. Perhaps embarrassed in front of Jack because his colleagues weren't able to access this important part of the puzzle that remained stubbornly locked.

'No offence, mate, but perhaps their best ain't good enough. Listen. I know a guy in London. We've been friends for years. I'd trust him with my life, and there aren't many I can say that about. Anyway, he's a self-taught hacker. One of the best around. He's helped me out on a couple of cases. Hell, if it weren't for Micky Knox I may never have tracked down my kid in the north of Scotland and rescued her from a particularly nasty villain.'

Da Silva's head half turned, then snapped back to the front as a car overtook them a little too close. He swore loudly at the other driver, calmed instantly and asked, 'What are you suggesting?'

'You borrow the laptop from the evidence room, Fed Ex it over the channel, Micky cracks the computer for you.'

'Are you out of your mind?' Even from side on Jack could see the man's eyebrows had lifted a couple of centimetres. 'I can't remove evidence.'

'Sure you can. All you gotta do is sign it out, replace it with another one of the same model, Bob's your uncle.'

'I can't believe you're even–'

Jack burst out laughing. 'I'm just joking, Zé. I know your techies will be having another go at it tomorrow. But they might fail again.' He held up a finger and said, 'I'm sure if I asked Micky to fly over and have a look – under your supervision – he'd jump at the chance.'

'I don't know about that. I'm not sure the budget would allow…'

'Forget it. Micky's got more money than you and me put together.' The dial tone was already playing as Jack called his friend.

Three minutes later and it was settled. Knox would book the next available flight to Lisbon and render whatever assistance he could to the investigation, no remuneration offered or expected.

'But you'll be in the Algarve,' said Da Silva once the call was terminated. 'How's that going to work?'

'Micky's a big lad. Well, he's not very tall, but you know what I mean. He don't need me around to hold his hand. If your team cracks it before he arrives, he's happy to spend a couple of days sightseeing.'

The last two minutes of the drive were consumed with Da Silva's opening up about the stresses of his home life. It came as no surprise to Jack, the signs were all there in the man's body language.

'I knew there was something up.'

'I always seem to be doing things that upset my wife. I try to be careful but she gets triggered by the slightest thing. Or maybe it's the constant demands of the job, me getting home late that she doesn't like.' He sighed. 'No matter what the situation, I'm always the bad guy.'

'Hmmm,' said Jack. 'My marriage was a disaster, but that was mainly down to me and my bad habits. It seems to me that you'd make a better husband than I ever was to my wife, God rest her soul.' He gave a wan smile. 'I'm sure the two of you will work it out eventually.'

'I thought the surprise gift of that cat would cheer her up. But it didn't exactly have the effect I was hoping for. It's clawing the furniture all the time. I fear the damn thing will drive us both mad.'

'Maybe you could try a dog,' said Jack in his best compassionate tone. 'I got one. Best decision I ever made. Apart from seeking custody of Skye, that is.'

'It won't be easy.' It seemed Da Silva hadn't been listening to what Jack was saying. 'But I think I might have to put her to sleep.'

'Your wife?' Jack just managed to keep the bobbling chewing gum in his mouth.

'No, the cat.'

'Blimey, you had me worried there for a second. Anyway, we're here.'

Da Silva extended his hand and Jack shook it firmly. 'Thanks for everything, Jack. And for asking your friend to fly over. I'm sure we won't be needing him though.'

'I reckon you're right,' said Jack. He poked his head through the open passenger window. 'I guess you'll be talking to Rosa Braga again tomorrow? Her mentioning Ahmad sounds like he's the key to this whole case. I'd be studying that fella inside and out. He rubbed me up the wrong way – even more than his Doctor Strangelove boss.'

'What doctor is that?'

'Never mind.' He had a hunch the Peter Sellers movie reference would be too obscure, but it was worth a shot.

'I will say this: it's a pity you won't be around to lend a hand over the next stages of the investigation.' Da Silva's lips formed a thin line.

Jack showed open palms. 'I'd love to 'n all, but my daughter's my main focus. I'm sure you lot can find the killer without me.' Jack tapped the bottom of the passenger door window frame. 'Keep me posted though, won't you?'

'Will do.' Da Silva's mouth opened and closed like a goldfish before he said, 'I've got to attend a press conference tomorrow night. One of the Deputy National Directors – the DNDs – will be sitting next to me, which will really test out my nerves. I don't mind admitting, I'm not looking forward to it.' He paused before adding, 'I've seen a couple of videos of you speaking to the media. I wish I could be half as confident as you.'

'You really went to the bother of checking them out?'

'Yes. I was looking for inspiration.'

Jack empathised with the man. It took Jack a few times in front of the camera before he figured out the best way to handle tricky journalists. He had no idea whether the Portuguese press were as tough as the Aussie brand, but he had no reason to think it was any different. He reached across and gave Da Silva a friendly pat on the arm. 'You'll be fine, sunshine. Just imagine you're talking to me when you look at the camera and that I'm agreeing with every word you say. And if a journo gives you a hard time, pretend they're a criminal.' He barked a short laugh. 'Which is often not far from the truth.'

'I'll certainly give those methods a try.'

As a weary Da Silva made his way home to his grumpy wife, Jack pushed the case out of his mind. He stood still to savour the moment of just being there. The evening was as hot in Lisbon tonight as it got back home in Yorkville, with the blessed difference of lower humidity. Still, sweat had dampened the back and armpits of his shirt. A dip in Mirabella's pool would be the perfect way to cap off the day. And later, he'd suss her out about assisting in the enquiry. On the drive back with Da Silva it dawned on him that her specialist skills might lead to a breakthrough.

The pool already had two occupants when he slid open the glass doors to the patio. Soft ambient lights around the edges of the pool created shadows in the canopy of palm fronds above. Skye shrieked when she spied her father, like she hadn't clapped eyes on him in years. Her little arms and legs thrashed away like the mosh pit dancers a younger Jack slammed against at punk gigs. All enthusiasm, no finesse. She sent thousands of droplets into the air as she splashed her way towards the ladder. Jack grinned to himself – they'd work hard on those swimming skills once he got her back to Yorkville. Jack looked on bemused as she inched her way to the ladder, then clambered up with ease once the aquatic part of the dismount had been dealt with. She had her wet body pressed up against him before he could lay a towel on the wooden sun lounge, arms squeezing his thighs.

'I didn't think you two would be back until after 8:00pm,' said Jack, looking into his daughter's eyes.

'Mirabella decided we'd seen enough.'

The hostess was also out of the water now, dabbing at

her hair with a towel. 'And maybe it's got something to do with you anxious to get home in case your father was here?'

Skye laughed. 'Yeah, that too.'

'You two finished swimming?' said Jack.

'I am,' said Mirabella. 'I've got some work to do before bed.'

'I'm staying with you!' said Skye. 'You can teach me the Australian crawl. Since you live there, you must be an expert at it.'

'Not sure about that. I'm a better boxer than swimmer.' He shadow boxed a power jab–rip–hook combination to demonstrate the point. 'Hop back in the water, love. I'll be with you in a minute. I want a word with Mirabella before she toddles off, OK?'

'Sure.'

With Skye traversing the breadth of the pool, holding onto a kickboard for dear life, Jack floated his idea. 'Could you look into the family ties of someone for me?'

Her forehead furrowed as she frowned. 'I'm not sure that's entirely ethical.'

'C'mon. Is shooting a woman on a tram ethical?'

She folded her arms across her chest. 'What is it you want exactly?'

Jack rubbed his cheek. 'That's the thing. I'm not sure. There's this bloke, Carlos Ahmad, works as a lawyer for a company called Entrega Rápida. I'd like to know if he's got relatives in Morocco. He claims he's of Egyptian heritage, but I don't trust the guy one bit. Da Silva told me his passport has him down as Khalid Ahmad, but he prefers to go by Carlos.'

'Is he a suspect in the murder?'

Jack shrugged. 'Could be.'

'Without his cooperation, I'm not sure I can get very far.

There *is* a branch of science that could help you, investigative genetic genealogy, but it uses DNA and only the police are allowed to do this kind of thing. I can't approach Ancestry.com or any of the other sites to hand over data to me. They would tell me to, how do you say it in English, take a hike.'

'We ain't collected the bloke's DNA since he's not charged with anything.' He reflected for a moment that he'd said "we" and not "they", made himself an honorary member of the Polícia Judiciária.

'Then that avenue's not an option for you.'

'Hmmm. Are there other ways?'

'Of course. Manual methods. But again, without the man's assistance, I'm not sure how successful I'd be. And searching Egypt and Morocco is going to be tricky, especially if the records are in Arabic. Although I do speak French, which would open up more doors on the Moroccan side.'

'Could you at least try?'

'I'll work on it for a couple of hours, but I'm not calling any people on the phone or anything like that. Just the normal searches. This is just as a favour – you still have to grant me that interview for my website, remember?'

'I haven't forgotten.' Jack tied the string of his boardshorts. 'Give me half an hour with the kid. I'll call Da Silva after that, see if he can pass on Ahmad's date of birth, stuff like that. It appears the guy's a clean skin as far as a criminal record goes, at least in Portugal. But who knows what you might find, right?'

'Yes,' she sighed. 'Anything's possible.'

AT 11:15PM and with Skye in bed asleep, Mirabella tapped on the door. 'Jack, you awake?' He was engrossed in a Peter James crime novel, right at the suspenseful part where the killer lay in wait, about to attack the unsuspecting detective. Her knock made him start. His heart began to beat faster as he said, 'Come in.'

He flicked on the bedside light and sat up straight. She stood in the doorway in a sheer nightie. The curves of her body stood out under the translucent material. As his eyes grew accustomed to the light levels he noted with relief that she had a bra and knickers on underneath.

'Got a minute?' she said, twirling her hair.

'Sure.' He put his paperback to one side and tugged the sheet up around his chest. He was sleeping in his customary attire – his birthday suit – and suddenly felt very exposed.

Mirabella strode softly across the carpet, sat on the edge of the bed without a trace of self consciousness. Jack's legs trembled under the covers. Other things were happening, too. He hadn't been intimate with a woman for many months, and her presence was creating a completely natural biological reaction. He gritted his teeth and thought about the boring minutiae of doing his tax return instead. The tactic wasn't working. She leaned over, smoothed a couple of wrinkles on the sheet and said in a whisper, 'I've got something you might like.'

He could barely bring himself to speak as he struggled to breathe. She smelled like he imagined the gardens of heaven did. He gulped twice before he managed to say, 'What…is it?'

From behind her back she produced a couple of printed sheets of A4. 'Voila!'

'Ahmad?'

She nodded. 'It wasn't easy, but I did manage to track

down a handful of people I suspect could be his relations in Casablanca.'

'Do they work for—'

'Vital Fashions?'

'Yes!'

She patted the bedsheets, narrowly missing his growing appreciation of her. She stood quickly. 'Come downstairs, I'll make us a coffee and we can go over what I found.'

## Chapter Seventeen

DRIVING to the Algarve proved a trickier proposition than he first anticipated. He'd never driven a car with the steering wheel on the left-hand side and he had to concentrate hard to avoid having a crash or running into the guard rail. On top of that, there were other inconveniences you could only get used to with practice, a luxury he didn't have time for. The seatbelt felt weird slung across his left shoulder instead of the right, negotiating intersections was a nightmare, and overtaking was so problematic he decided not to attempt it. At home he had no compunction nudging the car up to 20 kph over the limit – on the Portuguese highways he kept it at 10 kph under. Which pissed off a lot of drivers behind his rented Opel, but he didn't care. He blocked out the abuse and raised middle fingers, clenched his teeth, and kept his eyes on the road.

'How much further, Dad?'

Jack smiled. At least it wasn't "are we there yet?" 'Not long, love. Just twenty-two minutes according to the GPS.' Jack noticed his knuckles were white on the steering wheel as he hugged the narrow coastal road, steep cliffs and crashing surf way below. It would have been smarter – and faster – to take the main highway, but he figured you could see boring highways in any country. Who knew when they'd be back in Portugal, if ever?

They had already been through the delightful towns of Sines, Vila Nova De Milfontes, where they had lunch and a refreshing dip in the Atlantic Ocean. Then brief stops for coffee and soft drinks at Cabo Sardão, Praia de Odeceixe and Praia da Bordeira. At the last stop the pair sat on an outcrop of red rock, sipping ice-cold colas, mesmerised by kite surfers below negotiating the waves and wind like sea eagles.

Jack's mobile rang in the console. He asked Skye to answer it and hit loudspeaker. 'Hello?'

'It's Zé. You sent me a text late last night.'

'Yeah. I got some interesting news for you. Turns out Ahmad wasn't being a hundred percent truthful with us. Mirabella cast her magic genealogy wand.'

'And?'

'Yes, his parents are from Egypt, he spent his early years in Cairo, up to the middle of high school. Then he moved to Portugal.'

'I hate to stop you, but we know all that.'

'Did you know his mother got divorced ten years ago? Then she married another guy – a Moroccan – whose son to a previous marriage is the chief financial officer of... drum roll...Vital Fashions.'

'What!'

'Yep. Go back and confront Ahmad and Alvarenga with it. I'd take Quintal along if I were you. She strikes me as a can-do copper.'

Da Silva ended the call in a mood of quiet confidence, and the road trip continued.

As the chequered flag loomed on the GPS monitor, Jack's jaw dropped as he saw the scale of the house behind the stone wall. The white paved driveway that led from the roadway to the edge of property positively shone. Their destination, a rambling eight-bedroom *quinta* with plenty of land, lay on the outskirts of Sagres, a historical town at the south-west tip of Portugal.

'Uncle Paulo must be doing all right with his architecture business,' said Skye. Jack grinned: the kid was learning to perfect the art of understatement.

Someone must have been watching them because a massive steel gate slid open slowly, revealing the mansion on the other side. Elegantly framed by white columns and crowned with Portugal's ubiquitous orange terracotta roof tiles, adorned with pergolas covered in bright purple and red bougainvillea flowers, the joint must have cost a fortune. Maybe even more than Mirabella's place.

In the baking heat of the late afternoon, Jack parked the rental under the shade of a spreading Jacaranda. 'We've got these trees Down Under, sunshine. Amazing purple blossoms, but you'll have to wait till October to see them.'

'Did they import them from Australia, like the gum trees we saw along the way?'

Jack scratched behind his ear. 'I don't think so. Something tells me they came from Brazil originally, but I wouldn't bet my life on it.'

'You like these trees?' came a male voice from somewhere outside the car. 'Remind you of home?'

Jack looked through his window to see a deeply tanned man of average height and pronounced dimples in a broad-brimmed hat. He knew from his Internet researches that this was his cousin Paulo. Instinctively, he shoved open the car door, leapt out and embraced the man like he was a brother. Because to Jack, that's what he was. The closest thing to a real brother he had. With both parents passing away some years ago and no siblings, this man, this beautiful, warm man, was the flesh-and-blood link to his Portuguese heritage. The son of his father's brother.

*His family.*

Nothing was said for at least a minute as both men embraced. Finally, Jack managed to say, 'I thought you were in Madrid until next Monday.' He let go and took one step back. He realised his eyes were moist. But so were Paulo's, so he made no effort to hide the tears. 'We were going to meet your wife and kids first, then you. What happened?'

'I couldn't wait,' said Paulo. 'I'll fly back to Madrid tomorrow. It's no big deal commuting between Spain and Portugal. Family is more important than business after all.'

A tug on the shirt sleeve. Skye looked up at the two men. 'I'm here, too, you know.'

Paulo picked her up like she was made of air and she squealed with delight. Jack noticed Paulo's massive arm muscles. Much too big for the head of an architectural company who presumably spent a lot of time behind a desk. Jack couldn't resist giving the biceps a prod. 'What's this, sunshine? Are you a bleedin' body builder?'

Paulo put Skye back on the ground and said, 'No. Boxing's my thing. I understand you like it too.'

There were no words. Jack could only shake his head.

---

A DELIGHTFUL BARBECUE dinner of pork, octopus and a medley of vegetables in his belly, an untouched glass of red wine in front of him, Jack had to pinch himself. After a miserable childhood, beaten by his father for the slightest thing, a mother marinated in cheap brandy and prescription tranquilisers, here was the family he wished he'd known. Peaceful, gentle, generous people. Sure, like everyone they would have their problems, but it was obvious that this was a loving home. And Jack would be damned if anything would ever stop him providing the same thing for his daughter.

'You don't like the wine, Jack?' said Paulo's wife, Linda. 'It's made from grapes harvested from our own farm.'

'I'd love to try it, but I gave up drinking a couple of years ago. Health reasons.'

'But you let me pour it for you?' said Paulo, incredulous.

'Oh, yeah.' Jack fidgeted in his seat. 'It's this thing I do. In a bar I'll order a rum with a coke on the side. I never drink the alcohol, but it's there as a reminder of how it used to control me. Now, I'm in charge.' He raised a glass of water. 'I'm sure the wine is wonderful. *Saúde*. Cheers!'

'*Saúde*,' said Paulo and Linda together.

Linda gathered plates, stacked the dishwasher and excused herself to check on the kids. Skye was already playing outside with her newfound cousins, a rambunctious boy with a gap-toothed smile called Cristóvão, who they referred to simply as Cris, and a girl with scraped elbows and knees called Maria. Their hysterical laughter rang throughout the house as the adults talked about their lives.

'I hate to bring this up so early in our…I don't even know what to call it…relationship?' said Jack. 'No, that sounds wrong.'

Paulo poured thick black coffee for himself and Jack. 'I know. It's very strange. But Linda and I are delighted you and Skye are here. Stay as long as you like.' He took a sip and smacked his lips. 'So, what was it you wanted to bring up?'

'The murder of the young lady on the tram.'

Paulo's lips bunched, then he said, 'Not a problem. Everyone's been talking about it. The story is all over the news. As a detective, yes, the case must interest you immensely.'

'Me and Skye were on that very tram. I saw it happen.'

'No way!'

'Now I'm kind of assisting the cops with the investigation.'

'How on earth have they kept that out of the news?'

'Well, I'm guessing your police force has much tighter discipline than I'm used to. To be honest, I'm surprised it hasn't leaked.'

'What about witnesses and suspects? They might leak it at some point, no?'

'Everything on the tram happened so fast, people ran for their lives. No one would remember me as being a passenger on that tram. As for suspects, they aren't likely to want to bring attention to the fact the cops have their eye on them, so they tend not to leak information.' Jack suddenly remembered something. 'A funny thing, though. There was mention in a news site from back home that an Australian – not named – was rumoured to have been a witness to the crime. Anything like that in the Portuguese press?'

Paulo shook his head before saying with half a smile. 'Perhaps the discipline in our police isn't as strong as you thought?'

'Hmmm. Maybe not. I'll be keeping a close eye on the bleedin' lot of them.'

The men decided to take the conversation out onto the deck to have some cold drinks and take advantage of the sea breeze cooling off the night air. Watching the kids kicking a football around, Jack thought there'd be no harm in asking. 'Have you heard of a company called Entrega Rápida?'

Paulo put down his bottle of beer, turned to Jack. 'Yes. They're quite well known in some circles.'

'Which circles?'

'Transportation. Delivery of large items, mainly. Construction companies we work with sometimes use them to ship building materials.'

'Know any of the people who work there? Gorge Alvarenga or Carlos Ahmad?'

A shake of the head. 'Do you know who's the head of Fed Ex or UPS?'

'Good point.' Jack folded his hands in his lap, smiled as Skye and her cousins fell about in the dirt, laughing their heads off. 'You know what?'

'What?'

'I'm actually glad you don't know anything about those guys. Gives me a chance to sit around for a couple of days and do nothing but enjoy the weather and the company of my new relatives.'

Paulo laughed. 'You are misguided, Jack.'

'Waddaya mean?'

'You won't be doing nothing. I've got plans to teach you a few lessons in the boxing ring.'

'Let's see about that, sunshine!' Even as he said it, the flex in Paulo's upper arm told Jack the man would be no pushover.

## Chapter Eighteen

THAT FUNNY LITTLE detective looks as nervous as hell. His pathetic red moustache twitching away like the whiskers of a terrified mouse. The freckles and receding hairline don't do him any favours, either. Hands touching his face constantly, eyes shifting up and down, right and left. He's absolutely shitting himself. Even with the Deputy National Director of the Polícia Judiciária there to hold his hand. What a loser.

How pitiful they are. Both of the useless fools, standing on the steps in front of their grand headquarters, a forest of microphones pointing at them. No doubt they've rehearsed their non-answers to deflect from the lack of results, to fudge the narrative of their hopeless investigation.

Can't blame them too much, though. I've covered my tracks well.

A stiff drink in a shot glass. Ginjinha, a patriotic choice for this occasion. Two more, perhaps, but that would do. Lots of things to do in the morning. A small sip, savouring the berry, cloves and cinnamon flavours of the infused liquor. A wine would be better for the stomach, but we're making an exception tonight; enjoy life to the full as the cops bumble through their TV comedy routine.

They've got *nada*. If they had half a brain between them, they would have pieced it all together by now, come to see me again. There would have been a pounding knock on the door. A menacing phone call to invite me down to the station for questioning, a search warrant to look at my home, my devices. Something!

I'm in the clear, they can't touch me. Murder weapon secreted away safely for now, ready to pick up and toss in the Tagus once the heat dies down. Careful to make sure no one paid the slightest bit of attention to me on the tram, or before I got on it. And they were all too frightened to look at me after I'd killed her. Scattering in all directions like marbles on a sloping floor as I pumped warning shots into the air. Best of all – no security cameras anywhere. All of which equals...*no arrest.*

But let's not get too cocky about it, not just yet. Maybe they'll announce the name of the killer live on air? No, no, no, of course they won't. That's ridiculous, because the killer is me.

And there's been no knock on the door. No phone call. No search warrant.

Another sip of the delicious ginjinha, feet up on the footstool.

OK, here we go. The important man in the more expensive-looking suit is about to speak. He's clearing his throat.

*Bring it, idiotas!*

PAULO STRETCHED his feet out on a black leather ottoman, pointed the remote at a large wall-mounted flatscreen TV, turned it on. Jack had only seen a bigger one in the Pelican Bar in Yorkville. 'You like football?' asked Paulo, momentarily taking his feet off the stool to open a packet of crisps and tip them into a bowl.

'Skye does, so she tells me. FC Barcelona. Is there a match on? I'll call her in from the garden if there is.'

'Yes, a European Cup qualifier. Us against Sweden. Should be a great game. Here we a...wait, they're going to a live media conference at the police headquarters.'

'Nice one.' Jack leaned back in the leather armchair, locked his fingers behind his head. His mood instantly dropped. The image of a fidgeting Da Silva in a crumpled jacket and poorly knotted tie didn't fill him with confidence. Hopefully, he'd find his mojo once the reporters started firing questions at him. The man to his right, square jawed and a head taller than Da Silva, on the contrary, appeared totally unruffled. The stony face of a career bureaucrat who he knew could handle difficult people with ease. 'Turn it up, please, cousin. I love a good press conference. I want to hear...oh...' He suddenly remembered the broadcast would be in Portuguese and he wouldn't understand a word of it.

Paulo laughed gently as his wife came into the living room and sat on the arm of her husband's chair. 'Jack thought he could understand Portuguese for a moment there.'

Jack made a mock-hurt face which quickly morphed into a grin. 'Maybe you could interpret for the ignorant foreigner?'

'My pleasure,' said Paulo. 'If I miss anything, I'm sure we'll be able to find a video online afterwards.'

Jack nodded. 'Sure. But I'm really only interested in the

big picture, so you can probably skip some parts you think are irrelevant.'

For the next fifteen minutes, Paulo frantically tried to keep up with the questions posed by the journalists and the answers given by Da Silva and the Deputy National Director. From time to time photos of the victim and the crime scene flashed on the screen together with a hotline number for people to call. It was a tough battle for Paulo, who struggled to hear what was being said as he relayed to Jack what he'd just heard. Towards the end, Jack said, 'Maybe don't interpret the questions from the media, just Da Silva's answers.'

Paulo sighed with relief, and the flow of his translating instantly improved. Da Silva was soon giving a summary, reading from a prepared statement, which boiled down to a reassurance that this was a targeted one-off incident and the public should feel safe using Lisbon's public transport system. The city remained one of the safest capital cities in Europe – if not the safest – and there was absolutely no need to panic. The police were pursuing a number of promising leads and he hoped to have the culprit arrested and charged in the near future.

Da Silva wound up his spiel with a final plea to the public to bring forward any information that could assist the investigation. Did they see the murderer on the tram or prior to him getting on? Could they provide a detailed description? Anonymity guaranteed for tips. Ten minutes later and the event ended with a nod and an *obrigado* from the DND. Jack, not entirely surprised, had learned nothing about the state of the investigation he didn't already know.

'What did you make of that?' said Linda. 'Are they any closer to catching whoever killed that poor girl?'

'Not yet,' said Jack. 'These press conferences are a thing

the police have to do. To make the public feel like something's being done, even if little progress is being made.' He dropped his voice to a whisper. 'Just between us, they have a couple of suspects in their sights, one in particular that I mentioned already.'

'From Entrega Rápida?' said Paulo.

'Yeah, him. And his boss too. The victim was about to publish the second instalment of an article exposing a company profiting from human rights abuses. Everything points to it being Entrega Rápida.'

'You think the company had so much to lose they had her murdered? On a tram, in the middle of peak hour?'

'Quite possibly.'

Paulo shook his head. 'It doesn't add up to me.'

'Why not?'

'Lots of companies gain from the misery of others. The EV in my garage has a battery that contains minerals mined by children working as slaves in the Congo. It's not even contested by the car manufacturers. But they are able to put enough distance between themselves and the product that they can get away with it. They shift the blame to China or wherever. It's horrible, but no one seems to care. The exact same thing could apply in this case with Entrega Rápida.'

'*Could* being the operative word.' Jack crossed his arms as the referee blew his whistle to get the teams ready for kick off. 'But we haven't seen the second part of that article yet. Perhaps it exposes more than she led everyone to believe in the first part. Perhaps something about individuals rather than the company as a whole.'

'Do you really think that's the case?'

Jack shrugged. 'Without any real physical evidence, I effin' hope so.'

## Chapter Nineteen

GRITTY SAND WORKED its way between his toes as he ducked and weaved. The sun beat down fiercely even in the early morning. Another couple of hours and the sand would have burned their feet, but at this hour it was nice and warm. A rip to the midsection from a heavy right hand hit home, making Jack gasp. Paulo's compact and fast technique surprised Jack. He'd expected a more lumbering pugilist, considering the big arms and chest.

He managed to avoid most of his cousin's pot shots, but the odd one got through his defences and stung painfully. There would be bruises all over his torso tomorrow. So far he'd shown restraint and concentrated on defending, letting Paulo do all the attacking. As he crouched and bent his knees to get under a whooshing left hook, out of the corner of his eye Jack spied a small crowd of maybe ten beachgoers who had gathered to watch the middle-aged men slugging it out. It was a workday, but this was tourist central, even at 7:00am.

Jack stood tall again, smacked his gloves together and

held them in front of his face. He bobbed and weaved, angled his head to be just out of reach of Paulo's exploratory punches, then flicked out a lightning left jab. Paulo must have been relishing his perceived advantage in being the aggressor, became complacent. The jab squeezed through the close guard, landing flush on his cheek. Paulo bawled an oath in Portuguese. Jack saw blood trickle from a tiny cut. *Nothing too serious, box on.*

'Good one, Dad!' Skye enthused from among the spectators.

What sounded like gleeful encouragement to their father came from Cris and Maria, although their actual words were a mystery to Jack. Whatever, it seemed to work, as Paulo cracked his neck from side to side and made come-on gestures with his gloves. His head moved back and forth like a cobra waiting for the exact moment to strike, then – *whack!* A thunderous right cross to the jaw that sat Jack on his backside in the sand. Jack cursed himself as he fumbled about on hands and knees; he should have followed up the jab with another and a straight right.

'Come on, sunshine,' said Paulo, failing spectacularly to replicate the cockney accent. 'You can do better than that.' He held out his hand and Jack leveraged himself up.

'How many rounds to go?' Jack mumbled through the pharmacy mouthguard. A poor fit compared to his usual one, but better than nothing.

Paulo consulted with his son, who looked at the screen of a mobile phone, gave the answer. Paulo looked back to Jack. 'This is the last round of eight. A minute left.'

Jack nodded and shaped up. 'Defend yourself, cousin.' No way this was ending with him being the last one to bite the sand. Time to channel his inner brawler.

'Same to you, *Bife*.' Paulo held his hands up high.

To Jack the word sounded like "biffer", a compliment which made him smile through the drool of his mouthguard. However it was half an hour later, when he had finally regained full consciousness, temples pounding and an egg growing above his right eye, that he discovered the word was no compliment, simply a nickname the Portuguese reserve for the English.

---

'DADDY, WHAT HAPPENED?' Skye's wide eyes loomed over the side of the bed.

'Simple, love. Your uncle knocked me out fair and square. I underestimated him and paid the price.'

'But…I thought…'

'You thought I was unbeatable?'

'Well, yeah…'

'I can take on lots of fighters and win.' He sighed. 'But not always, sweetie.'

'You're taller than Uncle Paulo. And older…I mean you've got more experience.'

Jack grimaced as he tried to sit up. 'Yeah, but…'

'Stay down, *Bife*.' Paulo leaned over the other side of the bed, gave Jack a nudge on the shoulder. 'You need to rest for a couple more hours. I'm calling a doctor. You should be checked out.'

'Yes,' said Skye.

'No,' said Jack. 'I've had worse hidings than this.' He probed the inside of his mouth with a finger. 'At least I've still got all the teeth I arrived with.'

Skye held a cold compress against her father's swelling eye. 'But how did he beat you?'

'What your uncle neglected to tell me before I agreed to this insanity was that he boxed in the bleedin' Olympics!'

Skye glanced up at Paulo, with one eye narrowed said, 'Is that true?'

'*Sim.* Yes.' Paulo smiled as if it happened only yesterday. 'It was twelve years ago, but it's true. I did fight at the 2012 Olympics.'

'Bleedin' heck,' said Jack. 'That was in London. My turf. I probably watched you on a TV in some bar or other. You're adding insult to injury now, mate.'

'Don't feel too bad,' Paulo said, a wistful look in his eyes. 'I didn't win a gold medal.'

'Well, at least there is some justice in this world,' Jack mumbled. 'You're a very clumsy fighter, sluggish on your feet. If I were ten years younger I would have–'

'Only silver.'

Jack pushed himself up onto his elbows. 'What? That's brilliant! Can I see the medal?'

'Dad, I don't get it.' Skye screwed up her face. 'You should be mad at him for hurting you.'

'Nonsense. We have an Olympic boxing legend in our family. It's an incredible honour for me that he knocked me out.'

Paulo called out to his son, who appeared in a flash, panting from running. He sent him on his way again, and in minutes the lad returned with the medal.

Jack slowly opened the box, took out the prize and held it in his hand, eyes closed in reverence. 'You've done the family proud, old son.' He handed the box back slowly. 'I think you were right about me needing more rest. Gimme two hours and I'll be up and about.'

A deep sleep ensued until he felt a pair of small hands

shaking him awake. Skye held his mobile out to him. 'I answered it, Dad. Hope you don't mind.'

'Of course not, love.' He did mind. He was having a nice and not entirely gentlemanly dream about DC Claudia Taylor, who, he suddenly realised, he missed very much.

'It's Detective Da Silva.' Skye skipped away; the other two children calling out to her was obviously more tempting than eavesdropping on her father's conversation.

Jack took the phone. 'Yeah?'

'Have you had a relaxing weekend?'

'I got beaten up a little bit.'

'What?' The alarm in Da Silva's voice was almost palpable. 'Have you called the local police?'

'Not necessary. All resolved thanks, Zé.' He took a sip of water from a sports drink bottle beside the bed. 'Now, what can I do for you?'

'I was going to ask you to come back to Lisbon to help with some interviews. The DND knows you've been assisting us. He even offered to pay you, rather handsomely, for your efforts. But...' Jack heard a cigarette lighter spark up, the first draw on a cigarette, 'since you were bashed up, I won't press you on it. Enjoy the rest of your holiday.'

'Wait, wait, wait.' The police offering to pay him put an interesting spin on things. One of the charities Sarah donated to was struggling for funds. A woman's shelter of some kind. He'd ask Sarah's sister Jocelyn for the details. 'How much exactly?'

'No. I withdraw the offer.'

'Look, I'm fine. I was involved in a...ah...sporting activity, during which I got injured. Slightly. I was exaggerating when I said I got beaten up. How much is your boss willing to pay me?'

'Two thousand euros for one week. The same amount if

we find the killer in less time. Whether it's down to your work or ours, you get the money regardless.'

'Deal,' said Jack. Skye would be in safe hands here on the *quinta* until he got back. 'When do you want me there?'

'As soon as you can manage it.'

At the end of the conversation, Jack gingerly rolled his battered body out of bed. Bruises were already starting to bloom on his stomach and chest. He grabbed his shorts, tried to pull them on, but his brain wouldn't cooperate with his legs. Shit. Maybe that KO blow was worse than we thought? He sat down for a moment, sucked in a couple of litres of air. He tried again, fingers shaking, again, unable to coax his feet into the leg holes. Driving back to Lisbon in this state was a dumb idea. He folded the shorts and placed them on a chair before getting under the covers again. He grabbed his mobile and was scrolling through his contacts to call Da Silva back to decline the offer when a soft knock came on the door.

'Yes?'

Paulo appeared in the threshold, hands on hips, in the company of another man. A short dapper fellow in smart casual business clothes. 'This is a friend of mine, Dr Emilio Soares,' said Paulo. 'I'd like him to–'

*Why didn't people listen?* 'I said I didn't...' He pulled himself up before the rant had a chance to build. He had to know how bad his concussion really was. 'I'm sorry.' He gestured towards the bed. 'Please, come in and check me over.'

The doctor whipped out a stethoscope, blood-pressure cuff and a mini pen torch. After subjecting Jack to a number of tests he gave his verdict. Full rest for 24 hours. If he was still having trouble with coordination, he recommended a full CT scan at the earliest opportunity.

'I need to drive back to Lisbon. Today.' Jack manufactured his most pleading expression.

'Why?' said Paulo.

'I just do.' Jack didn't want to divulge the real reason in front of the stranger, although he was sure Paulo could guess it was to do with the murder case.

The doctor laughed. 'No chance. It's not just yourself you need to consider, but other people on the roads. Wait until tomorrow, at least. I'll come back after lunch and check you over again. My feeling is that by then you'll be OK to drive.'

'Looks like you're not going anywhere for the moment,' said Paulo.

Jack pushed his head back into the pillow. 'Fine.'

## Chapter Twenty

JACK STOPPED TWICE on the drive back to Lisbon to swallow five aspirins. He wasn't sure if the coffees from roadside cafés he drank in any way counteracted the effect of the painkillers, but he didn't care. It was his one surviving vice and he wasn't giving it up for anything. Dr Soares had given him the all clear to drive, although he cautioned Jack to stop and call Paulo the minute he sensed any weird symptoms. Or, if he was more than halfway to Lisbon – Mirabella. Fortunately, the throbbing pain in his head and the muscular aches in his stomach and chest didn't qualify as weird symptoms – they were the collateral damage boxers suffered as part and parcel of the sport. Mild drugs were more than enough to deal with those inconveniences.

As he got closer to the outskirts of the capital, even with the increasingly heavy traffic, Jack felt he was finally getting the hang of driving on the wrong side of the road. Not that hard, really. Most of the world did it, no problem. He changed his mind about how easy it was when, fifty kilometres from the Vasco da Gama bridge, he veered across onto oncoming traffic, thinking he was in his proper lane. The blaring of the driver coming at him head on was so loud, even through closed windows, he had to pull over and take some deep breaths. The rest of the trip he focused so hard on driving that his headaches seemed to get worse. Some internal mantras to convince himself the pain wasn't real helped him get across the finish line.

He returned the car to the rental agency near the airport, gave the key back with a shaky hand and took a taxi to Mirabella's house. A change of clothes and a shower, more coffee and a little meditation were in order before the late-afternoon briefing with Da Silva.

'Why are you here?' said Mirabella, confusion knitting her brows as she opened the door for Jack. 'And where's your daughter?'

'I left her with her cousins. They're getting along like a house on fire.'

'You're not worried about leaving her there without you? You must be aware of the case of the young Irish girl who disappeared from the Algarve. She's never been found.'

Jack sighed. The saga of the little blonde girl made headlines twenty years ago and occasionally made a reappearance when so-called new evidence was found. 'The thought had crossed my mind. But she couldn't be in better hands.' He recounted the epic battle with Paulo. 'To paraphrase Mr T, I pity the fool who tries anything with him around.'

Mirabella stared blankly, the cultural reference missing by a mile. 'Meaning?'

He filled her in about his cousin's phenomenal sporting achievement at the Olympics. Then he asked the logical question, 'Why didn't you tell me about that?'

She shrugged. 'You and Paulo have a lot to learn about each other. Why should I spoil all the surprises?'

'Why? To spare me the indignity of being knocked out.'

'So that explains the bruise on your cheek. But,' she finally ushered him inside the house, 'you don't look very upset by it.'

Seated at stools in the kitchen, Jack explained something that not many outside the fighting fraternity would understand: that being pummelled into next week by your champion relative is nothing to be ashamed of. She agreed with that assertion. She didn't get it at all.

'I ain't got too much time to chat. Da Silva's waiting for me at the station and the day's nearly over.'

'What are your plans for after this meeting?' He wasn't sure, but he thought he could detect a hint of an invitation in her question.

'No plans. I'm prepared to sit out a long briefing, but it could be over quickly, depending on what's come to light since the press conference.'

'If you get back early, I thought you might like to go out to dinner in the city. Just adults for a change? Maybe catch a fado show?'

'What's that?'

'A traditional style of singing that started here in Lisbon. I think you would like it.'

'Sure,' he said, hoping like mad the briefing would live up to its name and be brief. 'I'd like that.'

'Call me when you know what's happening.'

'Will do.' The sooner he got there, the sooner he'd return.

*Showered, changed, gone.*

'BLEEDING HECK,' Jack blinked hard. 'Micky! No one told me…'

Micky Knox rose from his seat, embraced his friend in a bear hug.

'Careful, now.' Jack flinched as the pressure to a rib made him think Paulo had done more damage than first suspected. He broke free from the embrace and took a step back. 'I'm a bit delicate.'

'What happened?'

'Long story.'

'Yes.' Da Silva rolled up his shirt sleeves. 'I'm afraid Mr Knox is not able to sit in on this meeting. He just dropped by for a quick chat to introduce himself. Which he's done. I've just received orders from higher up to limit his involvement to the computer, nothing else. He will be back tomorrow morning to attempt to gain access to the victim's laptop, under the supervision of our head of IT, however he will now have to leave.'

Jack thought the Portuguese detective's treatment of Micky was a tad dismissive, however he realised it was only natural his friend's role would be a limited one. He shook Micky's hand, promised to call him after the briefing and arrange an immediate catch up, his tentative arrangement with Mirabella relegated to the "maybe later" file.

'And I want your word, Jack,' continued Da Silva, 'that you will keep the contents of tonight's discussions confidential.'

'Fair enough,' Jack agreed. Sure, he'd already shared information with Paulo, but he was family and Jack's gut told him the guy was solid. Not to mention smart and therefore a solid sounding board.

With Micky out of the room, the conversation among the small lead team, which included Quintal and Rebelo, first turned to the increase in the number of witnesses following the press conference. 'We now have a general description of the killer from several people,' said Da Silva, spinning a pen on the table. 'Fortunately, they seem to be in agreement. Unfortunately, the description is as follows: male, average height, dressed in dark clothing – hoodie with long sleeves rolled down and trousers despite the warm weather. Also a dark cap. No logos on the clothing, and if there were, no one is remembering them. No remarkable facial features, tattoos, piercings, nada.' He pressed a button on a remote control and an image appeared in the TV monitor behind Da Silva.

The team let out a collective sigh. The AI-generated image could be anyone. 'This is the problem with today's world,' complained Jack. 'Everyone on their effin' mobiles all the time. I guarantee whoever sat right next to this bloke had their eyes glued to a screen.'

'True,' nodded Quintal. 'I worry for the future of humanity. However, we have to deal with the situation as it is, not wish for how we would like it to be.'

There was a hint of admonishment in her tone, but it was a lot easier to wear than one of Paulo's punches. 'On the positive side,' said Jack. 'If the killer is a paid hit-man, which I highly suspect, then we're better served focussing on motive, rather than means.'

Da Silva clicked his device again, and the large wall monitor filled with images and names of the people in their sights – suspects and witnesses. Pointing at the gallery, Jack said, 'The professor. He was identified early on by Detective Rebelo. Any more out of him? You were going to follow up with him at his home on Friday after he wasn't in much of a mood for talking on Thursday.'

'You've got a good memory,' said Quintal, the corners

of her mouth drawn down in an appreciative frown. 'Indeed, we did drop by his home Friday morning. He wasn't there. We waited for a while, in case he had popped out for some shopping or whatever, but Catarina thought something might be up after an hour had gone by. She rang the university, and it turned out he was back on campus.'

'A fast recovery from his inconsolable grief, one would think,' mused Jack aloud.

'Yes,' agreed Quintal. 'Miraculous. And suspicious.'

'What did he have to say for himself?'

'He said he was denied the extra time off because he had suffered a couple of bouts of illness earlier in the year and had used up all of his leave.'

'Sounds plausible,' said Da Silva.

'We double checked with the university's administration,' said Rebelo. 'They didn't want to divulge anything to begin with, but Detective Quintal got them to cooperate. Turns out he was telling the truth.'

Rebelo said, 'He still had a lot of redness around the eyes, and his mood was pretty low. I got the impression he would have preferred to stay home.'

'Unless he's desperate for the money, he could have taken leave without pay,' said Jack. '*If* he was grieving over the victim as much as he claimed.' He took a sip of water. 'The guy's full of shit. He's a very good looking dude. Probably shagging half the female students in his department.'

'I doubt that,' said Da Silva. 'But I'm not liking him as a suspect. What would he have to gain by her death? We've got no evidence the two were ever in a relationship, that he was in love with her or that he was jealous of someone else. Where's the motive for this man?'

Jack shook his head. 'I can't see one at all.'

Rebelo offered more information. 'Perhaps there was

something between them but it was kept secret. Detective Lisbon was onto something, though. Grosso does seem to have a reputation for being a lady's man around the campus.'

'Among whom?' said Jack.

'Students. Random chats we had with people walking the hallways revealed he has slept with quite a few women he's taught over the years.' She pressed the button of her pen a couple of times before a glare from Da Silva made her stop.

Jack made to stand up. He felt like pacing as he ruminated the information he was learning, but the stabbing pain in the ribs kept him in his seat. 'Let's not forget the mother. Farooq shared all her personal stuff with mum. If the professor was involved in any way, the mother would know about it.'

'Jack's right,' said Da Silva. 'Without more than baseless rumours about a professor who may get a little too friendly with his students, I'm inclined to keep a more relaxed eye on him from now on.' He spun in his chair to look at the names and photos on the screen, then back to face the others. 'We have more likely suspects to deal with.'

Jack said, 'Did you manage to get another audience with Alvarenga and Ahmad after what Mirabella discovered about the Moroccan connection?'

A shake of the head. 'They have left the country.'

'What the…'

'They are currently in Paris but the unfriendly woman on reception advised they'll be back in a few days. With no charges, we cannot hold them here in Portugal.'

'Did Rosa Braga reveal anything else?' said Jack. 'You and Quintal were going to grill her again.'

Da Silva's face fell. 'The Ministry of Foreign Affairs has blocked us from speaking to her.'

'You're kidding me! That's political interference, isn't it?'

'Yes it is. And I'm pissed. I don't know how the machinations of government work. The DND passed the message onto me, but there's a caveat. And it all hinges on one thing.'

'What?'

'The laptop. Specifically, whether or not it contains evidence that Farooq had found what you have labelled "the Moroccan connection". In other words, if she stumbled upon something that implicated Ahmad through his stepbrother, we will be given the green light to pull in whomever we deem fit for questioning. Warrants will be issued immediately and the Ministry, as the expression goes in English, can go fuck itself.'

Jack leaned back in his chair, observed the broad, approving smiles creeping across the faces of Quintal and Rebelo. Jack's gut told him Da Silva only used profanity as a last resort.

The lead detective looked at Jack with a squinting left eye. 'Let's hope your friend Micky can, how do you say, deliver the goods.'

Jack smiled. 'Me too. I'd like nothing better than to pay another visit to those smug pricks with a warrant in my hand.'

Rebelo coughed. 'Excuse me?'

Jack gave a small frown. 'I meant in Zé's hand.'

## Chapter Twenty-One

'ARE you feeling confident about hacking into the victim's laptop?' Jack swirled ice around in his whisky, put the glass down and drank his cola instead.

'I was when you called me and asked for a hand.' Micky stared back up the street at the lovers walking hand in hand down the narrow Rua dos Remédios that ran through the charming heart of the Alfama district. Da Silva had highly recommended this tiny bar, a joint that had seating for only a dozen customers. He promised it would be an authentic Lisbon dining experience. Jack reserved judgement as he perused a stained menu with only a handful of dishes on offer.

'Not now?' Jack followed Micky's gaze up the street. The approaching pair of lovers weren't in the flush of youth. In fact, they were well into their fifties at least. They leaned into each other as they strolled slowly along the cobblestones. Perhaps a little tipsy, perhaps simply intoxicated by each other. There was still hope for Jack.

'It's a MacBook Pro.'

'And?'

'Depending on the encryption software protecting it and a few other factors, I might have a chance. They're famous for being hard to crack.'

'But not impossible, right?'

Micky took a sip of Sagres beer, a brew made, strangely, in Lisbon and not the town it was named after. 'Correct. But I'm not offering any guarantees. I mean, if the might of an entire police force with all their forensics tools can't get into it, why would I succeed?'

Jack raised his soft drink. 'Because you're Micky Knox, that's why.'

'Look, it will give in to cracking eventually, even if it's not me who does it.' With no pre-warning Micky switched the subject. 'Did you know McNair's Gym has closed down for good?'

'No way!' Jack sucked in a lungful of the warm night air. 'Why?'

'Not enough punters. Bigger, fancier gyms are drawing the younger generation away. And the old breed are dying off. That's one version. Another is that the mysterious owners simply decided they needed the cash for some other venture.'

'It's a travesty either way.' Jack stared at the amber tones of his untouched whisky over ice. The bare-bones boxing gym where he'd spent so many years as a young man was an institution on his old patch in South London. It was where he learned his array of pugilistic skills, and quite a few dirty street-fighting tactics as well. He'd had loads of raw talent as a youngster, got special coaching from the man Jack would eventually send to meet his maker. He didn't have as much talent as cousin Paulo it would seem, but enough to be a serious contender for a title. He had made it to the last round of the Great Britain middleweight championship for under twenties. But he'd gotten too confident, lost a fight he should have won easily. He stupidly let his guard down and the other kid took full advantage, knocked the absolute shite out of him. After that, Jack's life spiralled out of control, and he only managed to claw it back by a miracle. Micky Knox had played a pivotal role in his salvation later in life. To Jack, Micky was capable of almost anything.

'It was open only a week ago. I trained there the day before Sarah's funeral, worked myself into a bleedin' lather. I can't believe it.'

Micky gritted his teeth and whistled. 'Everything comes to an end, Jack.'

'Yeah, but McNair's, Micky?'

Micky shrugged. 'Even McNair's, mate. People will find an alternative.'

'Yeah. At twice the price for half the bleedin' service.' Jack grabbed the laminated menu, ordered cod and chips. Which, as was the standard about town, came with rice for a double carb hit. Micky ordered the same.

While they ate, Jack told Micky about everything that had happened since his arrival in Portugal, leaving out the details of the suspects and the key witnesses. Once upon a time, when he was a bent copper working for the London Met, he would have revealed all to Micky, betrayed a superior's trust just for the hell of it. Not anymore. Da Silva said don't blab, and that was that.

'You attract trouble like a dog turd attracts flies,' said Micky, picking the bones out of his fried *bacalhau*. 'Unbelievable.'

'Please,' said Jack, raising his knife and fork. 'I'm eating!'

'Sorry.' Micky slugged more of his beer. 'If you won't divulge the details of the investigation, you can at least tell me more about this Mirabella woman. Sounds like you've got a thing for her. Even if you haven't said so in as many words. Your expression changed when you was talking about her. Your face softened, which isn't something one would normally say about your beaten-up old mug.'

'You know I'm not good at talking about this kind of thing.' He forked up a heap of rice. 'So I won't. Next question?'

'How's Skye getting on?'

This was a topic Jack was only too happy to talk about. Micky had taken a shine to the kid. They got on like old friends when she and Jack came to stay at his St Albans home. Jack had a feeling the guy almost considered himself to be her godfather. Jack would never admit it to Micky, but that role was reserved for his Yorkville CIB colleague, Aden Trevarthen. Jack rambled on about his wee pride and joy; Micky listened attentively as he chewed, smiled and laughed along. And if there was too much detail in the telling of the story, if Jack was laying it on too thick about Skye's prodigious intellect, charm and good manners, Micky made no comment about it.

'Sounds like the kid's gonna do all right with a devoted dad like you looking after her.'

'You're not often right, mate, but this time you are,' Jack said with a lopsided smile.

'My treat for tonight, OK?' Micky pulled a handful of high-denomination euros out of his pocket as the waiter came to collect the payment. 'But be realistic about the kid, wontcha? She's not far off entering those difficult teenage years. Remember what you was like at that age. Probably a right bleedin' handful.'

'You wouldn't have a clue what I was like, Micky. I'm twenty years older than you.'

'You know what I mean. Hormones start raging, your head's all over the place. Moody, snappy, even a touch rebellious. You and me wouldn't have been much different at the same age.'

Jack grunted.

'All I'm sayin' is, be extra careful as she gets older.'

While Micky was talking perfect sense, Jack's eyes remained fixed on the wad of cash in his mate's clenched fist. Secured with a couple of rubber bands the roll looked like some drug dealer's takings. If Micky was into anything dodgy, Jack had no intention of asking. Let sleeping dogs lie and all that.

'Where to now, Jack?'

He consulted his watch. Getting on for 23:00. 'I'm beat and it's late. I'm heading home and I suggest you call it a night, too. You've got a computer to crack tomorrow.'

Micky waved one hand dismissively as the other stuffed the money back into his pocket. 'I've heard Lisbon has some wild night life, and I'm keen to party on. Maybe meet a nice local lady.' He paused. 'Like you have.'

'Steady on, mate. There's nothing going on between me and Mirabella.'

'As you say,' said Micky with a cheeky grin.

They strolled in silence until the road flattened out and they reached the end of the Alfama district. Micky sparked up a cigarette within view of an imposing pink stone building with Museu do Fado plastered across the entrance. Mirabella had suggested a night out listening to fado. Must be awesome stuff if it had its own museum, Jack mused.

Micky and Jack hopped in separate taxis, one heading to the party district of Bairro Alto, the other to his temporary digs in Belém.

At 23:45, Jack tiptoed his way across the tiled floor,

shoes in hand. Ten years ago he would have been crashing into furniture, pickled to the gills after a night out with a mate. Now, he was like a Ninja who could visit every room and steal the silverware with no one knowing.

'Jack?' Mirabella's tousled head popped up over the back of the couch. 'Are you interested in listening to some fado?'

'Oh, you're up.' *Ninja skills must be lacking.* 'Are you serious? Nothing's gonna be open at this hour.'

'I know a place that's open till 02:00am.'

Jack scratched his chin thoughtfully. 'That's a tempting offer, but I want to be alert tomorrow. My friend flew in from London, and he's helping out with the murder enquiry. I'd like to be in my best form.'

'I think you are in pretty good form as you are.' Her voice was husky from sleep.

*Why are you doing this to me?* was what he wanted to say. Instead he said a simple, 'Thanks.'

She sat up slowly. 'I've got a couple of old DVDs in that cabinet over there. Compilations of Lisbon's best fado singers. We could watch that?'

Jack was in no doubt now. The woman had designs on him. But the image of Claudia Taylor in the back of his mind, memories of the sound of her voice, held him back. 'How about tomorrow?'

'Sure.' She folded up the sheet she had covering her, put cushions she'd been using for pillows at either end of the sofa. She flashed him a forced smile. 'Let's do that.'

Before he turned in for the night, he had to ask the question. 'Were you sleeping on the couch waiting for me to come home?'

She smiled sheepishly. 'Maybe. I'm worried about–'

He leaned across, kissed her on the cheek. 'You're an absolute treasure.'

As he walked up the stairs he felt her eyes burning into him. He'd have a chat with Claudia tomorrow, ring her on the pretext of being concerned about his dog Daisy. It wouldn't be a lie; he did miss the pooch. He'd had some direct messages from Aden Trevarthen with updates and photos. Aden and the dog were having a ball together. But it was the best excuse he could think of for contacting Claudia. If he didn't get the vibes he was hoping for as he spoke to Claudia, lovestruck hostess Mirabella might just get what *she* was hoping for.

## Chapter Twenty-Two

'HE'S CRACKED IT,' said Da Silva triumphantly as he shook Jack's hand. 'We've got into Farooq's laptop.'

'Already?' said Jack. 'How?'

Da Silva's russet moustache quivered. 'What do you mean how! You're the one who brought us Senhor Knox. Whatever methods he used, they worked, and he has kindly shared them with our IT department. I'll be recommending an ex gratia payment to him.'

'You're going too fast, sunshine. Slow down. It's barely gone 09:30. Surely he couldn't have got you a result already?'

Da Silva shook his head. 'I'm as amazed as you are. He came in an hour and a half ago, bleary eyed and unshaven, smelling slightly of alcohol. To be honest, I immediately doubted your competence, Jack. Your friend looked like a homeless man who'd staggered in off the street. I must say, though, despite his appearance, he retained his enormous charm.'

Jack shook his head. 'He's made of tough stuff, is our

Micky. Still young enough to stay out late partying and come to work the next day to get the job done. And a gentleman into the bargain.'

Quintal gave a perfunctory knock at the open door before she and Rebelo entered the briefing room. The women said their good mornings, placed takeaway coffee cups on the table, handbags on the floor, and pulled up chairs.

'Catarina,' said Da Silva. 'Please contact the DND's office, tell him we have the evidence he requested. Ask him to organise warrants to confiscate the personal devices of Gorge Alvarenga, Khalid "Carlos" Ahmad, and also Rosa Braga.'

'Yes, sir.' She walked out of the room, phone pressed to her ear.

'Excuse me,' said Jack, leaning forward and resting his wrists on the edge of the table. 'Isn't that a bit premature? You've only just got into the victim's laptop. Surely…'

Da Silva beamed back at Jack. 'Salma Farooq, fortunately for us, had her files meticulously organised and labelled.' He paused, reached under the table and plonked printed-out files in front of Jack and Quintal, and one where Rebelo had been sitting.

'First, we have the completed second instalment of her exposé. In it, as we expected, she names Entrega Rápida as the company hinted at in the first instalment.'

'You've read it?' said Jack.

'Yes. She doesn't hold back. Of course, a lot of her quoted information came from "unnamed sources" inside the Ministry of Foreign Affairs, and Entrega Rápida could dispute the claims.'

'Would the article alone be enough to initiate a police investigation into the company's activities?' said Jack.

'Perhaps, perhaps not. But either way, publication of the article's conclusion would've done enormous damage to the company's reputation.'

'Enough to have her killed to suppress the story?' said Quintal. 'Then why didn't they steal her laptop and destroy the evidence altogether?'

Da Silva shook his head. 'That's an excellent question. Unfortunately, I don't have an answer.' He looked at his team, manufactured an optimistic smile. 'However, we have found other material that we can use to our advantage.' He patted his pockets like he was looking for cigarettes, then gave up.

Rebelo rejoined the group. 'DND's office is onto it sir,' said Rebelo. 'We can expect the warrants to be prepared and signed by 2:00pm.'

'Excellent.'

'Are Alvarenga and Ahmad back from Paris yet?' said Jack.

'They're booked on a flight arriving tomorrow morning.'

'Did their lovely secretary tell you that?'

'No. She refused to divulge the information. In fact, it was Micky Knox.'

'What?!'

'I asked him if he could access an airline's manifest, and to my shock, he did.'

Jack lowered his voice to a whisper. 'You can't be serious about this.'

Da Silva folded his arms. 'As a heart attack, I believe is the expression. Senhor Knox assures me he got in and out quickly and undetected.'

'A minute ago you were questioning his bona fides because he came in looking like a tramp, now you've got him hacking airlines' effin' databases? I gotta give you credit, Zé, you've got a set of enormous balls on you.' He flashed a look of apology at the women. 'Sorry, ladies.'

The four detectives paused the conversation for a moment to flick through the pages Da Silva had printed out, eyes boggling. All except Jack's – the text was entirely in Portuguese.

'I can't read any of this.' Jack threw his hands in the air.

'I'll explain, step by step,' said Da Silva.

The salient sections, highlighted in bright yellow, contained a series of emails exchanged between Rosa Braga and Salma Farooq.

'Braga accused Ahmad of standing to gain five million euros on the back of the deal with Vital Fashions. He was going to split the money with his new boss, Alvarenga. The weird thing is, the value of the transportation contract between the two companies, while still profitable, was a lot less than five million.'

'Then how does it add up to a sound business deal?'

'It doesn't,' said Quintal. She pointed at a highlighted section on the third page of the printout. 'This email claims the extra payment was a "door opener", paid for by a corrupt Moroccan official. It was to secure Alvarenga's agreement to provide special treatment for other Moroccan companies.'

'Who,' said Jack, 'presumably, paid a fee to the corrupt Moroccan official to grease the wheels to get them into the program.'

'Precisely.' Da Silva nodded sagely.

'Tell me,' said Jack. 'Do you have more than accusations made by Rosa Braga? Any corroborating emails between Entrega Rápida and the Moroccans?'

Da Silva pursed his lips. 'Not yet. Once we confiscate

Alvarenga's and Ahmad's devices, I'm sure we'll find the kompromat.'

'Sir,' said Rebelo. 'Can you remind us, when is the contract between the two companies going to be signed?'

'At the end of the month. And I'm already guessing your next question. Has this five million euro payment, or should I say bribe, been paid yet?'

'That's exactly what I was wondering,' said Rebelo.

'According to the email from Braga on page…' he licked his fingers and flicked over a couple of sheets… 'six, the money is set to be transferred the day before the deal enters into effect, being the 29$^{th}$ of June.'

Jack stood gingerly, his ribs still aching. 'This is all well and good, but is there anything originating from Ahmad's or Alvarenga's email accounts? So far, all we've got is your mole Braga passing stuff on third hand.'

'I knew you'd say that.' Da Silva couldn't have looked more smug if he'd tried. 'Look at the last page.'

Jack's eyes narrowed. A screen image of an email. But it made even less sense to Jack than what he'd seen so far – this one was in Arabic. 'Enough already, Zé. I feel like I'm waiting for Hercule Poirot to do the big reveal.'

'It's a shot Braga took on her mobile phone. She happened to be in Ahmad's office while he was called away to a meeting. He carelessly left this particular email open. Braga told Farooq in a message how lucky she was to snap the photo, because seconds after she took it the screen saver came on, which would have required entering Ahmad's password to log back on. Which she, of course, didn't know.'

'But what's written in Ahmad's email?'

'We had it translated as a matter of urgency, by three independent accredited translators to make sure we got it right. All translations say the same thing. It's from an elected senior official in the Moroccan coalition government, a gentleman called Nizar Bensaid. It confirms that Carlos Ahmad would receive the promised five millions euros in a Panamanian account he had nominated. It ends with a note of thanks for Ahmad's efforts.'

A tap on the door interrupted them. Bernardo Horta stood there with a serious look on his face. Jack feared something had gone wrong. Then, Horta beamed as he waved two pieces of paper. He blurted a round of rapid-fire Portuguese before he realised Jack was present. Rebelo quickly interpreted on Horta's behalf. 'Great news. The warrants for the confiscation of the devices of Rosa Braga and the men from Entrega Rápida have been expedited based on the contents of the laptop.'

Horta handed the papers to his boss. Da Silva clapped his hands. 'Right. It's a show of force. And a chance for Jack to have a look inside the Ministry of Foreign Affairs' beautiful palace. We're all going.'

———

THE WELCOME AT THE MINISTRY, housed in the spectacular Palácio das Necessidades, wasn't the warmest Jack had ever witnessed. He kept his distance, standing behind the three legit detectives and two more cops in uniform brought along to do the heavy lifting. He happily let the others bear the brunt of the animosity from the belligerent gatekeeper in reception. Finally, a young man in a suit and long dangly lanyard appeared and guided them along a maze of corridors before admitting them into Braga's office. She looked up in shock.

Again, the opening exchanges took place in Portuguese,

however Jack could guess by the players' body language what was going on. Da Silva displayed the warrant in his outstretched arm like the Sherrif of Nottingham come to collect taxes from a peasant. He held his jaw firm but spoke to her in the politest of tones. She nodded, stepped away from her desk. The two uniforms unplugged her computer tower, keyboard and monitor, plus a couple of other peripheral devices, bagged them up and took them away.

Back at the station, things became a lot clearer to Jack, as Da Silva insisted Senhorita Braga speak in English. He calmly and thoroughly explained she wasn't in trouble or suspected of anything, but she could insist on someone being present with her for moral support. She declined the offer.

'I'm not very strong in English,' she said, a touch disingenuously.

'Somehow, I doubt that,' Da Silva countered. 'But if you insist, we can set it all up with interpreters, and the process will take twice as long as it should.'

Braga frowned deeply. 'OK, I will try.'

'Thank you.' Da Silva offered a smile as warm as the afternoon sun. 'Your cooperation could help us convict a killer.'

Braga nodded slowly. 'I've told you everything I know. I spoke to those two just yesterday,' she pointed at Quintal and Rebelo, standing with their hands behind their backs like soldiers at ease on the parade ground.

'I know you did. However, I don't believe you told them everything. In fact, I know you didn't. And I can understand why.' He tapped a pen on the table. 'I have to inform you that we have broken into Salma's laptop, and we've found strong evidence that links the second part of her magazine story directly to Carlos Ahmad. That evidence is a photo I presume was taken with your mobile and sent to her in an email.' He pushed a photocopy across to her. 'Am I correct?' She looked at the image and nodded.

Braga placed her head in her hands, soft sobs escaped from between her fingers. Jack slapped the table hard with the palm of his hand. 'I fail to see why you're crying!' he growled.

He heard gasps from Da Silva and the women behind him. The poor girl before him *was* frightened, as Quintal reported yesterday, but this was a horrific murder case and tough talk was justified. If they wanted a result, going softly with Braga wasn't going to help matters. 'Please confirm for Detective Da Silva you sent the email to Salma Farooq.'

'*Sim.* Yes.'

'That's better. Now,' he dropped the intensity a fraction, 'why are you scared? Are you worried about losing your job?'

She nodded rapidly. '*Sim.* I will lose my job for sure now. The way you took my computers away like that, they will think I am a criminal, involved in Salma's murder.'

'Nonsense,' assured Da Silva. 'On the contrary, they will thank you for exposing their previous employee as a criminal.'

'Perhaps you are frightened of Ahmad himself?' said Jack, now going full friendly good-cop. 'Do you think he could do something to hurt you?'

Her head jerked up and she directed a stare at Jack, then shifted it to Da Silva, to the two women standing by as onlookers, then to Jack again. 'What do you think?! You suspect him of murdering Salma. Of course he could hurt me.' She glanced at the ceiling and said, 'He is a horrible man. Always rude to me. I hate him!' Her chest heaved, struggling to regain her composure. Jack poured her a glass of water; she took it and guzzled greedily.

'He will be arrested, whether he's guilty of murder or not,' said Da Silva. 'On corruption charges. Along with Alvarenga, if we can prove he had knowledge of the bribe. Was he in on it?'

Braga's eyes bulged. 'I can't say whether he knew or not. I just know Ahmad's email to Nizar Bensaid suggested he would split the money with Alvarenga. If that is confirmed in writing elsewhere, I cannot say.'

Da Silva leaned back in his seat, arms folded. 'Is there any other information you can offer us?'

She pursed her lips in thought. 'No. And you won't find anything extra on my computer either.'

'Your mobile phone?'

'No.'

'I believe you. However, since we've started the process, we intend to finish it. The devices, including your phone, will be returned to your employer some time tomorrow.'

'I need my phone. Why are you keeping it?' Her eyes pleaded.

'Surely you can get by without it for a day.'

A knock on the door. Horta held out a late-model Samsung, addressed Da Silva. 'We've got everything we can off this. She can have it back now.'

Jack smiled at Rosa Braga, her face stained with tears. 'Your lucky day, sunshine.'

## Chapter Twenty-Three

'ARE you getting closer to solving the case, Daddy?'

'I'm just helping them out. It won't be *me* solving the case. You won't see me on any press conferences, my name won't even be mentioned. It'll be like I wasn't even there.'

'You know what I mean.'

'I think the killer will be arrested soon, love. I'm sworn to secrecy until told otherwise, but, yeah, I think it should be wrapped up in a couple of days.' He deliberately omitted the fact he'd be playing a pivotal role in trying to coax a confession out of Ahmad. If Jack could get him to tell the cops where the murder weapon was, it would be case closed and back to the Algarve for a deserved rest with Skye.

'I hope so.' She paused, her small breaths like those of a puppy. 'But don't worry about me. I'm having a lot of fun with Cris and Maria, Tio Paulo and Tia Linda.'

'Tio and Tia?'

'Uncle and Aunty. I've already picked up a few other words.'

Jack smiled, turned his face towards the sun as his feet

dangled in the cool water of Mirabella's pool. 'You'll be fluent before we leave.'

'Ha ha! I doubt it. Portuguese is so hard.'

He didn't need telling. None of it made sense to him. 'Are you sure you're doing OK without me? I can drop all of this consulting detective malarkey any time you say.'

'No, Daddy. You have to catch the bad guy first. Tio Paulo promised me if anyone tried anything, they'll get beat up so bad that what he did to you will look like a kiss on the cheek.'

'Did he now!' Jack fought hard not to burst out laughing. The kid really was in the best hands possible.

'Yeah. He's nearly as funny as you, Dad. Can we have them over to visit us in Australia?'

A dragonfly landed beside Jack on the edge of the pool, its wings twitching as it walked around looking for who knew what. Its wings began to beat until they disappeared in a blur. The insect took off and flew behind the hibiscus hedge. 'Of course.' He mentally estimated the tens of thousands of dollars an extension on the two-bedroom farmstead would cost. Accommodating the four members of the Lisboa family in the house in its current state would be a tight squeeze. Perhaps not all of the money paid to him by the Polícia Judiciária would go to Sarah's charity after all. Either that or the guests could stay in a big tent. 'We've got plenty of room.'

She gave a short, sharp squeal of delight. 'Awesome!'

'Did you go to the beach today?'

'You bet. If I lived here I would go every day. The water is so cool and clear.'

'Was my blood still visible in the sand?' Jack laughed.

'No, silly. You weren't even bleeding. Not much, anyway.'

He realised he hadn't mentioned Sarah for the duration of the call. Neither had Skye. He looked at the heavens for advice. Bring it up or not? The dragonfly returned, landed on Jack's knee. A sign? He took a deep breath. 'How are you feeling, love? I mean…overall.'

'You mean about mum?' The kid could see around his less-than-fancy footwork better than any boxer.

'Ah, yeah. I guess.' For a man who could make the meanest of criminals quake in their boots, this "feeling and emotions" territory was tough going for Jack. 'Did you sleep OK last night?' was the best he could come up with.

'I did cry before I went to sleep, Daddy. But I think it's getting easier each day. I…" She lost it, started sobbing again.

'That's it, young lady. I'm coming down. Paulo might be able to fight off an army, but I'm still your father.' What did that even mean? He hadn't been there for years; he'd offered no emotional support, and now all of a sudden he was what, father of the year?

'No!' The crying stopped. 'You will not come down.' She was channelling Sarah now: decisive, commanding, let's face it, bossy. 'I'll be fine. That poor lady got killed on the tram and I'm still alive. You have to make sure she gets justice, Dad. It's what you do best. Even better than your blocking technique.' She gave a broken laugh.

The sound of the sliding door punctuated the trilling hum of cicadas. Jack turned to see Mirabella, her lime green one-piece bathing suit hugging her body, as she slowly walked towards him. Walking was the wrong word, he realised. Sashaying, dammit. That's what she was doing. He looked away from her, bore his eyes into the solid green mass of the hibiscus hedge, and pressed the phone close to his ear. 'Listen, sweetheart, I've gotta go.'

'No worries. Tia Linda is calling everyone to dinner. At least that's what I think she's doing.'

A soft splash as Mirabella dived in.

'I'll call you tomorrow. Wish me luck with catching the crims.'

'Don't you mean toe-rags, Dad?'

'Yeah, them 'n all.'

He ended the call, slid the phone back under the banana lounge and pulled out the Peter James novel. He had three chapters to go. It was one of those slow burners but the pace had picked up and the thrilling conclusion was upon him.

'You more interested in that book than talking to me?'

Jack placed the book on his lap, saw Mirabella's face framed by his feet. Droplets of water cascaded from her hair, nose, lips. She placed her hands on the rim of the pool, pushed herself up and out of the water with the ease of a gymnast.

'Actually, I'm getting to the really good part. I think I've worked out who the killer is, but I'm not sure. It's often a lot easier in real life to play detective than with these tricky novels.'

Standing over him she said, 'I overheard some of that conversation. If the police think the case will be solved soon, that means you'll be leaving me for good. I need to pin you down for the interview you promised me.'

The woman was persistent. Tempted to postpone the conversation so he could finally finish the novel, he decided against it. If he left without having done the interview, he'd be mired in guilt for breaking his promise. 'I consider myself pinned.'

She smiled, two rows of gleaming teeth and a full-lipped

mouth. 'Wonderful. I'll go and get out of these wet bathers and we can do it right here beside the pool. Agreed?'

Jack gulped. There was so much double entendre in her words, but he doubted she was even aware of it. Or was she?

Ten minutes later she reappeared in a dressing gown. She had an iPad tucked under one arm and in the other hand balanced a tray with a couple of cold drinks on it. 'Let's sit at the picnic table over there.'

Jack leapt to his feet, gallantly took the tray from her. Once seated, she said, 'This shouldn't take too long.'

'Great.'

'Then perhaps we can go out to listen to fado?'

'No. Then I finish my book.'

'Then fado?'

'Let's see.'

Mirabella turned on the iPad and wasted no time switching to interviewer mode. She addressed Jack like he was a perfect stranger she had only just been introduced to. She asked some questions she already knew the answers to by dint of her profession, like when and where he was born. Then she followed up with open-ended questions that required Jack to be more expansive in his responses: what was his childhood like, how did he get drawn into boxing. What led him to join the police academy and then apply to the London Met. How he met his Jamaican ex-wife, now sadly deceased.

Up to now, plain sailing, and Jack was able to give more or less honest answers.

After that, they arrived at a period of his life he would rather forget. And admitting the truth to Mirabella could lead to the dormant cold case being resuscitated. True, the interview was only going to be published on her website blog to drive business, but still...

The bad times began with the murder of Alex Gallagher six years go. A murder Jack committed with no compunction whatever. He couldn't talk about that, though. No chance in hell. And so, turning his back on his honest-cop persona, he did the only thing he could do. Lie. One awful porky after another, until the story moved from the awkward stuff to the part where he touched down in Brisbane, Australia, and resurrected his career as a beat cop.

'Interesting you went back to uniform, Jack. Why was that?'

'That was the rule back then. I had to take a demotion to constable. I was told I needed to get some experience of life on the street in a new country before I could even think about applying to become a detective again.'

'And you certainly got that. Didn't you stop a bank robbery when you were off-duty and unarmed?'

Jack blushed. 'My, you have done your homework.' He shrugged, took a drink to slake a sudden parching thirst. 'Yes, I was fortunate the bank robbers were a pair of numpties.'

'Sorry? Is that some gang or other?'

Jack coughed. Another sip. 'It means idiots. Actually, I think they were spaced out on drugs. Violent bastards.' He'd choked one of them to death with an ethernet cable. He left that part out. Also the bit about being in the bank with the purpose of exchanging dirty stolen English pounds for Australian dollars. 'Luckily, the special ops guys turned up en masse at the end of the day and tidied everything up.'

'All the hostages survived, thanks to you, correct? I've read news articles about it.'

'I guess my training was good enough to...do you think we can move onto another line of questioning?'

Mirabella smiled. He realised he'd used a police term – line of questioning – but it was unlikely she got the connection.

'Sure. Tell me about Skye?'

What seemed like a slam dunk question at first required some fast thinking to avoid admitting he was a deadbeat father for most of her life and had only turned it around recently. Again, he reached deep into the lie drawer for an answer. 'Her mum and I, well, we didn't get on so great. Clash of personalities 'n that. We agreed it would be best for the girl if I gave them both some space. It seemed to work, 'cos she loves me now when she didn't so much before.'

'I guess you rescuing her from a gang of kidnappers made you a hero in her eyes?'

'Yeah,' he laughed awkwardly, 'I guess.' He omitted to say the kidnapping was connected to the murder he'd committed, basically that it was his fault it happened at all. And that Skye had been snatched in broad daylight when, like a fool, he got sucked in by a diversion created by the kidnappers. At that point, Jack thought he was the dumbest copper and the worst father on the planet – worse than when he was a stumbling drunk on the take.

Fortunately, the conversation turned to a series of murder cases Jack had solved in Australia. 'I was only able to crack those cases with the assistance of my hard-working teammates at the Yorkville CIB.' No way he'd let her paint him as some ego-driven glory seeker. He would always make sure his colleagues shared in the success, even if the media painted him as the main man. 'My partner DC Claudia

Taylor, in particular, played a major role in most of those cases.'

'And what made you want to seek out your roots here in Portugal?'

Jack ran his fingers through his hair, short but in need of a trim. 'I never had much family life growing up. My parents were disconnected, to put it mildly. Once I knew Skye would be living with me permanently, I started to get these feelings I never had before. My father told me nothing about his own family in Portugal. It was all a big mystery. On mum's side, my relatives were a bunch of wastrels and I wanted nothin' to do with them. But the connection with a foreign country where they speak a language I don't understand, that sounded kinda…romantic.'

Her eyebrows rose a fraction. 'And that's why you contacted me?'

He reached under the table, brushed a fly away from his knee. 'Yeah. Good old Internet, hey? What can't it do?'

'Were you satisfied with my services?'

*Aha! Now we get to the nitty-gritty. The testimonial she wants for her business. Not that she needs it to make more money. 'As they say in Australia, bloody oath, I was.'*

'Is that a yes?'

He nodded. 'An emphatic one. It also doesn't hurt that my new-found relatives are wonderful people who have shown us nothing but kindness and…'

'And love?'

'Yes. I think you're right, it is love. On a deep level. The minute I saw my cousin, I knew he was family and the emotions just kinda poured out.'

'Ooh, I'll be putting that bit in. So, Jack, it seems you've accidentally become involved in a high-profile murder case here in Lisbon. Can you tell me about that?'

'No. Can you turn the iPad off please?'

She reached across and pressed a button. 'What's wrong?'

'By some bleedin' miracle, the press haven't gotten wind of my role in the case. And Da Silva wants to keep it that way. He knows that you know – thanks to the information you found out about Ahmad – but it has to stop here.'

'What if I promise not to post this on my blog until someone is arrested and convicted of the murder? Would that be a fair deal in exchange for getting your perspective?'

'Hmmm. I guess you already know the extent of my involvement, and there's nothing I could do to stop you from publishing.'

She stared at him pensively for a moment, eyes narrowed and lips pressed together.

'Wot!'

She shook her head. 'Nothing.'

'No. You were thinking something just now. Tell me.'

She put a finger in her mouth. 'Maybe I'll tell you after the show. What time is it?'

He glanced at his watch. 'Just after 8:30.'

'Great. Go and put on your best clothes and I'll take you to see something you'll never forget.'

He sighed inwardly. Her wily moves would be put on hold. For now.

## Chapter Twenty-Four

SHE'D EXPRESSED a desire to relax at the show tonight with a couple of drinks, which set Jack's alarm bells off again. With inhibitions lowered, she'd be a different proposition again. Or was he imagining it all? Dammit, he could never read women unless the language was clear and unambiguous. Which it hardly ever was.

He paced up and down outside her front gate waiting for her, chewing furiously on a stick of gum. The sun had set some time ago and it was already dark. He enjoyed the long days afforded by daylight savings in the northern hemisphere. He'd miss them in Australia. For a while, at least, until he again got used to the fairly uniform length of days in his town in the tropics.

She'd been gone five minutes, ostensibly to find a better pair of earrings than the ones she'd first picked. Any longer and he'd call the thing off and get back to his novel. As he paced, his foot caught on a piece of grit and scraped it along the cobblestone.

*Or did it?*

He lifted his foot. Nothing.

There was someone else here in the shadows. Surely not Mirabella playing silly games, hiding behind the bushes? He wouldn't put such behaviour past her.

'Who's there?' said Jack, the muscles under his shirt flexing, fingers twitching. The streetlighting in this part of the suburb was lousy to the point of being non-existent. He extracted his mobile, found the torch app and switched it on. He crouched, waved the thin beam of light under the lower foliage of the hibiscus hedge that abutted the brick wall surrounding the house. Then he swept it in an arc in front of him, left and right.

Satisfied there was no one there except insects, he pocketed the phone.

Then he heard the awful crunch of something hard across the back of his neck. His knees buckled as he fell to the ground, the arcing pain crippling him. Instincts screamed: *roll over and get out of the way, there's another swing coming.* He did, and the clang of an iron bar – a tyre lever perhaps – against the cobblestones echoed in the deserted street. A miss, thank God.

At ground level, he made out the outline of the boots. Black, thick soles. Doc Martens. Footwear favoured by thugs. He rolled back to the original spot as another blow rained down, missing again, but not by much. Blood from that first blow now flowed freely: his face was wet, the sticky mass matting in his hair, trickling into his eyes. He roared as loud as he could, like a beast; perhaps the noise would frighten the man off or alert someone nearby. *Mirabella.* Shit, the attacker would beat him senseless, then get stuck into her when she arrived at the gate.

He rolled again and again, the bar missing each time. *Clang, clang, clang.* And then – it didn't miss. Cracking into his lower leg, thankfully the back of a well-muscled calf, then skimming off to connect with the ground again. Still, it hurt. Everything hurt like hell. *Why didn't I just fly home to Australia instead of coming here?*

The onslaught was unrelenting, matched only by Jack's desperation to avoid the blow that would stop him for good. He hatched a feeble plan. The next roll away would become another in the same direction, like a barrel tumbling down a hill. *Put some distance between yourself and the attacker, try to stand up and defend yourself.*

The attacker was a big man, he could sense it. Jack smelled the aggression, the adrenaline pouring off him. The next swing came, and Jack was off, spinning like a top. The man grunted, swore an oath in Portuguese.

Guessing there was maybe five metres separating them, Jack prised at the cobblestones, summoned every Newton of power his fingers could burn, and prised a white block from the pavement. He clambered to his feet, unsteady, wobbling, aching in every fibre of his being. 'Come and get me, you fucking toe-rag!' he thundered.

As Jack was praying that his defiant words would scare off the maniac, the man took up the challenge, advanced with the steps of a seasoned brawler. Not necessarily a skilled fighter, but a vicious and merciless thug. Eyes now accustomed to the darkness, Jack could see the mugger stood about half a head taller and carried a lot more bulk. By the straining of his black leather jacket, it was more fat than muscle.

A car turned at the bottom of the street, high beam engaged. It illuminated the man for a second before it turned off into another street and all fell dark once more. Jack's hunch was confirmed: the man was leaning towards the pudgy side. If not for the crowbar, Jack was sure he could have knocked him out with a couple of hard punches. But this was not a fair fight. Even though the geezer had a firm grip on the weapon, Jack knew he had the bloke's measure. *If* he could throw straight.

'Come on then,' he bellowed again. 'I'm waiting, you fat fuck!'

The man laughed derisively. Jack could barely stand up and blood poured from the back of his neck; he was like an injured wildebeest calf begging to be picked off and devoured. When the snarling brute got to within a metre, Jack summoned all his strength, wound up like a baseball pitcher and unleashed. He blinked blood away as the white chunk of calçada, the size of a packet of budget smokes, hurtled through the air.

Then came the sickening thud of rock on bone and the clatter of the dropped tyre lever.

*'Aargghh...Filho du puta!'*

Bullseye.

Jack slumped to the ground as the sound of groans and plodding, heavy boots disappeared up the road.

---

'JACK! WHAT HAPPENED TO YOU?' Mirabella leaned over and touched him on the shoulder as he sat slumped on the pavement. 'Is that blood?'

'It ain't bleedin' sangria.'

'You can joke at a time like this?'

He turned his head on an angle. 'Always.'

'You still haven't said what happened.'

'A bloke attacked me with an iron bar. Got me a couple of times, as you can see. But I clocked him in the head with one o' them paving rocks. He dropped the weapon and hobbled off. And,' he showed open palms, 'that's about it.'

'Oh my God! That's terrible. Should I call an ambulance?'

Jack found the strength to stand. 'What is it with you people, always wanting to call an ambulance? I didn't get hit in the head this time. I'll be fine.'

She stammered a reply that Jack couldn't make out.

'Just get me back into the house.'

'You've got a gash in the back of your neck.'

'Listen, let me clean it up, then we can make a judgement call on it, OK? First,' he pointed north, 'go and grab that tyre lever for evidence, and the loose cobblestone if you can find it. You got a handkerchief?'

'Yes.'

'Use it to pick up the evidence, drop the lever and the rock in your front yard, then come and help me back into the house.'

Instructions carried out to the letter, Mirabella offered her elbow for Jack to lean on as he hobbled back up the driveway. It turned out the whack to the leg was causing him more grief than the one to the neck. At least for now. A handful of strong painkillers would be needed if he had any hope of getting to sleep tonight.

She led him into the ensuite bathroom, pulled the polo shirt up and over his head. He offered no resistance. He leaned against the marble sink as she dabbed the blood away from his neck with a face washer.

'Good news,' she said, 'The cut is shallow. No stitches required for this.' As she pressed a sticky bandage against the wound, he winced and suppressed the urge to cry out. The skin may be cut superficially, but something deeper – muscle or tendon – had suffered more serious damage. Not life-threatening, but there would be some lasting soreness. The back of his leg, absolutely caning, as they would say in Australia, would be every colour of the rainbow by the morning.

'I guess I don't need to tell you I'm not exactly feeling it for a night on the town, right?' said Jack.

'Of course.' They looked at each other in the mirror, her face a portrait of understanding. She took the liberty of resting her chin on his shoulder, he didn't protest. She said, 'Are you going to call the police about this? I don't like the thought of people getting attacked outside my house. This has always been a safe neighbourhood.'

He nodded his head slowly, regretting it as the pain throbbed in his neck. He fished out his mobile, put in a call to Da Silva.

'Yes, Jack? Everything all right?'

No point leading with any preamble. 'I was attacked outside Mirabella's house. Any chance of getting a squad car to park out the front and keep an eye on things for a while?'

'Are you OK?'

'He hit me twice, I got him once. He ran off crying like a baby.'

'I'll send a couple of uniforms around immediately.'

'Thanks. And send someone to pick up a couple of pieces of evidence. The guy might have been wearing gloves, I couldn't tell, but there'll be DNA on the rock I chucked at him. It's got his blood on it.'

Da Silva let out a phew sound. 'This has to be the work of Alvarenga and Ahmad.'

'Ya think?!'

The sarcasm was lost on Da Silva. 'Absolutely. Who else? Where you are staying is an affluent area. Crime like this simply doesn't happen there. This was definitely no random attack.'

Jack ended the call, Mirabella prepared chamomile tea and a cold compress for Jack's neck. To his delight, both treatments made him feel better. Or perhaps it was the way she tended him like a nurse. She left him to rest on the sofa while she searched for an elusive music DVD. 'Aha! This is the one. Camané.' She popped it in the stereo, took a seat in the armchair nearest Jack.

As they listened to the haunting melodies, recorded with minimal acoustic string accompaniment, Mirabella started to explain the meaning of the music, about the unique Portuguese notion of *saudade*, how it was all about emotions, but Jack cut her off. Not to be rude, but because he was enraptured by the man's voice and the haunting arrangement. 'Maybe let me listen to it all the way through, and then tell me the background to it all. I promise, I will find it fascinating, but for now, I just wanna hear it.'

She frowned for a second, and Jack instinctively understood why. She loved her culture and she wanted to share it. But then she smiled. 'Your are right. No need to analyse it. Just feel.'

Three songs in and his eyes closed. He slept on the sofa for close to ten hours. When he awoke, Mirabella was gone. She had left a short note. *Thanks for listening to my music.*

## Chapter Twenty-Five

THERE WAS ALWAYS plenty of trash to pick up in the hip Lx Factory restaurant precinct nestled under the 25 de Abril bridge. The popular eateries created a biomass of food scraps that gave off a sweet, rotting odour. He was used to it though; after years collecting garbage his nose barely registered the stench. The man whistled through crooked teeth as he wheeled the rubbish bin closer to the rumbling truck.

In the early morning, the sun beat down with a ferocity. All he could think about was the beers he was going to guzzle with his pals around the card table tonight and the money he would win. Arch rival Fernando won a packet off him last payday, leaving him short of money for cigarettes. He vowed to get revenge tonight. He'd been watching videos on the Internet about how to cheat at poker without getting caught. He'd been practicing various techniques, and was sure he'd get square tonight.

Once the bin was emptied into the grinders, he rolled it more or less to the spot he'd taken it from. He went to grab hold of another one when he saw something odd out of the corner of his eye. A couple of centimetres of hollow metal tube poked through the compacted soil of a concrete planter box. The tub sat under a colourful mural commemorating the Carnation Revolution of 1974 and was usually full of bright flowers. Despite being a burly binman, he was a softy at heart, and often stopped to admire the blooms. Today he looked with more attention because the flowers were gone.

'Edu, come and look at this! You won't believe it.'

'Piss off, I'm busy.'

'Seriously. You have to see this!'

Edu, a recent immigrant from Angola who loved to boss his simple-minded partner around, switched off the engine and clambered down from the driver's side door. 'What is it, for goodness sake? I was listening to my favourite song on the radio. If it's not interesting, I'm going to knock you senseless.'

The man didn't register the warning. He waved Edu towards him. 'Come here, quick. It looks like a pistol.'

'What?'

'A pistol,' he said in a hushed tone. He bent down, plucked it from the dirt and gave it a shake. He held it up by the end of the barrel with thumb and forefinger, dangling it in the air.

'You're such a dumb-arse, Tonho. You don't have to hold it like that.'

'Yes I do. I've seen how the cops do it on TV. To avoid contaminating the evidence.'

Edu slapped his mate hard on the shoulder and laughed. '*Idiota*. You're wearing gloves.'

'Oh, yeah.' Tonho swapped the grip to a more comfortable one. Then he aimed it at his workmate, looking at the point of the barrel and squinting.

Edu held his hands up in front of his face. 'Oi! What the hell are you doing, *cabrão*? It could be loaded!'

'Sorry.' Sufficiently wounded by being called a bastard, Tonho lowered the weapon and held it by his side. His eyes widened, a realisation dawning. 'Hey! We're only five minutes away from where that poor girl was killed the other day.' He gawped at the gun in his hand. 'You don't think…?'

'I do think.' Edu's eyeballs bugged out. 'Yes, it could be!'

'Is there a reward?' A glint sparkled in Tonho's eye.

Another slap, this one across the chest. 'It doesn't matter, *idiota*. We have to hand it over. It's our civic duty.' He pulled out a beat-up old mobile phone. 'I'm calling the cops to report it.'

## Chapter Twenty-Six

JACK WINCED as he hobbled up the last couple of steps to the entrance of the Polícia Judiciária. Despite icing the injuries before settling down to watch Mirabella's fado DVD, bruising on the back of the leg, as well as his neck and shoulders, bloomed blue, purple and black. On top of getting outboxed by his cousin, this was turning into a holiday to remember for all the wrong reasons.

So far the Farooq case had intrigued him from a professional point of view. Last night's attack, no doubt instigated by Alvarenga and/or Ahmad, made it personal. If the thug they'd paid had been even fractionally better at his job, Jack wouldn't have survived the assault.

Da Silva waited for Jack outside the Entrega Rápida building, a look of serene patience on his face as the visiting detective shuffled along. Even with a body wracked with pain, Jack could appreciate the fact it was another classic summer's day. Mainly because he was still alive. Porcelain blue skies stretched from horizon to horizon, sunshine warmed the skin and a breeze blowing off the Tagus kept things fresh.

'Any developments since last we spoke?' said Jack. 'Has a guilt-ridden killer come forward and confessed yet?'

'Sadly no. But we think we've found the murder weapon.' No good morning, no how are you. And a total lack of animation about the find.

'You don't sound too excited about it,' said Jack, rubbing at the back of his neck.

'It won't tell us who the murderer is. Initial tracing on the database revealed the gun was first purchased legally in Italy five years ago. The original owner is dead and there's no way of determining how the hell it ended up in Lisbon. My guess is the killer obtained it in the slums of Cova da Moura.'

'Where's that?'

'Believe it or not, favelas aren't just found in Brazil. We have them here, but on a much smaller scale. Cova da Moura is a drug trafficker haven in the north-west of the city. If you wanted to get your hands on an illegal gun in Lisbon, that would be the first place to look. Even so,' he inclined his head and shrugged, 'I'm only guessing. We will ask locals if they know anything, but it's the type of area where they don't like the police and it's safer for residents to keep their mouth shut.'

'Who found the gun?'

'A sanitation worker found it by chance. It was almost completely buried in a flower box just five minutes from the murder scene.' Da Silva chuckled. 'Apparently the man was reluctant to hand it over. He wanted a souvenir.'

'That's one way of hiding a weapon I've never heard of.'

'Me either. I think the killer was in a hurry to get rid of

it and the flower box was an opportunistic solution. It's actually in an area that gets a lot of foot traffic through it. He must have been very sneaky when he placed it there.'

'A bleedin' magician.'

'Indeed. The killer may have intended to retrieve the gun later and dispose of it properly.'

'Either that or he was confident it would never be traced back to him and had no intention of going back for it.'

'Both scenarios are plausible.' Da Silva agreed. 'The gun will be analysed for DNA, of course, and to confirm it actually *was* the weapon that fired the bullet that killed Farooq. We are only assuming at this stage. Unfortunately, this pistol was contaminated by soil, which won't make the ballistics team's job an easy one.' He levelled his gaze at Jack. 'Listen, are you sure you're up for this? I mean, you were beaten up pretty badly last night and have barely had time to recover. It would be no shame for you to pull out and forget about the case.'

Jack hunched his shoulders. 'I've suffered worse hidings.' And it was true. He'd been beaten to a pulp in London years ago and spent days recovering in hospital. He'd been an easy target then, drunk to the gills and unable to defend himself properly. 'And if the attack was instigated by these two fuckers, I wanna be there to see them squirm as I...I mean you...put the blowtorch to their feet.'

'I don't know about Australia, but here in Portugal we do not employ torture when questioning people.'

'I didn't mean it literally,' said Jack, frowning.

Da Silva grinned. 'I was joking. Anyway, there shouldn't be a repeat of that silly game where they made us wait.'

'Are you sure they're even here, Zé?'

'Positive. I rang and made an appointment.' He waved a piece of paper in front of Jack's eyes.

'Is that what I think it is?' said Jack.

'That depends. What do you think it is?'

'An arrest warrant?'

'Correct.'

'So, the evidence on the computer was enough to proceed with an arrest? Micky will be pleased as punch.'

Da Silva flashed a sly grin. 'It is enough to charge Ahmad with corruption at the highest level. A five year jail term at least. I'm hoping he'll roll over and rat out his boss.'

'I'm more interested in the murder,' said Jack, unable to hide the disappointment in his voice. 'Financial crime's boring, innit?'

'I tend to agree. But this is a start.' He pointed at a couple of waiting police vehicles parked on the side of the road. 'Once I give the signal, those officers will be upstairs to confiscate the computers of every employee in the building. If there's anything on them that incriminates the company in this murder, we'll find it.' He winked. 'Come on, let's see what they've got to say.'

No offer of coffee, not even water. A mood of brooding malevolence hung in the air, both men unsmiling. Even the ancient wheelchair pilot, Marco, wore an expression that could curdle milk.

'I'm not happy about this interruption,' said Alvarenga, wiping his spectacles with a cloth before putting them back on again. He dismissed Marco and asked him to make sure they weren't disturbed by anyone. 'We are only just back from Paris and have barely had time to unpack. We have a business to run, and the way the Polícia Judiciária have been treating us is appalling. Bordering on harassment.'

'Come now, Senhor Alvarenga. This is just our second visit. You can hardly call it harassment.' Da Silva ran a thumb and forefinger down his moustache, tapped his chin a couple of times. 'For a tough businessman, you seem to have rather a thin skin.'

Jack keenly observed the two men across the table. He could imagine smoke pouring out of their ears as the detective toyed with them. This entitled pair thinks nothing and no one can touch them, no matter what crimes they commit.

'By contrast, my colleague here,' Da Silva gestured towards Jack, 'has thick skin. But, as tough as he is, it still isn't thick enough to withstand the force of tyre lever blows. He has suffered incapacitating injuries to his neck and leg because last night he was attacked in the street without provocation. Yet here he is, unbowed.'

Alvaranga and Ahmad were both shaking their heads. Jack thought he could spot a trace of nervousness creeping into their body language now. He paid attention to their hands, unable to keep still.

'You don't want to make a comment on that?' Da Silva prodded. 'No denials?'

'Denial of what?' Ahmad gripped the edge of the table, white knuckles visible. 'Are you suggesting we had something to do with a man attacking Senhor Lisbon?'

Jack stood, leaned over the table 'You know the police are close to finding the evidence that will send you to prison, and you panicked. You naively thought employing a thug to kill me would work in your favour. Well, guess again!' He yanked back his collar. Twisting his body hurt like mad, but he didn't care. 'Look at this, you son of a bitch. A couple of inches to the left and it would have been game over for me. And,' he thundered, 'who said it was one man?' He felt Da Silva's strong hand pulling at his forearm. He tugged it loose from Da Silva's grip, squared his shoulders. 'Huh? You paid someone to do this to me.'

'Please, take a seat, Jack.' Da Silva turned to the two men opposite. 'His behaviour is a little unorthodox, but Detective Lisbon has a valid point. Neither of us mentioned just now how many had assaulted Jack, nor the gender.' He screwed up one nostril. 'I agree with Jack. I suggest one of you is behind this atrocity. Or both of you.'

Jack was on his feet again, stabbing a finger at Ahmad, whose eyes were as wide as manhole covers. Then he shot a withering glare at the CEO. 'I don't care if you're old and you've got no legs, you toe-rag. I'll rip your fucking arms off to make it all nice and symmetrical.'

Ahmad cowered in his seat, yet still managed to splutter, 'Detective Da Silva, please. Do something about this man. I'm going to lodge a serious complaint to your superiors about this.'

Before Da Silva could stop him, Jack had leapt across the table and Ahmad was in a headlock. Jack knew exactly how hard to apply the hold to cause maximum pain but cause no lasting harm. The lawyer whimpered like a beaten dog under the pressure.

Da Silva yelled out, 'Jack! That's enough for now.'

Jack gasped with exasperation, released his grip. He slapped his palms together, hobbled around the table and resumed his seat.

Ahmad rubbed his burning ears while Alvarenga glowered, spat something out in Portuguese.

'English only,' said Da Silva firmly.

More Portuguese. Jack could only guess Alvarenga was giving Da Silva the equivalent of *go fuck yourself*.

'English only, or we will not leave your office and I will not allow you to leave.'

'You can't behave in this way,' Alvarenga said, switching back to English. 'Can he do this, Carlos?'

Ahmad stopped rubbing his ears, looked up with tearstained eyes. 'No.'

'I cannot believe you just sit there and let this... animal...carry on without restraint.'

'Hey, I stopped him, didn't I? And I guarantee he won't lose his temper like that again. Will you, Jack?'

'Nah. I've got it out of my system.'

Da Silva addressed Alvarenga with open palms. 'I'm giving you one last chance to admit you organised the attack on Detective Lisbon. You'll no doubt be interested to learn that the man who did your dirty work has left behind traces of blood. And he was stupid enough to abandon the iron bar he used to hit Detective Lisbon. We've expedited the DNA and fingerprint analyses and have already identified the man who carried out the attack.'

Jack grinned as the two men opposite squirmed. The fast-tracked tests had indeed been done, but whoever the samples came from remained a mystery. The expressions of anxiety on the men's faces said the bluff was working.

Jack decided to throw in a little subterfuge of his own. 'I actually got a good look at the man, even though it was dark. Once the cops haul that bloke in, I've been given permission to interview him. I'll probably adopt my go-to physical strategy, like I used on Carlos here, except with a bit more vim and vigour.' He laughed. 'It's amazing how easy it is to get the truth out of someone when they're handcuffed to a steel chair.'

Alvarenga and Ahmad exchanged a look of apprehension, then the CEO whispered something in his lawyer's still-red ear. He turned back to Da Silva. 'Honestly, I don't know what else to tell you. Take me down to the station and I'll swear on a lie detector if you like. I know nothing about the man who attacked Detective Lisbon.'

'Neither do I,' said Ahmad. 'We'll both come down to the station.'

'Well, well,' said Da Silva joyfully. 'That is wonderful news, isn't it Jack?'

'Uh huh.'

The two men sitting opposite breathed a sigh of relief, the tension in their faces disappeared. But only for a moment.

Da Silva pulled out his phone, barked an order. He hung up and brandished the arrest warrant, went into a long spiel that Jack later learned was the announcement that they were under arrest on corruption charges. The more serious charge was levelled at Ahmad – abusing his position in the Ministry of Foreign Affairs to collude with a foreign government and a private company for personal gain. Alvarenga was charged with being an accessory to corruption. The second part of the speech was Da Silva reading Alvarenga and Ahmad their rights. During the unfolding drama, Alvarenga affected a look of defiance, Ahmad's eyes welled with tears and his lips trembled.

Three minutes later Detectives Quintal and Rebelo marched into the office, jaws set, cuffed Ahmad but not Alvarenga on account of his being wheelchair bound and posing zero threat. Marco was called upon to steer Alvarenga's wheelchair and accompany him to the station after the CEO successfully pled the case that he needed the old fellow for "emotional support." Jack sat back in his chair, enjoying the show as it played out. The only part he didn't like was the soft treatment of Alvarenga because of his missing legs. Copping two beatings in the space of a week was a fair price to pay to witness this fascinating spectacle.

When only he and Da Silva remained in the office, suddenly quiet as a library, Jack said, 'What next, boss?'

'We haul away their equipment and tear every device apart. I won't rest until I find proof those two are linked to Farooq's murder.'

'And I won't rest until I get a couple of ibuprofen down my gullet.'

Da Silva shook his head and said, 'Come on, Rocky. Let's find a pharmacy.'

## Chapter Twenty-Seven

DA SILVA HAD GONE ABOVE and beyond, bless him. Not only did he obtain for Jack a bagful of over-the-counter painkillers, he threw in powerful prescription ones left over from when he was recovering from a spinal fusion operation. The extras were able to switch off neurons the supermarket variety couldn't get near. One every three hours and there was very little pain to contend with. Except when he moved. His stomach growled as the sun hung almost directly overhead. The thought of more of those custard tarts made his mouth water. He'd limp to the store a couple of blocks away and buy a boxful once he'd finished the phone call.

In the sun lounge by the glorious pool, he sluiced down another pill with lukewarm coffee as Skye rambled on about her day. She was still having a ball with her second cousins: swimming in the ocean, riding bicycles, exploring the beaches, even fishing. Her laughter-filled narration overloaded his heart with joy. No mention of Sarah so far. He guessed her not mentioning it was Skye's way of portraying stoicism. He had visions of her sobbing herself to sleep at night, though.

'And how about you, Dad? You haven't been on the news like back in Australia when there's an investigation happening.' She paused then said, 'Are you sure you're telling me the truth about this? Maybe you're just hanging back to stay close to Mirabella?'

He sat up straight, knocking over a glass of water with his ankle. 'No, honey.' He scowled as the pain in his calf scored a brief victory over the pharmaceuticals; his movements needed to be slow, but it's not easy stopping reflex actions. 'There's nothing going on between me and her. Seriously, love. How could you even think it?'

'I dunno.' He pictured her shrugging. 'She's very pretty. And she seems to like you a lot.'

'Yes, she is pretty. But I'm not…I don't…can we talk about something else?'

'Like I said before, how come you aren't on the news?'

'Because, officially, I'm not involved in the case. I'm just helping out with advice 'n that.' He decided to keep quiet about yesterday's attack. The kid would freak out and demand he leave Lisbon immediately. But with Ahmad and Alvarenga in custody, he felt the risk to his person had been negated. 'Check the news tonight. My friend Zé will be making an announcement.'

'You found the killers?' she said, her voice going up a register.

'No, love.' He scratched his ear as he thought how best to explain it. 'Well, yes, but the police had to arrest the men on other charges, to keep the pressure on until they can prove those men murdered Salma Farooq.'

'OK. I'll make sure Uncle Paulo turns on the TV and

interprets for me. Does this mean you've finished helping the police?'

'Nearly. They might want me to sit in on an interview or two, but maybe not. If no requests come in tomorrow morning, I'll take a bus down to the Algarve. Done and dusted.'

'Yes!'

Mirabella would make the offer to drive him, he was sure of it, but he wanted a clean break. He did the interview for her website, and now they were square. He'd stubbornly resisted the temptation of her very tempting flesh, but not without a great deal of internal struggle. If he was going to be totally honest with himself, if Claudia Taylor wasn't hovering in the back of Jack's brain like the dragonflies that hung around the swimming pool, he and Mirabella would have consummated their mutual attraction. And more than once.

'Tio Paulo wants to talk to you dad.'

'Sure, put him on.'

'Jack.' He could hear the concern in the man's voice. In the background he heard him tell Skye to go outside, the kids were waiting for her on their bikes. 'OK.' Back to Jack. 'You need to come down soon.'

'I'm probably coming on the bus tomorrow. Is something wrong?'

'We've heard some noises coming out of the bedroom. Crying, talking to herself. I think...maybe you need to come down straight away.'

Jack gnawed his knuckle as he thought about it. Skye wasn't at any risk, her mourning period would go on for some time, it was normal. And she was a tough cookie. 'Listen, I'm still a bit sore after you KO'd me. Gimme one more night here, then I'll be down on the first bus I can get a ticket on tomorrow. Hang on a minute, I'll do it now and call you back.'

Inside the mansion, Jack pulled out his laptop, logged onto one of those godawful aggregator booking sites. The morning buses were full, so he had to settle for the 2:00pm. A connection in Lagos along the way. Maybe, just maybe, he'd finally get to finish that Peter James novel and start the Ian Rankin one. He flicked a text to Paulo with the arrival details when Mirabella appeared at the bottom of the stairs. Again, ready for the pool. It seemed she was never out of skimpy gear.

'Finished with Entrega Rápida?' she said, pulling up a stool at the breakfast bar next to Jack.

'Not quite.' He made a lip-zipping motion. 'I'm still bound by the confidentiality thing.' He smiled as he realised how nonchalantly he shared information with a twelve-year-old girl but not an adult. There was a fundamental difference – he knew he could trust Skye. 'Da Silva will be making an announcement tonight. I *can* say this: you're work on the genealogy side helped out big time.'

'Wonderful!' She hopped off the stool, pulled a jug of iced water out of the fridge, poured glasses for each of them. 'Are those guys behind the attack on you last night?'

'I can neither confirm nor deny. Make of that what you will.'

She curled her bottom lip and asked, 'What were you doing on your laptop just now?'

'Glad you asked.' He drained half the water. 'I'm going to have to say good-bye, Mirabella. I've booked a bus down to Sagres for tomorrow afternoon.'

She screwed up her eyes so tight Jack didn't know whether she was going to laugh, cry or scream. None of the above. She unscrewed her eyes and said, 'Oh, OK.' She took her drink and ambled out onto the patio. Jack heard a loud splash as she dove into the water, more splashing as her arms and legs drove her up and down the pool.

Whether her behaviour was sulkiness or not, Jack wasn't sure. He picked up his phone again, googled the time in Yorkville. 9:15pm on a Thursday. Taylor would still be up.

'Hello, stranger?' She sounded excited to get the call.

'Hi.' He paused for a moment. Should have rehearsed it in his head, had at least a couple of things to say.

'Everybody misses you,' she blurted. He'd forgotten how she took the stress out of their conversations by refusing to allow silences. 'Aden and the dog, in particular.'

'Not you?'

'I said everybody, didn't I?' she chided. 'Which of course includes me. I guess the only people not missing you are the criminals of Yorkville.'

'Are those criminals giving you lot a hard time?' he chuckled, but quickly stopped as he saw Mirabella hauling herself out of the pool. She placed a foot on one of sun lounges, slowly patted dry the inside of her upper thigh. Jack pressed his mobile to his ear and took to the stairs. He'd finish the conversation in the guest bedroom.

'Actually, it's been very quiet,' said Taylor. 'We feared with your departure, the worst of the worst would come crawling out of the woodwork. But we've been spared murders, rapes, break-ins. The crooks have taken a holiday the same time as you!'

'I can't believe it.' He closed the door behind him and snibbed it shut.

'It's true. Nothing apart from a couple of domestic disputes. Kylie Smith and I handled one of them, Semmens and Wilson the other. No charges laid because the wives refused to turn on their husbands.'

Jack sighed. 'Some things will never change.'

'No they won't.' Jack heard the sound of a kettle whistling. 'Like you.'

'Meaning?'

'There's been a sensational murder in Lisbon, and you've not said a word to me about it.'

He readjusted his pillow, groaning with the effort of turning over.

'What was that noise? Sounds like you've hurt yourself.'

'Claudia, you ain't gonna believe this.' Over the next thirty minutes he poured out the details. From the horrific crime on the tram, meeting his new family members – including getting knocked out by his boxing champion cousin – to the random attack on the street. What he did leave out was the fact he was living under the roof of a highly desirable woman who, he believed, had designs on him.

'I knew it!' she cried. 'The news said there was an Australian on the scene, but no one knows who it was. You can't keep out of strife, can you?'

'Keep it under your hat, Claudia.'

He heard the footfalls of Mirabella as she passed his door, presumably on the way to her own bedroom to get changed out of her wet bathers.

'I've been helping the local cops out.'

'What!'

He explained about the travel blogger who visited North Queensland and introduced Jack to the Portuguese people. To his shock, he was already well known in certain circles. The police all knew of him.

'This is unbelievable,' she enthused. 'I wanna know everything. I promise not to blab. Who knows, I might even have some ideas.'

The idea wasn't crazy. Claudia had solved a number of crimes, even though Jack usually got most of the credit. At the end of the long story his voice has turned croaky. He excused himself for a minute, went to the bathroom, stuck his head under the tap and drank for ten seconds to slake his burning thirst.

'I'm back. Now, as a neutral observer thousands of miles away, what do you make of all that?'

'Those guys the cops arrested, the ones whose names both start with A…'

'Alvarenga and Ahmad.'

'Yeah, them. They're crooks, Jack, but they're not behind the murder. Their deal with the Moroccan firm was already public knowledge. Ahmad could not have guessed that the woman Brago…'

'Braga,' corrected Jack.

'Gimme a break! I think I'm doing pretty good keeping up with these names.'

'You are,' Jack conceded. 'Go on.'

'He could never have suspected she was lucky enough to get a look at his open e-mail admitting to the corruption. That discovery may have given them reason to have her bumped off, but not an exposé that accused them of engaging in dodgy practices. Much bigger companies than Intrigue-a whatsaname have been doing the same thing for decades, and flourished.'

The same thought nagged the back of his mind – and Paulo had voiced the identical theory – but Jack so wanted the pair to be guilty. 'Then who is behind it?'

'No idea. I'd be pushing those other suspects, the ones with more personal motives. That slum area you mentioned where it's easy to get guns – I'd be turning that upside down looking for a link with the murder weapon. Find who sold the gun, find the buyer.'

'Da Silva said the folks there don't talk, and they don't like cops.'

Claudia burst out laughing. 'Nobody likes cops, Jack. That's no excuse not to try.' She sipped something, probably one of those flavourless herbal teas he hated.

'Yeah, all that makes sense. Unfortunately, the lead detective on this case has it in his head only Alvarenga and Ahmad can be responsible.'

'Change his mind. Or maybe the prosecutor there will see it's all supposition and force him to dig deeper.'

'I'll have one more word with Da Silva before I head outta Lisbon. But who bashed me in the street then, Claudia? If it wasn't Alvarenga and Ahmad's doing, then whose?'

'Is it entirely beyond the realms of possibility it was a random assault?'

'Crime stats for the area suggest it's unlikely.'

'Yeah, but not impossible. The world's economies are tanking, people are getting desperate, even in so-called safe areas.'

'I guess. The bloke only spoke Portuguese. There was no warnings to back off from the case…you might be right.'

'In this case, I think I am. A professional hired thug would never have dropped a crowbar with his prints on it.'

Jack rubbed his calf, throbbing worse than ever. 'Makes sense, I guess.'

Then came the suggestion that took his breath away.

'I want to fly to Portugal.'

'What?' He wasn't sure he'd heard correctly.

'Inspector Batista's given me the all-clear for a two-week break.'

'That's two senior detectives out of the station. Are you sure you didn't misunderstand him?'

'Not at all. I've got it in writing. Like I said before, things are quiet here in the old home town. You know the drill, Jack. Yorkville CIB can ask for relief officers from Cairns to help out if needed.'

Jack rubbed his cheek for a moment, contemplating this turn of events.

'Hello? Are you there? Do you want me to come or not?'

His heart screamed *YES*. His mouth drawled, 'Yeah, OK. I guess that'd be all right.'

## Chapter Twenty-Eight

WHEN HE AGREED to attend to a live fado concert, her smile lit up the room like a firework. He couldn't have got a better response than if he'd dropped to his knees and opened a box with a ring in it. When he added the rider that his pal Micky Knox was accompanying them, the lights in her eyes seemed to snuff out like a candle in a stiff breeze.

'Why does he have to come with us?' she asked, frowning hard. 'I wanted it to be just you and me.'

'Because he's one of my best mates, innit. He's flying back to the UK tomorrow and I don't know when I'll see him again. Maybe never.'

'What about when you'll see me again?' she pouted. 'Once you've finished your holiday, it will be all over.'

Jack shrugged his shoulders, regretted it instantly as a sharp pain zinged through his injured neck. 'You've got more than enough money to come for a visit Down Under. You can stay at my place with me and Skye and the dog. *Mi casa, su casa.*'

'That's Spanish.'

'But you know what it means, right?' he smiled.

'Of course. The Portuguese version is almost the same. *Minha casa é sua casa.*' She touched her forefinger to her lips. 'You know, I can put my business on hold for a while. Actually, I can run it remotely if I set everything up properly. Maybe I *will* come for a visit.'

She wouldn't, of course. None of his UK friends, few that they were, could be arsed undertaking the journey to Australia. *It's too far*, they all whined. *I'll be jetlagged for days.* It was like he lived on the moon.

And so, later that evening, Jack and Mirabella took a cab up to the lively Bairro Alto district. Drinkers spilled out onto the streets, conversations in different languages punctuated the sound of pop music pumping from a plethora of bars. The smoky aromas of grilling fish and other meats filled the air. Mouths watering, the pair grabbed beef kebabs and fries, ate them standing at an outdoor bar table. She tried to coax information out of him about the case, but he refused to be drawn on the subject. Or on any subject, for that matter. 'Since you won't talk,' she said, 'it's time to listen to some fado!'

After wandering the streets for less than five minutes they reached the café Mirabella had pre-chosen among the masses of entertainment options. Jack's initial fears about the potential carcinogenic atmosphere inside the venue subsided immediately. Smoking rules were lax in this city, and he'd imagined a dark and dingy room, cigarette smoke climbing to the ceiling and choking his lungs. As he stepped inside he took an appreciative deep breath – there wasn't a wisp of cigarette smoke in the air.

In muted lemon-yellow lighting at the rear of the café stood a curly-haired woman cloaked in a tassel shawl with an intricate floral design. She crooned a mournful song as the spell-bound audience hung on her every word. On a stool to the right of the singer sat a serious young man with a curtain of straight black hair obscuring his eyes, strumming and plucking at a 12-string guitar. To her left, a man with an appalling combover kept the beat with thumb and forefinger on a double bass. The singer's eye-acting was superbly hammy, her long fingers waved expressively as she gave it everything she had. Her powerful contralto, reinforced by a tremendous vibrato, bounced off the white stucco walls and echoed inside the room. Jack imagined she was narrating the tragic tale of a fisherman lost at sea, or a broken-hearted lover unable to bear being cheated on who threw himself off a cliff. Or maybe it was about Ronaldo missing a penalty in the World Cup? What the hell did Jack know?

Mirabella standing by his side, he looked towards the bar, the back of a familiar head standing out from the crowd. Micky Knox, wearing his favourite Fulham FC jacket, sat on a stool by the bar, cradling a beer. Next to the beer, a straight shot of what looked like rum, and a Coke in a tall glass, all ready for Jack's arrival. Thoughtful to a fault. Jack steered Mirabella towards the bar, whispering, 'There's Micky. You're gonna love him.'

Micky completely ignored Jack as he shook her hand, bowing low. For a second Jack thought the man was going to kiss her hand, but he held back by an inch. He looked up and gazed into Mirabella's widening eyes. He spoke loudly enough to be heard above the music but not so loudly as to incur the ire of the paying customers. '*Bom dia.* Jack has told me all about you. I must say, you are even more beautiful than he described.'

Jack's fingers twitched. He could slap Micky for that lie; he'd not said a word about what she looked like. And, although it was a cringey remark, Mirabella wasn't embarrassed or offended in the least. On the contrary, the corners of her mouth stretched into a smile so broad it threatened to split her face in two. By most of society's standards, Micky was a much better looking specimen than Jack. His face didn't bear the ravages of a long boxing career like Jack's did. Hardly a mark or a scar, his skin smooth and clear. Features classical, symmetrical. And he possessed one of those goofy lopsided smiles many women found magnetic.

Without letting go of Micky's hand, Mirabella turned to Jack and said, 'Are all of your friends as handsome and charming as this one?' She ended the sentence with a flick of her hair and a titter. *My God, she's flirting with him now.*

Jack felt an enormous burden lift from his shoulders. Micky could draw the heat away from him. But then came a realisation. He had grossly exaggerated in his own mind the level of Mirabella's attraction to him. Right now, she was acting with Micky the same way she had with Jack. This was her default mode. Coquettish, to the point of being what some might call a prick tease. And perhaps there was an innocence behind it all and there was no sexual endgame. *Don't be naïve, Lisbon. Of course there's an endgame.*

The trio found a spare round table a couple of metres from the singer and her accompanists and quietly absorbed the music until there was a break. Micky got the next round in, and the next three after that. Two hours later, he and Mirabella were tipsy verging on drunk, and Jack was loving it. He was mostly a spectator when there was a chance to talk between songs, the two strangers like a couple who had met on a dating app and whose low expectations were exceeded by the pleasant reality of their hook-ups.

Around midnight, Jack passed the untouched rum to Micky, who slammed it down. He took his leave of the pair, both expressing their desire to party on hard, probably until the sun came up. Micky had an iron-cast constitution when it came to cutting loose; Jack didn't know about Mirabella. Fingers crossed, Micky takes her back to his hotel room and then Jack could put her out of his mind altogether. If they consummated the friendship, Claudia could fly over to catch the end of Jack's vacation without worrying that Mirabella would throw a spanner in the works.

He began slowly wending his way down the steep and narrow streets of Bairro Alto, limping and wincing as he walked. He dismissed the discomfort and soldiered on: he hadn't had a proper walk for a while, let alone a run, which was what he really craved. A long, 10km loping run along the embankment of the Tagus. It was a pleasure he'd have to forgo this trip, although he might recover enough for a slow trot along the beaches of the Algarve.

The encounter with the mugger had left him a little antsier than usual. When people got close behind him in the crowded streets his muscles involuntarily stiffened as he prepared to defend himself. It was nonsense, of course. No one was going to king-hit him in public. Lightning would not strike three times. He reached the sprawling Praça do Comércio in twenty-five minutes instead of the fifteen it would take a fit Jack Lisbon.

He waved down a taxi and levered himself into the back seat. He pulled out his mobile, set to silent for the fado performance. He'd missed a call made by Raquel Quintal two hours ago. She left a message. He listened. *Hello Jack. Detective Da Silva has been involved in a car accident. He is in the hospital and has suffered serious but not life-threatening injuries. Please call me in the morning.*

His mind started racing as the taxi made its way to Belém. He was tempted to call Quintal now, but he resisted the urge. There was nothing he could do for Da Silva other than pay a token visit and bring a bunch of flowers. He came to a compromise decision. He fired off a short SMS to Quintal. Not his fault if she was asleep and didn't have her phone on silent.

His phone jangled within seconds of him sending the message.

'What happened to him?' he said.

Quintal explained the chief had been t-boned at a junction on his way home from the office this evening. Luckily, the car that ran into him struck the passenger side. Nevertheless, he suffered brain swelling after his head smashed into the airbag when it deployed. He was in a medically-induced coma, but the doctors expected to bring him out of it in a couple of days.

'Anything else?'

'Yes. I would like you to stay one more day to assist us.'

'How? I don't know what else I can do?'

He heard a complaining, tired female voice in the background. Jack spoke no Portuguese, but he interpreted the tone of the words as: *hang up and go back to sleep.* Quintal shushed the woman firmly, then said to Jack, 'With him out of action, I've been put in charge of the case. I hate to admit it, but your presence gives me confidence. Just between us, Da Silva can be a little...soft...on suspects.'

'I noticed that. But, like I said, I'm pretty much cooked.'

'I believe Da Silva mentioned a fee for your assistance?'

Jack had forgotten about the promise he made to

himself, to earn the dough then send it to Jocelyn for Sarah's charity. 'He did mention it, yeah.'

'Still interested?'

'I could be.'

'The Deputy National Director made it clear to me the offer is still on the table, but you have to complete the week, like Zé told you.'

'OK. I'll be there. My daughter won't be happy about it, though.' Disingenuous, Lisbon. She's fine without you. 'Any point checking in on Zé?'

'It won't make him any better.'

Jack got his wallet ready to pay the driver as he pulled into Mirabella's street. With luck, she wouldn't be home when he got up in the morning.

He wanted to ask Quintal so many questions about the status of Alvarenga and Ahmad, if she was seriously considering other leads, but he decided to leave it until the briefing. He was keen to see how she ran the show after being asked to step up. His gut told him she'd make a better lead detective than Zé, but as always he reserved judgement.

'I guess not,' he said. 'But I've read that you can speak to a person in a coma and they can hear what you're saying to them.'

Quintal chuckled softly. 'I doubt it. A lot of fully conscious people I speak to aren't able to process what they're told.'

'I know exactly what you mean.' Jack nodded, even though she couldn't see his agreement. 'See you at 8:30am?'

'No. Seven. I have some ideas I want to discuss with the team as early as possible, get things moving. I believe we need to branch out in different directions, not concentrate on two suspects just because we want them to be guilty. I would like to hear the perspectives of as many officers as possible. To be honest, Alvarenga and Ahmad are in massive trouble for corruption, but the murder...it will be very hard to prove it was them.'

'Will someone be there to let me in at that hour?'

'Don't worry about that, my friend. I'll pick you up at 06:15 sharp. Text me the address.'

Jack was right. She would make a better lead detective.

## Chapter Twenty-Nine

THE SHRIEK of the phone alarm shattered his dream. He slapped the mobile quiet, eyes opening through the crust of sleep. Still lying flat on his back, he stretched his arms and legs to their full extent, relishing the tension then the relaxation of tendons and muscles. There were no sharp pains anywhere now, just dull aches from the blows he'd sustained. He sat up and drank the full glass of water he'd left on the bedside table, the usual early morning thirst slaked. With the back of his wrist he wiped his lips, then felt the sheen of sweat that coated his brow. The REM stage of sleep must have come right at the tail end of his slumber because the visions were still fresh and technicolour vivid.

In the dream he was a young man again, fighting the lad who'd killed off his hopes of pursuing a professional boxing career. But this time Jack *wasn't* KO'd in the championship fight. He *didn't* drop his guard at the crucial moment. He fought a flawless fight, sending the other guy to the canvas in the second round. A total inversion of reality. What could have been, but was destined never to be.

Staring in the mirror at his bleary eyes, the swelling above the left testimony to his cousin's prowess, Jack smiled. So what if that dream never eventuated for him? It had for Paulo, and that was all right for the Lisbon/Lisboa clan.

A squirt of spearmint toothpaste on the travel toothbrush, up and down, round and round. There was another reason to be grateful: over the years of fighting, in the ring and on the streets, by some miracle all his teeth remained intact. He didn't deserve his blessings: successful career, a home of his own, a daughter he never thought he would see again. *You are one very lucky bastard, Jack Lisbon.*

He downgraded that assessment to "standard" lucky bastard after the twentieth and final lap of Mirabella's pool. He pulled himself up the ladder, every fibre burning from the effort. The calf was still too tender to risk even a light jog, so he'd opted for a swim instead. Out of practice, he'd be feeling the effects for a day or two.

On the positive side, Mirabella hadn't come home yet. He imagined her curled up, sound asleep in Micky's arms back at his 5-star hotel. Just before flicking out his reading light last night, he'd received a couple of images on his mobile: selfies of Micky and Mirabella, drunk as skunks. They wore big grins, eyes glazed over from who knew what substances, their fingers splayed in peace signs. There was even one Mirabella must have taken – Micky on stage with a microphone in his hand, gob wide open like one of those laughing clowns you drop ping pong balls into at the fair. The lad was mad on karaoke and had a decent singing voice. Put a few drinks into him and you've a job getting the microphone off him.

A hot shower to soothe the muscles followed by a breakfast of buttered toast and two double espressos and he was ready to meet his foreign colleagues for one last hurrah.

Jack closed the gates behind him at precisely 06:13am. In the early dawn light he made out the police vehicle on the other side of the street, Quintal behind the wheel. She called out of the open window, 'Come on. We don't want to be late.'

The woman was the antithesis of Da Silva in so many ways. Not that he was a bad operator, the two cops just had different approaches. Confidence personified, she bent the car to her will like a veteran rally driver, haring along the roads with scant regard to traffic rules.

They arrived fifteen minutes ahead of time. Jack took a seat at the back of the small auditorium while Quintal fussed about at a lectern, arranging a drink bottle and shuffling papers. Once it seemed all who needed to be there had arrived and the room fell silent, the new lead investigator cleared her throat. She spoke for about a minute in her native tongue, eliciting a variety of murmured responses from her colleagues and a blank stare from Jack, before she switched to her perfect English.

'Extensive searches have been and are being carried out on all the devices confiscated from Entrega Rápida. Not one shred of evidence has been found – so far – on any of them. Alvarenga and Ahmad have been released on bail.' She called out three names, told those officers to pay a visit to the company's offices and speak to each and every employee on the premises. 'Tell them the company they work for will sink when their CEO and top legal man are convicted. Appeal to their sense of right and wrong, their consciences.'

Jack smiled. Good tactic. If he was going down the gurgler due to a crook's misdeeds, he'd do everything he could to make sure they paid the ultimate price for it.

She called out four more names. 'I want you to take two

squad cars and comb the Cova da Moura area: north, south and east. Leave the southern sector to me.'

A uniformed officer started to protest, but Quintal was having none of it. 'Yes, I know we are not welcome, but remember we now have the gun used to kill Salma Farooq. It's a Heckler & Koch VP9, originally sold in Italy. Guns of this type have been used in a number of robberies in the outer northern suburbs this year, all of them traced back to the Cova da Moura neighbourhood. There's a good chance this one came from there too. Show the residents photos of the victim and every suspect on our list, plus the photofit of the killer.'

She rattled off a couple more names, told the officers to make follow-up calls with chief suspects Oliveira and Phillipson, arrange visits. Don't let up. Five more were tasked with door-knocking Farooq's apartment block and calling the phone numbers of all residents registered as living there. Make note of apartments where no one answered; they would be visited at night. Somebody – other than the witness Andre Ferreira – may have seen something. Once they were done there, they were to canvass the streets in a radius of one kilometre around the apartment building. Finally, she called out Rebelo, Horta and Costa, instructed them to speak to half a dozen or so people who had called in overnight and who reckoned they got a good look at the shooter. These tips seemed credible, because the witnesses claimed to have seen the man not far from where the murder weapon was found outside the Lx Factory – information which had not yet been made public.

'And that's all we can do for now. Once you're done with your assignments, hit your desks and dig into all the files we've put together on this case. Attack them like you're the victim: a researcher with determination. Boring work, yes, but the kind that very often leads to discoveries. Any questions? Portuguese is fine. I'll relay anything important to Jack.'

Again, to his surprise, the assembled officers respected their visitor and stuck to English. Some spoke at a level much lower that the detectives Jack had been working with, but fluent enough to get the message across just fine.

In the car with Quintal, Jack said, 'Everyone got a job except me.'

She raised an eyebrow as the engine roared to life. 'Isn't it obvious?'

'Not to me.'

'You've heard of good cop, bad cop? Today it's bad cop, worse cop.'

'I think that was the name of a movie.'

She gave a disappointed pout as she gunned the car out of the parking lot. 'And I was sure I'd thought of it all by myself.'

———

'WHY ARE WE HERE?' Jack watched his step as he and Quintal trod carefully around piles of broken bricks, tiles and random debris. Even though the streets were empty, loud voices and radios playing thumping hip-hop rang out behind barred-up windows. The small, crumbling houses had needed painting ten years ago. Now, they looked only fit for demolition. The air stank of dope, stale urine and underlying menace. 'I thought you'd assigned four cops to comb this area?'

'Yes. And with us, it makes six.' She snapped out a couple of words into her phone, listened intently to the reply. She switched it off, stuffed it in her jeans pocket and looked back to Jack. 'The others are on the job. Like I said, we're taking the southern section. It happens to be where the nastiest bad guys live. One man, Jeremias, is known as the major gun supplier. That's who we'll be talking to.'

'You don't look too worried about it?'

Quintal's shoulders were squared, her jaw set like granite. 'Why should I be?' she patted her armpit. 'I've got a gun in case things go, how do you say, pear shaped?'

Jack grinned. The woman was well up to speed on English slang. 'Yeah, but I ain't got one of those.'

'Aren't you a tough guy, though? A champion boxer?'

'More of a brawler. A scrapper. Not much technique. I've done most of my fighting in the streets.'

With a sweeping hand she gestured at the decrepit streetscape like she was advertising washing powder on the television. 'Even better. This place is crawling with street fighters.' She shaded her eyes from the morning sun for a moment as they stood before a fork in the serpentine road. They were still climbing, and Jack was glad of the rest, his calf throbbing a little. 'Now, what I want you to do is let me do the talking.'

'All of it?'

'I'll give you a cue when it's your turn. We're actually not cops today.'

'What, like undercover?' He stopped to let a hunched over woman stagger past them in the narrow alleyway. 'I wondered why you were dressed so casual.' Instead of her usual crisp black pants, white shirt and navy-blue jacket ensemble, Quintal sported tattered blue jeans and a faded pink top under a light cotton jacket. If not for the concealed weapon in her armpit, she probably would have left the jacket off, such was the warmth of the day.

'Exactly. Here's my plan.'

AS INSTRUCTED, Jack stood next to Quintal, legs spread wide and arms folded high across his chest. He affected his best disdainful snarl as she spoke to a heavily muscled black man in a mesh singlet. Jeremias. Greying dreadlocks poked out from a black, red, yellow and green rastacap. He had deep scars on both cheeks. Book-ending him on fold-out chairs were two other black dudes: one with a shiny bald head, the other in a baseball cap and sporting a thick beard. All three were living kaleidoscopes of tattoos, their chests, arms, legs and necks shaded in blue and green. They lounged in their seats like lizards, taking small sips from brown beer bottles. A white bulldog with a pink nose snoozed on the end of a chain, clearly unperturbed by the unexpected drop ins. Jack suspected that, let off the chain, the dog would be quick to action to defend its owner.

Quintal and Jeremias exchanged a dozen or so softly spoken sentences in Portuguese before Quintal, pretending to be a crooked lawyer with criminals for clients, made her move.

'Mr Jones here,' she said, 'is looking to buy a pistol for his own protection while visiting our country.' The sudden switch to English made Jack stop analysing the three toughs. His part in the play was coming up next.

'Why?' said Jeremias. 'He looks like strong man. Not need weapon.'

'He has enemies here. Enemies who want to kill him.'

'Then why this *bife* not go home?'

Quintal sighed in mock exasperation. 'Because he is setting up a business here. One that is not exactly legal, if you understand me.'

Jeremias nodded slowly, eyes closed.

'He may need more weapons to make sure that he is protected properly.' Quintal looked at Jack. 'You tell them.'

'Ah...yeah,' said Jack. 'If the business proves successful, I will want to purchase more pistols. For my men. I hear you have some in stock?'

The man shook his head, the swishing dreadlocks shooing away a couple of flies. He took a pull from a bottle of beer then said, 'I know nothing about that.'

'A shame,' said Jack. He held out a tight roll of cash bound with a rubber band. Quintal told him there was three grand in the wad. 'Because I'm prepared to pay above market price. I'm particularly interested in the Heckler & Koch VP9. A contact told me he bought one off a man in Cova da Moura. If that's not you, I'll give you five hundred to tell me where I can get them.'

'This nothing to do with the girl killed last week?'

Jack waved the question away. 'A tragedy, but nothing to do with me. I arrived in Portugal after it happened.'

Quintal added, 'I've heard a rumour the police are looking for a Glock, not a H&K.'

Jeremias held up a finger. 'One minute.'

He went inside the ramshackle building behind him. His two companions laughed and joked while the boss man was away. A few moments later Jeremias brought out an object wrapped inside a bath towel. Jack frowned and nodded with appreciation. The man placed the bundle in Jack's outstretched hands. 'The price is 950 euro. One full clip included. No refunds.'

Jack clocked Quintal to his left, grinning. There would be no arrests for selling guns illegally. At least not now. Too dangerous without backup on hand. This was an evidence gathering expedition.

Jack placed the bundle on the ground. 'And another five

hundred to tell me who you sold the last one of these bad boys to.'

Jeremias's nostrils flared. 'Why you want to know?'

'A colleague of mine was shot with one. We think the shooter may have bought the gun in this area.'

'I no rat on customers.'

Jack licked his lips. 'A thousand.'

The man narrowed one eye. 'I still no say. But I give you, how do you say, a clue. The man say he hate cats.' He burst out laughing as he patted the twitching snout of the sleeping dog. 'So does Bennito here.' All three men laughed heartily.

'If you need a lawyer, let me know.' She held out a piece of paper with a bogus phone number on it.

From the back of his pants, Jeremias produced a huge pistol that resembled an old-fashioned .44 Remington Magnum. 'This is only lawyer I need.' He made a childlike wave with his fingers curling. 'Bye-bye now!'

As they made their way back to the vehicle, picking their way through the trash, Jack suddenly stopped. 'What's the penalty for illegally selling guns in this country?'

'I'd have to check, but it would range from fines to lengthy imprisonment, depending on the circumstances. Last case I recall a guy got five years due to previous convictions.'

'I've got an idea. If your uniforms working this area can get an ID on the shooter from photos, then—'

'No.' She slapped a hand against her thigh. 'Why didn't I think of it before!'

'What?'

'I'll tell you on the drive back to the station.'

## Chapter Thirty

QUINTAL FINISHED SPEAKING to one of the uniforms over the two-way radio, hung up the receiver with a clunk. 'Our officers aren't getting the positive reception we did. If you can call having a Magnum waved in your face positive.'

Jack unwrapped the towel, turned the chunky pistol over in his hands. 'It's only to be expected. No joy at all?'

Quintal turned her head to the side and frowned. 'Nada. But the day's still early.'

'You gonna swoop on Jeremias later?'

'Would you?'

'I'm in two minds about it. He could be a useful contact for any undercover work you might carry out in the future. To be honest, though, I'm stunned at how easy it was to buy this.' He held out the gun, barrel pointing up.

'Hey! Put that down. You'll scare people.'

Jack complied. 'Sorry. But, if it were up to me, I'd raid the bloke as soon as this case is solved. You don't want these weapons on the streets. I know money talks, but he was way too eager to make the sale.' He wrapped the gun in the towel, stowed it in the footwell. 'What was the idea you were going to tell me?'

'I was planning to set up a raid on Jeremias and his gang when we returned to the office, but I think we should offer him a deal. Information on the shooter for us turning a blind eye – for now – to his activities.'

'Smart. Has he been in jail before?'

She nodded as the car pulled up at a set of lights. 'Yes. He's somehow managed to avoid going back for six years. I'm not sure how loyal he'll be to the customer once we demonstrate the pistol used to kill Farooq was the one he sold.'

'But there's no evidence to prove it, is there?'

'He doesn't know that.' She was about to expound on the matter when her mobile chirruped in the centre console. A short and animated conversation ensued. She ended the call and executed a tight U-turn through the intersection, other drivers honking their horns. 'It's Da Silva.'

'What about him?'

'He's awake.'

---

THE DOCTOR OPENED the door to the private ward and ushered Jack and Quintal into the room. An elfin woman with pale skin was sitting by the side of the bed, holding Da Silva's hand.

'Raquel and Jack! Thanks for coming by.' For a man not long out of a coma, the detective's voice conveyed a lot of optimistic energy. He inclined his bandaged head towards the woman in the chair. 'This is my wife, Gloria.'

'Pleased to meet you.' Gloria stood, held her small hand out. Jack shook it gently. 'Zé has told me so much about you.' She glanced at Quintal. 'Nice to see you again, Raquel. It's been a long time since you came to see us.'

'Yes it has,' said Quintal. 'Too long. Listen, we can come back another time if you two would like to be alone for a while.'

'Nonsense,' said Da Silva. 'I'd like to have a word about the case.'

Gloria grabbed a small clutch handbag from the floor, tucked it under her arm. 'Please,' said Quintal, snaking her arm around Gloria's thin waist. 'Don't leave on our account.'

Da Silva's diminutive wife wouldn't hear of it. 'I'll come back later tonight. He's in good hands.' She pulled a tube to one side and hugged her husband carefully, gave him a lingering kiss on his swollen lips. As she stepped away she wiped a small tear from her eye. Whatever domestic problems the pair had at home, Jack got the impression they weren't insurmountable and the marriage had every chance of surviving.

With Gloria gone, Da Silva wasted no time getting down to brass tacks. The status of the murder investigation was his first question. Followed by the linked corruption charges against Ahmad and Alvarenga. He spoke more quickly than was his wont, Jack thought, like he was running out of time. Quintal had spoken for two minutes, barely got warmed up, when Da Silva fell asleep, his breathing like a rusty ratchet. A thick line of drool ran from the side of his mouth. Bleeping on a machine intensified. Quintal stood in a hurry, told Jack she was going to speak to someone. She was back in under a minute with the floor duty nurse and the same doctor who brought them here. The doctor read the monitors connected to Da Silva, whipped out a stethoscope and assessed the unconscious patient. In a serious tone he told the visitors Da Silva needed urgent attention and they should vacate. He promised to keep Quintal and Gloria updated on developments.

As they left the hospital, Jack had an uneasy feeling deep in the pit of his stomach. Da Silva wasn't going to make it.

---

DESPITE THE EMOTIONAL knife twisting in his gut, Jack did his best to put some sparkle in his voice. 'Guess what, sweetie?'

'You're at the front gate?' she said expectantly.

'No. But I'll be there tomorrow.'

'Promise?' said Skye. 'No more excuses?'

He took a steadying breath. 'A hundred percent. No matter what else happens, I'm on that bus. But there is something else.'

'What?'

'Claudia's coming.'

'No way!' said Skye, incredulous. 'When?'

'In a couple of days. She wants to fly over and have a look around Portugal. And what better time than while we're here, hey?'

'She can stay with us on the *quinta*.'

'Let's not get ahead of ourselves,' Jack cautioned. 'We have to ask Tio Paulo and Tia Linda if it's all right with them first. It's not for us to decide.'

A sigh. 'I guess.'

'Even if they say no, she can stay nearby in a hotel or a short-term rental.'

'I suppose that would be all right too.' A pause, like Skye was trying to filter the information, make sense of it. 'You know what, Daddy?'

'What?'

'I can't wait to meet her!'

'I'm sure she feels the same about you.' He rubbed the swelling over his eye, beginning to throb again. He terminated the call, asked Quintal if there were aspirin in the glove box. She leaned over, popped it open and pointed at a jumble of items. 'Somewhere in there. Can you swallow them without water?'

'Like they do on American TV? I never understood how they do that.'

She pulled into a petrol station. 'I guess that means there's no water in there. Fill the tank while I'm inside, would you?'

She was already striding away before he had time to reply. When the nozzle clicked, he replaced it on its holster, jumped back in the car and checked his SMS messages. Micky had texted him, and so had Taylor. His mate had written a note of effusive thanks for "setting him up" with Mirabella. She was a firecracker and now he thinks he's in love. The cocky git thought the honey trap had been laid out just for him. Next, Taylor's confirmation of her flight, arriving in Lisbon in three days with a connector to Faro in the Algarve. Jack shook his head, marvelling at how quickly things can happen when you least expect it.

'Put that toy away. I've got some treats.' Quintal slid into her seat and handed Jack a plastic bag full of service station junk food. Among the goodies, the only thing he was interested in: a bottle of flavoured water. He chugged three aspirin and instantly felt the psychological relief. So much so that he was ready to attack the gummy bears and apple muffin.

'No coffee?' he said.

'Their coffee sucks. I know where they serve real good stuff.'

'Where?'

'Around the corner from Fernanda Brito's place. I'd like a word with her before I draw up the proposed deal with Jeremias.'

'You think she knows more than she's letting on?'

'Horta and Costa are the only ones who have questioned her so far. No offense to them, but they've not got much experience. Time to shake it up a little.'

## Chapter Thirty-One

'DO you mind if we conduct the interview in English?' said Quintal, nodding her thanks at the waiter who was bringing her a caramel latte. Jack sipped his own unembellished espresso, unable to fathom why anyone would want to adulterate a perfect product.

'*Por que?* Why?' said Fernanda Brito.

Quintal nodded at Jack. 'For the benefit of our special investigator from…Scotland Yard.'

Jack coughed up a couple of crumbs then swallowed hard on his pastel de nata. Even going down his throat like a jagged rock, it tasted delicious. The meeting at the quiet café had got underway with Quintal cleverly avoiding introducing Jack by name. The notorious blog post had spread so wide, he wouldn't have been surprised if Brito knew of him. *Scotland Yard, indeed. Well done, Raquel.*

'Are the Portuguese police not good enough to find the bastard who killed Salma?' said Brito, in perfect English. She offered a paralysed smile as she blinked repeatedly.

Quintal sipped her coffee, wiped away a thin froth-moustache. 'Nothing unusual. Police forces around the world often assist each other in high-profile cases. My colleague here has expertise in certain areas I'd rather not go into, but his results are excellent. It's been ten days since the crime was committed, which has us worried. We need to try everything. You wouldn't expect less for your best friend, would you?'

Her shoulders slumped as she stirred a sugar into black tea. 'No. I apologise.'

Jack smirked. Quintal's got the woman apologising – for nothing. Unbelievable.

'Please,' Quintal placed an iPad on the table. 'Scroll through these faces, tell me what each of them means to you, what they meant to Salma. Are they hiding something? Can you think of facts you may have forgotten to tell the other officers you spoke to?'

'OK,' said Brito, pulling the phone towards her.

Jack already knew who was in the rogues gallery. The addition of Jeremias was a Hail Mary, although Brito did stop and stare at the man's face, scratching her head and frowning as she did so. Once she got to the end, she scrolled back and gave her thoughts on them all. Anita Oliveira: an unhinged drunk who could easily have paid for a hitman. Caspar Phillipson: an egotist who couldn't cope when Salma dumped him. However, he was vain enough to hook up with another fairly quickly and his period of juvenile moping was short-lived. As far as Brito knew, the man was in a relationship with a new woman from Australia or New Zealand, she wasn't sure which. Editor Marina Ventura: she was an encouraging figure in Salma's life; appreciated her work but there was no interaction apart from the professional. Professor Grosso. Salma didn't talk about him much.

'Why's that, do you think?' said Jack. 'He has a reputation for being a ladies' man around campus. Salma was a very attractive young woman, bound to catch his eye. In fact, he was her mentor on the thesis she was writing.'

Brito delivered an apologetic look. 'Salma and I may have been best friends – we've known each other since kindergarten. But her brain...' she made a hand gesture, spread out fingers imitating an explosion around her head... 'it was on another level compared to me.'

'Meaning?' said Quintal.

'Meaning she rarely spoke about her studies, except in really general terms.'

Jack leaned forward. 'You work in a bank, is that right?'

She replied with a tiny nod.

'Isn't that related to her research, the articles she wrote?'

Brito knotted her lips. 'Not really. My work's boring. Adding up, subtracting, balancing the debits and credits at the end of the shift. She was into the high-up stuff that I can't even begin to understand.'

'So she never mentioned the professor at all?' said Quintal. 'I find that hard to believe.'

A shake of the head. 'No, she did mention him occasionally. And always good things. She needed an extension on the thesis because of the article taking up a lot of her time, and he granted it. She thought very highly of him.'

'Never said he was trying to hit onto her?'

A blank stare. 'Why would he hit her?'

Jack realised it was a mistake to use the slang term. 'Sorry, I meant he never asked her on a date, tried to get... romantic with her.'

'Ah, yes. Now I know what you mean.' A pause while she sipped her tea. 'Again, no. I think he was very respectful of her. She was a strong believer in no sex before marriage.'

'What about the men from Entrega Rápida?'

'Hmmm. Yes, she was a little bit worried they might make trouble for her. Senhor Ahmad had made some vague threats, but she thought it was about getting her kicked out of university.' She stared at the wall for a moment, then looked back to Jack. 'She would not have imagined they would kill her! I mean, this is Portugal, not some…I don't know…wild west town.'

One card left in the pack, thought Jack. He took the iPad, scrolled to the image of the mole in the Ministry, Rosa Braga, turned it around and tapped on the screen. 'What about her?'

'I don't know who she is.'

'She fed information to Salma about Entrega Rápida.'

'She did?'

Jack sighed. 'Please, Fernanda, there must be something. She was your best friend. If she didn't talk much about her studies or job, what did the two of you talk about?'

Brito smiled, although tears gathered in the corners of her eyes, trickled down her cheeks. 'That's just the thing. We've known each other so long we didn't need to share common interests. Just being around each other was enough. She made me laugh with her stories about her mum, her dad back in Morocco.' She wiped a tear away. 'And lately, about Vasco.'

The detectives exchanged a look of bewilderment. Quintal said, 'Who's that? A family member we don't know about?'

'Kind of. It's her cat. And…oh my God! What has happened to him?'

Quintal placed a hand over Brito's wrist. 'It's OK. My boss took him home.'

Relief relaxed her face, the lines around the woman's eyes disappeared. 'Thank God. I meant to go and get him, but with everything that's happened I forgot…I'm so glad he found a home. Salma rescued him from the streets two weeks before she died. She wasn't supposed to keep pets in her apartment, but she did anyway. Always looking to help.'

A small detail blazed in front of Jack's eyes like a neon sign. 'But didn't she stay at your apartment the night before she died?'

'Yes.'

'How could she have left him on his own in a small flat?' Jack was incredulous. 'One of the detectives reported she had to empty a very full litter tray, the place stank, and the beast was starving.'

Brito shook her head. 'No. That's not right. Salma said she gave the key to someone and they were going to come and take care of Vasco. I wonder what happened?'

'Who was it?' said Quintal firmly.

'I don't know the name.'

'Think!' roared Jack. He glared at Quintal. 'Remember what Jeremias said. The guy who bought the gun said he hated cats.'

'But the cat was alive.'

'Sure. Left to starve.'

'Wait, wait,' said Brito. 'I can't remember the name. But I do know where he works.'

## Chapter Thirty-Two

CATARINA REBELO HAD ARRIVED AHEAD of time. She stood alone, enjoying a nervous, sneaky cigarette at the entrance to the Pingo Doce supermarket. The suspect's place of employment stood three blocks from Salma Farooq's apartment building. Rebelo shuffled her feet, from time to time glancing through the shop window. Even though the suspect had no criminal record, due to the nature of the crime committed, Quintal had ordered armed backup. A team of officers from the Special Operations Group was only minutes away.

The two-way radio sparked to life. Quintal spoke to a crackling male voice on the other end. She listened for a minute and a half, said *obrigada* and hung up. She turned to Jack, face set like cement. 'That was officer Luca Mendes.'

'The efficient officer who handcuffed me on the tram?'

'That's the one. He and other officers have found enough evidence at his apartment. Pictures of Farooq on his walls, defaced with bullets and blood he drew with red crayon. Ferreira was stalking the victim's every movement.

A map with the route she took to university, the magazine's office, the Entrega Rápida building.'

'Holy shit,' said Jack. 'Why did he do it?'

'No idea. Perhaps Ferreira was obsessed like Oliveira was with Phillipson, but on a totally different level.'

'Or he was on Entrega Rápida's payroll?'

'I like the first theory,' said Quintal. 'Why would he have drawn a circle around the company's address?'

'Good point,' agreed Jack. 'You'll get those arseholes for fraud and corruption, yeah?'

She nodded quickly, then felt for the reassurance of the service pistol holstered under her jacket. 'I know you would love to, how do you say, make the collar. But I'm afraid you have to stay right out of this one.'

Although barred from taking part in the arrest, Jack was happy to remain in the passenger seat of the squad car. He'd had enough adventure for one trip. He had his mobile ready in his lap to take a video of the unfolding drama. Something to show Claudia and the family in the Algarve. Skye would love it. Jack tipped a finger to his forehead. 'Best of luck.'

Quintal clunked the door closed, hitched her pants and began to cross the street. Jack had the mobile up and was already filming the action. When Quintal was halfway there, a noisy commotion erupted at the entrance of the supermarket. A couple of pensioners were arguing next to a upturned pull-along shopping trolley. One man pointed at broken eggs and spilled milk on the ground, yelled at the other, who wasn't taking a backward step. They both had their fists up, ready to duke it out. This was a distraction that needed to be defused before it alerted Ferriera something was brewing.

Rebelo crushed out the cigarette under her heel, held her

ID up to the men, barked words at them. Quintal was doing the same, but with more elements of threat in her body language. The old fellas kept arguing until Quintal got right up in their grills, pointing her finger at them like a poisoned dagger. The message hit home. One old geezer snatched at the trolley and waddled off in one direction, his opponent in the other. But it was too late. A crowd of onlookers had emerged from inside the store, others appeared from outside. Maybe twenty bodies having what the Aussies call a sticky-beak. Jack could see Quintal giving instructions to Rebelo, who nodded and hightailed it down the side of the building, most likely to stop the suspect fleeing via the rear exit. Quintal elbowed her way through the crowd and marched inside. Big strides, like an angry sheriff looking for an escaped outlaw.

In the distance, Jack could make out the faint wailing of sirens. He had no idea if it was the tactical guys on their way, or first responders attending to something else. But, in reality, it made no difference.

On the screen of Jack's mobile, a large male figure appeared like a flashing meteorite. He rounded the corner of the building – on the opposite side of the building to where Rebelo had gone – and sprinted down the main street like his life depended on it.

*Andre Ferreira was on the run.*

Without hitting the button to stop filming, Jack dropped the phone in the console. He levered his injured body out of the car as quickly as the pain would allow. This was going to hurt for days, but there was no option.

*He had to give chase.*

The suspect had a number of advantages: a younger body, fear-driven adrenaline giving him extra speed, local knowledge of the streetscape, and there was an almost one-hundred percent probability Ferreira hadn't been attacked with a tyre lever recently. Jack's injured calf stung in dozens of places, like acupuncture gone horribly wrong. His neck and shoulders throbbed in agony. But he didn't care. Something deep inside took over, masked the pain.

As he ran, Jack called out the only thing he could think of. '*Stop! Police!*'

Ferreira turned his head quickly, without breaking stride, and put on the afterburners. Jack called out again. The suspect continued in a straight line for forty or so metres before making a sharp right turn. The man was out of sight for about ten seconds before Jack ducked down the same street. Ten seconds is a long time in a chase scenario. In this case, enough for Ferreira to disappear among a row of parked cars and shady trees.

But only for a moment.

Jack saw the flashing heels, about thirty metres ahead. No more calling out to the man – just run.

Twenty metres now.

Jack was gaining fast.

Fifteen metres.

Ten.

Five.

He could hear the man's ragged breath, like a ruptured air hose. No natural or developed fitness: until now it was pure adrenaline that had kept him going.

Two metres now.

One.

He steeled himself for the takedown. Power surging from the glutes and quads to launch into a flying rugby tackle. Jack's right shoulder – the uninjured one – crashed into Ferreira's left leg a couple of centimetres below the knee, propelling him forward. Jack heard a sickening crunch as the man's face ploughed into hard concrete.

He lay there panting and gripping the suspect around the legs with all his might as Ferreira struggled in vain to get himself loose.

Half a minute later, he heard two doors slam as Quintal and Rebelo jogged to the scene from their car. Quintal helped Jack to his feet as Rebelo applied a set of handcuffs to Ferreira. The suspect spat, blood and a tooth landing on the ground. He growled a series of furious oaths as Rebelo recited what Jack imagined was the fact of his arrest and his rights, whatever they may be in this country. Portugal was a nice, humane place, so Jack assumed the folks here had a shitload of rights. Sometimes, like now, that was a pity.

On the ride back to the station, Jack said to Quintal, 'I want you to take credit for the collar.'

Quintal laughed. 'What? The famous detective gone all shy now?'

'No...I...well...'

'Don't worry. I was teasing. No one except me and Catarina saw anything. We'll be keeping your name out of it. I'll say I brought him down.'

Jack eyed her up and down. 'I reckon you could have 'n all. You're certainly big enough to tackle plenty of villains.'

This time she laughed even louder. 'You have no charm whatsoever.'

He arched an eyebrow. 'Whaddaya mean? That was a compliment.'

She reached across and patted his forearm as she pulled into the parking lot. 'And that's exactly how I'm going to take it.' She killed the engine. 'Want to sit in on the interview? There's not much point. This will have to be conducted entirely in Portuguese.'

'I'll give that a miss. I want to get back to my kid, you know?'

Quintal called a taxi for Jack. While they waited, she started to talk about the ex-gratia payment for his assistance, but he cut her off. 'I'll email you an account number where you can send it. It's a charity.'

'Of course. It's your decision what you do with it.'

They said good-bye and shook hands. Then she said in Portuguese what Jack imagined was "*To hell with it*" and pulled him in for one the fiercest bear hugs he'd ever experienced from a woman. Sitting in the back seat of the cab, he wondered if he'd have to add cracked ribs to his long list of injuries.

## Chapter Thirty-Three

WITH HIS FEET UP on the stool and the television playing a local soap opera of dubious production values, Jack looked out the window onto the yard. The children were playing football on an enormous lush lawn. Skye ran rings around her cousins as she hammered another goal into the net. Only this time, she didn't. The ball sailed to the right of the upright and caromed off the brick wall. Even from where he sat, Jack could tell it was a deliberate miss. To give the others a fighting chance. Normally a smile would come naturally, pride in his daughter would surge through his heart. But not now.

'Did you hear me, Jack?' said Quintal.

'Yes,' Jack whispered. 'It's still sinking in.'

A minute ago, he learned Da Silva's condition had deteriorated. Gloria was contacted and asked to make a horrible decision. Switch off his life support or wait it out a little longer. The doctors said there was virtually no hope of him making a recovery; the swelling on the brain is irreversible.

'What about the driver of the other vehicle?' Jack

picked at a scab on his elbow, the healed-over graze a reminder of his tackle on Ferreira. 'Was she drunk? Will she be charged with anything?'

Quintal sighed. 'It seems the traffic light failed. She was driving on a green light, and so was Zé. No driver was at fault. The traffic cameras confirmed what happened. It's a tragedy.'

Jack shook his head. Da Silva was a good man, giving his job everything while trying hard to mend his failing relationship, and perhaps on the path to success in that endeavour. First Sarah gone too early, now Zé. Not to mention Salma Farooq. Life was a beautiful thing, but she could be so, so cruel. Every day alive was a blessing.

'Tell me about the prosecution. What's happening?'

'Full steam ahead, as they say.' She started to explain, then said, 'You could just read about it in the newspapers once the trial starts, you know.'

'You bet I'll follow it.' He readjusted his numbing feet before they went completely to sleep. 'But I want the inside information. Considering I was part of the team that helped catch the killer.'

Quintal pretended to find explaining developments tiresome, but Jack knew she was being disingenuous. She would now take Zé's place in the Polícia Judiciária hierarchy, and do a better job than him. Ferriera was denying his guilt, which would make for a much more interesting trial. Forensics on the pistol was inconclusive, and his lawyer was making the most out of that. However, Jeremias was prepared to testify he sold the gun to Ferreira in return for not being prosecuted for trading in illegal weapons. The ballistics proved the bullets inside Farooq's body came from the gun the sanitation workers found.

'Sounds like an open and shut case,' said Jack.

'We've circulated Ferreira's photo, and now witnesses from the tram are coming forward claiming they did see him on the day.'

'It doesn't help that the bloke looks so…average.' Jack jumped slightly in his seat as the football banged into the windowpane. The glass didn't break, so he was guessing Skye hadn't kicked it this time.

'True,' agreed Quintal.

'So if he's pleading not guilty, I guess you're no closer to getting a true motive?'

'No. He had notebooks in his apartment, filled with rants about Farooq ignoring him, poems – terrible ones – professing his love for her. He's a classic obsessive fan.'

'I guess Vasco the cat is lucky Ferreira didn't come back and finish him off?'

'Very lucky. And also lucky Da Silva took him. I offered to take the cat from Gloria, find another home, but she won't hear of it.'

Before she ended the call to attend to another matter, Quintal told Jack he could call her anytime for updates on the case. She trusted him to keep everything confidential, as he had done so far. Jack thanked her, but doubted he would take up the offer. This case had left him drained, physically and emotionally. Time to reconnect with Skye and his new family.

But first, a call to Jocelyn in South London. He told her he'd won a bundle of money at the Estoril casino and wanted to donate it to Sarah's favourite charity. She burst into tears. 'Oh, Jack. I've hated you ever since I knew you, but…oh, I don't know. Wait one minute.' He heard a clunk as she set the phone down. A couple of minutes later. 'You there?' She gave the name of the women's shelter in Croydon. He jotted down the details. Tomorrow he'd email the shelter to get an account number, then pass it on to Quintal.

He reached across to grab the mug of tea that was now stone cold when he heard Linda's voice calling from the kitchen. 'Someone's here to see you, Jack!'

He put the tea down and went to stand, when a familiar face walked into the living room. And Skye, clutching the woman's hand and beaming like it was Christmas morning.

'Look, Dad! It's Claudia.'

'I can see that, sunshine.' He was stretching it a bit. The truth of the matter was that Detective Jack Lisbon of the Yorkville CIB, tears spilling down his cheeks, could barely see anything at all.

## Next in The Fighting Detective Series

vinci-books.com/cold-shot

**As the Yorkville CIB investigates a brutal murder, they uncover dark secrets surrounding the victim, a failed NHL hopeful with a long list of enemies.**

Keep turning the pages for a free preview…

A free prequel novella...

vinci-books.com/takedown-free

**Get the explosive prequel to The Fighting Detective series, absolutely free.**

## Cold Shot: Prologue

IN THE FADING light of the late afternoon, the world outside sweated in jungle-green lushness. Amongst the tropical foliage that framed both sides of the road, signs advertising tonight's exhibition ice hockey match hung from light poles. As the Melbourne Mavericks' team bus ferried the players to the newly built Yorkville Entertainment Arena, Jonas Eriksson stared out of the window. A massive billboard showing a collage of players from both teams loomed ahead. He should have been pleased to see it up there; only three representatives from each franchise had been chosen for the promotional photoshoot. Still, a grunt of displeasure escaped from under his breath. They'd spent all day at the photographer's inner-Melbourne studio, and for what? You could barely make out Eriksson's face, pushed to the back of the collage with the younger, more attractive men at the front.

Wounded vanity aside, he was pumped for tonight's match. Whatever life's circumstances, the game was everything to him. If anyone lived and breathed hockey, it was Jonas Eriksson.

Tonight's opening match would be the first of three encounters with the Glacier City Hawks, an outfit of try-hards from a flyblown province no one outside of Canada could even find on a map. His own team, the Mavericks, comprised roughly half Australians and half imports. They stood a good chance against the Canadians; beating them would give Eriksson immense pleasure. He'd played in a Swedish youth team that nearly won the World Junior Championship – scored a hat trick – only to be narrowly beaten by Canada in the final match in a penalty shootout.

The coach had spent thirty minutes at the hotel giving the team a rousing pep talk, working himself into a lather in the process. There would be more of the same in the changerooms once they got to the arena. That type of thing had little impact on Eriksson, no matter how stirring the speech. He was practically impervious to manufactured hype. The thought of beating the Canucks at their own game was motivation enough.

As the bus rolled around a sweeping bend in the road, there was no conversation among the players. Coach Raff had his scarred, bald head firmly stuck in one of those political biographies he liked to read; his teammates were either glued to the screens of their mobiles or listening to music through earbuds. Eriksson did neither; instead he visualised himself scoring goals and slamming the opposition into the boards. In his mind's eye, the Mavs had thrashed the opposition 10 to zip, the Canucks left to lick their wounds. The toot of a car horn yanked him out of his dreaming.

He stretched and yawned, body stiff from sleeping on a too-hard hotel bed. Or maybe it was age catching up with him. The average retirement age of hockey players was 36, and he was already 38.

He absently rubbed away a light coating of his condensed breath from the window glass. It looked like rain was coming. Clouds grey and menacing. The rain would be heavy, maybe a tropical storm. It would be a welcome relief from the oppressive heat they had endured the last couple of days in Yorkville. Made a change from Melbourne's miserable summer, but only a madman would settle in these steamy parts voluntarily.

In many ways Far North Queensland reminded him of Florida. Hot, humid, coastal. He remembered playing a couple of forgettable matches in the southern American state, against the Panthers and the Lightning. It wasn't long after the last game against the Panthers in 2011 that a horrific shoulder injury sent him crashing out of the National Hockey League.

Only after a year of tortuous rehab was he able to put the skates back on and hit the ice. But he'd lost much of his once mighty mojo; despite herculean efforts, he was unable to get back to his best form. Always in the back of his mind lurked the fear of reinjuring the shoulder, so he stopped playing like a man given days to live. He got all cautious and, if he was going to be completely honest with himself – timid.

The Boston Bruins dropped him, and the other franchises wouldn't touch him. All that was left to do was to scratch out a living as a journeyman player in the Euro leagues. It wasn't the worst option in the world for a Swedish guy. Then, after a long slump, none of the European teams wanted him either.

Now, here he was, in Australia, where ice hockey ranked marginally above competitive marbles as a serious sporting pursuit. On the positive side, a genius sports psychologist in Melbourne had helped him reacquire his mojo. Over the last year, his former fearlessness had come back, but he was smart enough to know that returning to the big league of the NHL was a pipe dream.

Another sign caught his eye, illuminated brightly by lights as the storm clouds gathered and dusk loomed. A simple warning: don't swim at the town's beaches unless you want to end up as a saltwater crocodile's lunch. The words were repeated in a number of languages. His mind drifted back to Florida again, the Everglades. Swap out crocs for alligators, southern drawl for Australian twang, and you could almost wake up in one place and think you were in the other.

His mobile buzzed. He didn't want to look at the message, but his eyes were drawn to the screen. The bus was a tourer, big enough for the players to have two seats to themselves if they wanted privacy. Eriksson wasn't much of a socialiser, so he almost always had an empty seat next to him. Not that any of his teammates wanted to share his company anyway. And that was fine by him.

Another glance at his phone. His heart nearly leapt out of his mouth. An American phone number, just like the previous one. His – *or her, or their* – demand had quadrupled. Because now it wasn't just a vague threat. The hard evidence had been produced.

Sixty-thousand US dollars by the end of the week or the photo would be released all over the internet. The details of how to make the payment would be sent tomorrow exactly 24 hours from now.

*Shit.*

He didn't have anywhere near that kind of money saved up. There was one chance to borrow it, but that was a long shot. Dammit, his life would be ruined beyond all repair if the image was made public.

The aircon in the bus was set to Siberian chill, but sweat dripped under his shirt. Heart thudding, he re-read the message, which ended with the instruction to open the picture file. In case he had any doubt about how serious the extortionists were. But there was no need to open it. He could already see in preview mode what it was. Jonas Eriksson, ten years ago, in Prague, shirtless, and with a joint hanging out of his mouth.

He wasn't alone. The other person in the photo wasn't wearing a shirt either. He was holding aloft a can of beer.

But there was more.

Both of them were surrounded by blocks of compressed heroin with a street value of over a million dollars. Money Eriksson never got his share of. As if that mattered now.

One thing puzzled him deeply. He had a pretty good memory, but he was stoned out of his head when the picture was taken, couldn't remember it happening. Was the other person in the photo being blackmailed, too? Eriksson imagined he must be. He'd try and contact him on the quiet, but it wouldn't be that simple. There had been no contact between them for years. Most puzzling of all, who took the damned photo?

He closed the message, switched off his phone, shut his eyes and took a deep breath.

Win the match first, deal with this shitstorm later.

## Cold Shot: Chapter One

THE TEAMS STOOD in straight lines either side of centre ice, dancing coloured spotlights creating a kaleidoscope for the spectators. A skinny, acne-faced young man belted out the national anthems of Australia and Canada in an off-key falsetto. The fact he had a tin ear and completely lost control of his upper register, where the notes wandered around like a drunk trying to cross a busy highway, had no bearing on the fellow's enthusiasm. Loud and proud and painful to listen to. As the last note of "O Canada" faded into silence, the crowd roared its approval of his raucous performance.

Skye Lisbon stretched her body around to speak into her father's ear as frenetic organ music burst out across the arena. 'He's the worst singer I've ever heard in my life.'

Detective Sergeant Jack Lisbon nodded sagely. 'Terrible, I agree.'

'But why did they clap for him?' She pursed her lips critically. 'I would have booed the guy off the rink.'

'I think he's got some kind of rare illness. He was in the

papers last week. A charity's been set up for him. Apparently he loves to sing, even if the talent doesn't match the passion.'

Skye's face crumpled at the news and she slunk back into her seat. 'Oh no! I feel terrible now.'

Jack squeezed her hand. 'You weren't to know, love.' He smiled warmly. 'I'll make a donation to the family on your behalf if it'll make you feel better.'

Hope lit up her face. 'Please do. Lots of money!'

'Of course.' He was about to add something, but a sharp, shrill whistle from centre ice and a voice to his left cut him off.

'Guys. Enough talking. Pay attention. It's about to start.' Detective Claudia Taylor's eyes burned with excitement as the referee dropped the puck onto the ice. Sticks flashed in a blur, one of them connecting with the puck and sending it to the opposite side of the rink.

Soon, just under 4,000 spectators were screaming for the Melbourne Mavericks. Everyone in Australia loves an underdog, and the Aussies were at long odds to beat the visitors. There were some fans wearing Hawks gear sprinkled about the stands, but they were clearly in the minority.

For a couple of minutes the action seesawed across the ice, with both teams taking shots but missing the mark. Each attempt was met with shrieks from the audience. Jack could barely contain himself, stamping his feet and applauding like he was back in his youth at a Clash concert. What little ice hockey he'd seen previously on the TV was nothing compared to the real thing. For starters, the game was faster than any sport he'd watched before. And you could also see the puck a lot more clearly. Blink at the wrong moment, though, and you could miss something. But even better than that was the physicality of the game. The men slammed into each other with ferocity; each thumping body check and crash into the boards brought a smile to the old boxer's craggy face.

With five minutes elapsed in the first period, the stadium erupted when a burly forward from the Mavericks directed the puck into the opposition's goal with a perfectly timed slap shot.

As the excitement subsided, Skye pulled out a program and a pen. 'Did you get the number of the player who scored?'

'Number 11,' said Jack. He pointed to the centre-hung scoreboard that offered a view to spectators in all sections of the stands. 'There's a replay.' They both paused to watch the slo-mo.

'Jonas Eriksson,' said Skye. She twisted her mouth and, with a flourish, made a mark on the program.

'What are you doing, defacing an important document?' Jack laughed. 'I'm sure there's a statute against that.'

'Don't be a wally.' Skye shook her head, thick curls bouncing. 'It's a souvenir, innit.'

Jack guffawed. 'Please don't talk like me.' Despite the words, his heart ached for the kid. She'd slotted into her new life in Australia better than he could have hoped for. He'd been a fish out of water when he arrived in a strange land with a suitcase full of secrets, which, touch wood, still remained buried. It wasn't easy finding his feet, but for Skye it had been a cinch. A bit of teasing about her British accent was all she had to put up with. She'd already been to a couple of sleepovers and was now begging Jack to allow her to host one. So far, he'd held out. The thought of a bunch of teenage girls running amok in his house sent his heart rate into overdrive.

Play resumed quickly after the first goal. The coaches

made some reshuffling decisions; players leaped over barriers to replace their teammates like sheep going over a fence. Things were happening so fast, Jack had no time to figure out what was what, but he couldn't care less. It was all about the experience for the town, and, like everyone else, he was lapping it up. Skye's small hand grabbed his wrist as she pointed at the rink with her other hand. 'Look, Dad! A fight.'

Now we're talking, Jack thought. A bit of fisticuffs. The entire crowd stood and yelled their approval as two players threw wild haymakers at each other. One tried to pull the other's jersey over his head to get the guy off balance. Their sticks remained on the ice, drawing a pursed-lipped nod of appreciation from Jack. A fair fight is a good fight. Whatever the players' disagreement, it ended with both sitting on the bench, cooling their heels a while.

The first period came to an end with a couple of blistering waves of attack on both goals, the Hawks managing to slot away a pair, taking a 2:1 lead into the break.

Taylor offered to brave the crowds, headed down the steep narrow stairway to grab hot chips and drinks for everyone, leaving Jack and Skye to dissect the spectacle they'd watched thus far.

'Claudia's getting right into it,' said Skye, popping the lid back on the pen, which she stowed away in her down jacket pocket. It was the first time she'd worn it since arriving in Far North Queensland in the middle of a summer that was exceeding the long-term averages in both heat and humidity. Jack, too, had to search high and low for a jumper to wear tonight. He finally found a sweater in his suitcase, still folded up from his last trip to England. Winter apparel wasn't a priority living in the tropics.

'I know. Very surprising. She normally has little interest

in sports.' He scratched his chin, trying to remember if there was a sport she followed. 'Actually, correction. No interest whatsoever. Except for jogging along the Esplanade and swimming laps at the pool, but that's just exercise and doesn't count.'

'Just between you and me, I think she's having heaps of fun tonight.'

'I think you're right, sunshine. Never seen her get so het up over entertainment. She can't sit still.'

Skye flashed a lopsided grin. 'Or maybe it's because she's out on a date with you?' The observation came with a small, pointy elbow jabbing him in the ribs. 'I know she likes you, Dad. Why don't you two just–'

'Give over!' He protested, feeling the temperature rise in his cheeks and a prickling sensation under his scalp. 'She's only here because Aden Trevarthen couldn't make it because he had to look after his sick kid.'

'That's two "becauses" in one sentence. Anyway, you knew that before you got the tickets, Dad.'

Jack popped a pellet of gum, gave it a good mashing, then said, 'Look, she's happy because she's enjoying the show, that's all.' He decided to push another line to steer the conversation into safer waters. 'You know, I think secretly she likes boxing, but ain't gonna admit it to me because she thinks watching it's not ladylike.'

A slow shake of the head. 'Don't be disingenuous, Dad.'

'Bleedin' heck. What does that even mean?'

'It means that, ah…'

'What are you two chatting about?' said Taylor, handing over two steaming buckets of hot chips and a couple of oversized drinks. She kicked her protruding handbag further under the collapsible chair before resuming her seat. 'Why is your face red, Jack? Not feeling well?'

'I'm perfectly fine, thanks. It's a reaction to the cold in here. I think you're a tad flushed, too.' He turned around to face his daughter. 'Isn't she, Skye?'

A shake of the head. 'No. She looks perfectly fine.'

No time for more chat as the players filed out onto the ice, again to the accompaniment of organ music. The announcer revved up the crowd with appeals to cheer as loudly as they could for the Aussie outfit, and the request was met with instant uproar. The teams quickly got into position and it was on again.

Jack's phone buzzed in his pants pocket. He ignored it, focusing on the match. He'd not had a night out in weeks, and he wouldn't let anything interrupt tonight's entertainment. The phone rang out, then the sound signifying a message had been left. Then it rang again. Out of the corner of his eye, he saw Taylor rifling through her handbag. She pulled out her mobile, the sound of its ringtone barely audible over the crowd noise.

Something's up, Jack thought, as Taylor pressed a hand over one ear and listened intently, her facial muscles tense. A look at the screen of his own mobile confirmed the calls had come from the Yorkville station. Then another from Constable Ben Wilson's personal number.

'What is it, Dad?' Skye's lips were drawn taut in concern. She glanced at Taylor to her left, then back to Jack. 'Why don't you answer your phone?'

'We're out enjoying ourselves, innit.'

'I dunno. Could be something serious.'

Taylor ended the call, reached across to Jack, tapped him on the wrist. 'There's some serious shit…' she blinked hard, then looked at Skye. 'I mean there's an incident in the outer suburbs. Home invasion, residents terrified. Uniforms are combing the area for the suspects. Inspector Batista wants a detective there.' She thrust her phone back into her bag. 'I'll go.'

'No.' Jack shook his head. 'Despite you apparently not being able to speak without swearing in front of a child.' He smiled at Skye, who rolled her eyes; she was used to hearing much worse from him, in the school playground for that matter. 'I'd like you to look after her for a while. I'm gonna take it.'

Taylor squinted. 'Why the enthusiasm now? You didn't even want to answer Wilson's call.'

He ran a hand through his short-cropped hair. 'I've been getting nothing but spam calls for weeks now. Crooks in the Philippines trying to rip me off with offers to buy solar panels or some such nonsense. They've been calling at this time of night.' He stood, drawing the ire of a woman in the row behind who screamed at Jack to sit down. He turned, glared at her, flashed his Queensland Police Service badge and she quickly shut up. Turning back to Taylor he said, 'Anyway, I'm pulling rank. You're staying to look after the kid. Ring me when the game's over.' As he descended the stairs, the crowd erupted. He looked up at the big screen. The Mavs had scored to level up at 2 apiece. In the car park he dialled Wilson and got the details. He hated to miss the match, but he hated missing the opportunity to nab violent offenders even more.

## Cold Shot: Chapter One

HE STEPPED CAREFULLY over and around the fragments of shattered glass. The sliding door from the balcony had been smashed in, presumably with the handle of the garden spade which was now lying in the centre of the living area. Jack knew this address; he and Taylor had interviewed one of the residents in relation to the murder of a pool hall owner. Her testimony and co-operation had helped seal a conviction.

'Over here, Detective Lisbon,' called Constable Kylie Smith, standing beside a seated woman with a slim, athletic build. Jack recognised the victim in an instant. Local independent sex worker Michelle "Misty" Roach. Thirty-eight years old, of Indigenous heritage, and highly popular with the local male population.

'What happened here, love?' said Jack in his best sympathetic tone, the one he reserved for vulnerable females. 'You can't stay out of mischief, can you?'

Head hung low, the woman, exposed shoulders bathed in a sheen of sweat, muttered something incomprehensible under her breath. 'I didn't catch that.' Jack flicked her softly under the chin, a feather-light touch. Misty looked up, blinking away tears. Out of the corner of his eye he saw Constable Smith compress her lips and shake her head slightly. It was frowned upon to touch people without a reason. Yes, he could have said something to get the woman's attention, but the action was instinctive and brought no reproving words, just a blank look.

'Three men broke into the house, threatened to beat up my customer just as he was putting his pants back on. One of them landed a vicious punch on him when he started to protest. Sat him on his bum and shut him up quick smart. Then they robbed him of his wallet and phone, took my money, too.' She waited a couple of beats. 'Well, some of it. Look, do I have to go over this again?' She flicked her large brown eyes towards Smith. 'I already told her everything.'

Smith nodded, placed a hand on Misty's back. 'You may have to repeat the facts several times, Ms Roach. Now, please tell Detective Lisbon what you told me. And add anything you might have forgotten and since remembered.'

'Take your time,' Jack encouraged. 'What you tell us while everything's fresh in your mind will help us catch them quicker.'

She shrugged her shoulders quickly. '*If* you catch them. Listen, I need a cigarette. There's a packet in the kitchen.' Misty folded bony arms across a voluptuous chest that defied gravity.

'You need a doctor after what you've been through, sunshine,' said Jack. He reached for his mobile. 'I'm going to call the paramedics, OK?'

She puffed out her cheeks and shook her head. 'Does doctor sound the same as cigarette? I'm fine. They didn't touch me. Just let me fetch my smokes.'

'I'll get them', said Smith just as her mobile phone chirped in her pocket. She made an excuse-me face and ducked into the kitchen. She gave "uh huh" responses to the other party, a moment later brought a packet of cigarettes, plastic lighter and glass ashtray, then disappeared again.

'I don't think bringing punters back to your place is such a good idea. When did you start doing that?'

A tear formed in the corner of her eye behind a curtain of blue smoke. 'Since mum passed away.'

Jack swallowed hard. He remembered Betty-Lou Roach as a kind-hearted woman. 'I'm sorry to hear that.'

Misty brushed specks of ash from her lemon-yellow sun frock. 'Well, that's breast cancer for you.' She sucked in a lungful, expelled a cloud. 'So, there's no need for me to skulk around hotels 'n that. Mum knew what I did, of course. Never approved, but she loved me all the same.'

Fighting off the urge to hug the woman, with his own ex-wife recently succumbing to the big "C", Jack focused on the task at hand. 'Please, Michelle. Time's of the essence. Can you think of anyone who would target you?'

'Ha! Just about half the crims in town. People know I'm a cash-based business. Shit's getting worse with break-ins in Yorkville. Getting to be as bad as Cairns. These arseholes think they can do whatever they like without having to face punishment. I'm just grateful we weren't stabbed or bashed to death…this time!'

Jack nodded. He could get into a discussion with her about the causes of the QPS's lack of resources, the upsurge in crime. How the leniency of the courts was to blame, soft-on-crime politicians, kids getting their jollies by running rampant and uploading videos to social media to get likes. But what would be the point?

'What can you tell me about the attackers?'

'Young, I reckon. Probably teenagers. Dressed in jeans, dark t-shirts. And they all wore those bloody bala-whatcha-callits.'

'Balaclavas,' Jack prompted.

'Yeah, them.' She paused for a moment, eyes widening. 'My client won't need to speak to you, will he? I mean, I gotta protect his privacy. I'm valued in this town for my discretion.'

Jack scratched the back of his head and pulled out a small notebook. 'Give me his name, Michelle. Another witness won't hurt our case when we take the perpetrators to court.'

'Ha,' she scoffed. 'As if he told me his real name. He was going to pay me an extra bonus, too, before he was robbed.'

'We're getting off track.' His sympathy was dipping and he had to check the edge creeping into his voice. In any event, they could trace the client later via phone records if necessary. 'Was there anything familiar about the offenders?'

She tapped ash furiously into the ashtray. 'I was too scared to pay much attention. They were big – at least they seemed big. Didn't say much. One of them barked orders at us, the others seemed to be doing what he said. The leader threatened to tie us up and give us a hiding if we resisted. Like I said, my bloke had already copped a punch, so he did as he was told like a good 'un.'

'Could you see any part of their bodies? Skin tone? Tattoos?'

'Could have been Indigenous or white. It was pretty dark, I just had candles going. Don't remember any tattoos on their arms. Again, like I said, it was dark.' She closed one eye as she concentrated. 'Geez, I'm not much help, am I?'

'Sorry to interrupt.' Smith appeared with an apologetic frown. 'Just had Wilson on the phone, sir. Constable Semmens called it in. He thinks he's found them.'

Jack stood to his full height. 'Thinks?'

'Three lads in a stolen late-model Camry tried to rob a service station out on Pramberg Road. They fit the description Ms Roach gave us. Still wearing their balaclavas, too. In this heat, can you imagine! Anyway, the manager was able to lock the front door, trapping the robbers inside the servo. He's hiding in a secure storeroom in the back, waiting for us to rescue him. He reckons he's safe there for now, but still scared out of his wits.'

'What's Semmens doing?'

'Waiting for backup. In other words – you and me. Trevarthen's home with his kid while his wife's working nightshift at the hospital. And Wilson's on comms duty.'

'No time to dawdle then.' Jack pocketed the notebook. 'Did Wilson say if there are customers stuck inside with these thugs?'

'Apparently not. At least he didn't mention it.'

'Which service station? There's two on Pramberg Road.'

'He didn't say.'

'Call him back, get him to ring me in…one minute. You stay here with Ms Roach.'

'I don't need babysitting now you've got them,' said Misty, reaching for her cigarettes. 'Call me when you've caught the bastards.'

Jack grinned. 'We don't know for sure it's the same perpetrators.'

'Of course it's the same boys!'

Jack shook his head. 'On the face of it, yes. But I've been around long enough to know not to make assumptions. I want someone here with you until it's confirmed a hundred percent.' He shot her his best disarming smile. 'Besides, Kylie makes a great cup of tea.'

'In that case,' Misty sighed and turned to Smith. 'I'll show you where everything is.'

## Grab your copy...
## vinci-books.com/cold-shot

## About the Author

Blair Denholm is a born-and-bred Australian crime fiction writer whose previous jobs have been as varied as translator, debt collector, technology researcher, banking and insurance consultant, and even car-wash attendant. Over the years he has lived and worked in New York, Moscow, Munich, Abu Dhabi and Australia. His life-long love of sports is reflected in the plots of The Fighting Detective series.

Denholm's flagship series, The Fighting Detective, stars ex-boxer Detective Sergeant Jack Lisbon and is set in the steamy tropics of North Queensland, Australia. The series features heavy doses of noir crime with a vigilante justice twist. So far there are eight novels and one prequel novella in the series, with more in the pipeline.

Denholm's debut novel, *SOLD*, is the first in a noir trilogy featuring the detestable yet lovable one-man wrecking ball Gary Braswell. The book was long-listed for movie adaptation by Screen Queensland in 2019. The other books in this series are *Sold to the Devil* and *Sold Dirt Cheap*.

Denholm has also written two thriller novels set in Russia. Captain Viktor Voloshin is a hard-boiled investigator who has to fight the establishment in order for justice to be served in his own special way. The first in this series, *Revolution Day*, was published in 2021, with the follow-up, *The Defector*, released in 2024. One more book will round off this series.

In 2024, Denholm signed on with UK-based publisher Vinci Books.

Blair Denholm grew up in suburban Brisbane, Queensland. After two lengthy stints in Tasmania, he now resides in the relatively cooler climes of the Southern Downs region of Queensland with his partner, Sandra, and faithful dog, Bruno.

## Acknowledgments

It wasn't by accident I chose the name Jack Lisbon for my main character. Having visited the beautiful and enchanting capital city of Portugal twice now, it was an easy choice to borrow the moniker for my own devious means.

I'd like to thank the lovely Anita, a woman Sandra and I met by chance and who enthusiastically showed us the best parts of Lisbon and surrounds, and later the glorious city of Porto. Also thanks to Bruno, our dependable and skilled driver in Lisbon, and now great friend. And finally, to the awesome Nebula Castelino, a reader who suggested the brilliant title for this novel.

If you ever get the chance to visit Portugal, make sure you do. You're sure to love it as much as I do.

www.ingramcontent.com/pod-product-compliance
Ingram Content Group UK Ltd.
Pitfield, Milton Keynes, MK11 3LW, UK
UKHW040230220126
467235UK00004B/66

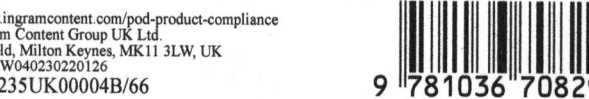